Praise for Tara Ratzlaff

"Ratzlaff debuts with an accomplished whodunit that combines solid prose, a winning lead, and plausible amateur sleuthing . . . This series is off to a promising start."

– Publishers Weekly

"The writer describes her writing as cozy mysteries because that's exactly how it feels. The story flows along effortlessly to its conclusion."

– Betty Lou Roselle, delcoculturevultures.com

"This debut volume of a new cozy mystery 'Native Prairie Mysteries' series has more unexpected plot twists and turns than a Kansas tornado and is a compulsive page turner of a 'whodunnit' murder mystery from start to finish."

– Midwest Book Review

"With the latest engaging addition to her Native Prairie mystery series, Ratzlaff once again delivers a wonderful sense of place and a marvelously entertaining community of characters readers will come to love."

—John A. Charles, The Poisoned Pen Bookstore
(in regards to *The Moth Wasn't Harmless*, Book 2)

THE
MOTH
BIT
BACK

Native Prairie Mysteries
Book Three

TARA RATZLAFF

CAMEL
PRESS
Kenmore, WA

A Camel Press book published by Epicenter Press

Epicenter Press
6524 NE 181st St.
Suite 2
Kenmore, WA 98028

For more information go to:
www.Camelpress.com
www.Coffeetownpress.com
www.Epicenterpress.com
www.tararatzlaff.com

This is a work of fiction. Names, characters, places, brands, media, and incidents are either the product of the author's imagination or are used fictitiously.

Cover design by Scott Book
Design by Melissa Vail Coffman

The Moth Bit Back
Copyright © 2025 by Tara Ratzlaff

Library of Congress Control Number: 2024952551

ISBN: 978-1-684923-16-8 (Trade Paper)
ISBN: 978-1-684923-17-5 (eBook)

I dedicate this book to my husband, who is responsible for what little knowledge I have acquired about native grass and wildflower seed farming. I'm so thankful many years ago he convinced me it was wise for us to leave our careers and take a chance on a farm.

ACKNOWLEDGMENTS

THANK YOU TO MY FAMILY AND friends who have been so supportive!

CHAPTER ONE

*Bottle Gentian is a bottle-shaped, bluish violet flower
that fades to white at its tip. It is found in wet prairies
and at the edges of woods.*

I<small>T WAS THE END OF</small> A<small>PRIL</small> and I was sitting in a dentist's wait-ing room on a beautiful, sunny Thursday morning, alternating between grimacing in pain and feeling proud, as I watched Faye Banning smiling and working with confidence behind the reception desk. She had come a long way in the last five months. In fact we all had since Nick Banning, my foreman/boyfriend, had introduced me to his half-sister when I surprised him and delivered a supper one evening in November. I hadn't realized how hard I had fallen for Nick until I saw him with his arm around another woman, and my soul had dropped with despair. To me it appeared all the secrets Nick had been keeping from me had culminated with another woman in his life. I was relieved when it turned out Faye was Nick's twenty-two year old half-sister from Oregon, who Nick had allowed to live with him when she needed a place to hide from her abusive boyfriend, Christopher. Nick had helped her move to California from Oregon previously but when Christopher was released after serving a short jail sentence for fraud, he found her in California and physically abused her once more. That incident put Christopher in jail again and Nick had returned to California to try and convince Faye to move to Arvilla, explaining his absence last fall. Although initially refusing, a month later Faye agreed, hoping Minnesota would be far enough away that Christopher wouldn't find her when his sentence was done. I sensed I wasn't yet getting the entire story—especially as Nick had never previously mentioned having a sister—but I had made the difficult decision to trust Nick knowing he was secretive about his past, although that didn't mean I wasn't itching to get to the bottom of things as I was an extremely nosy person.

My name is Carmen Karlaff and my family and I have been operating a native grass and wildflower seed farm for thirty-five years. Our farm is located about five miles from Arvilla, a small town in northwest Minnesota, with a population of around 2,500. Arvilla is approximately thirty miles east of the North Dakota border and twenty miles south of the Canadian border. Although I don't notice it, I've been told our close proximity to Canada gives our speech a Canadian accent. Our operation is more than a farm, as not only do we grow and harvest the seed; but we also clean, package, market, and ship our seed all over the United States. We sell the majority of our seed to wholesale seed companies who in turn combine the species we grow, along with species from other growers, into seed mixes that are used for projects such as prairie restorations, gravel pit reclamations, and roadside plantings. However the primary use of our seed is government conservation programs such as the conservation reserve program and wetland restoration projects more commonly known as CRP and WRP respectively. We also at times buy in species we don't raise to make our own mixes and sell them direct to customers in northwest and north central Minnesota, and eastern North Dakota. Additionally we have three small cabins we rent out that are built on one of our native prairies for birdwatchers and anyone interested in observing native prairies and whatever type of wildlife that may decide to show itself. We had a soft opening last fall and had rented out one cabin which went well. This spring most of the cabins were rented, and starting in June all three were booked well into October. We hoped to make tours of the farm available at some point, but between checking on guests, cleaning cabins, selling seed, getting ready for burning season and the normal spring farm activities, farm tours may have to wait until next summer, if ever.

In the meantime I was in a dentist's office wanting to be anywhere else as I was too busy to be sitting here, unfortunately my tooth felt otherwise. I had been enjoying a huge bowl of buttered popcorn last night while watching a movie at Nick's when I bit an un-popped kernel. I didn't think too much of it at the time, but when my hot coffee hit the tooth this morning and I couldn't drink it, a visit to Judith's Dental Office was in order, especially when an hour later the pain hadn't yet subsided and my tooth was throbbing. I was fortunate and Judith said she could squeeze me in. Although anytime a medical professional is squeezing you in amongst their other appointments, you knew a long wait was going to be in order. So in the meantime I was enjoying watching how confidently and efficiently Faye was handling patients and phone calls. When I first met Faye she was painfully thin, skittish, slumped as if trying to hide, with stringy blond hair hiding her face. Years of dealing with an abusive boyfriend who did everything in his power to convince her she was worthless, including beating her if she dared to express herself had left her a shell of a person. The past five months away from Christopher, along with Nick's encouragement and a job she was proficient at had worked wonders. Faye's starved angular features had softened with the addition of some weight. That, along with gaining a few good friends and a beautiful shoulder length bobbed haircut, had enabled her to regain confidence. My musings were interrupted by Jill Farris, the dental hygienist, who told me the dentist was ready for me and led me down the hallway to an examination room.

"I am so thankful Judith was willing to squeeze me in this morning," I said to Jill.

"She does a lot of that, in fact last night she had my dad here after hours fixing a tooth that was infected," Jill responded with a smile, "but it can make for long days."

"Wow, that's dedication," I said as I walked in the examination room.

"Good morning Carmen, did you have trouble with a tooth this morning?" Judith greeted me as I sat down in the dentist chair. Judith Lansing was in her early forties, average height, and blonde hair going prematurely gray, with a bit of a stoop from many years of leaning over a dental chair.

"I think I cracked or broke it eating popcorn last night." I told her pointing at the left side of my mouth.

"You wouldn't be the first. I'd have a lot less business if people could stay away from popcorn," Judith said smiling. "Why don't you open your mouth and I'll take a look."

She poked around in my mouth while I closed my eyes and tried not to think about the bill. Dentist visits are never inexpensive.

"Well, you are in luck. It's not a broken tooth, only a tiny fracture. I should be able to repair it. I'll bond it together with a plastic resin to fill in the fracture—basically a filling. It should take care of the problem."

"And if it doesn't?" I asked.

"Then a cap may be in order, which is much more expensive."

"Then let's hope it works," I answered thankful my checkbook wouldn't take too much of a hit—today anyway. "How are things going for you?" I asked as she got the tools ready for my procedure.

She stopped, looked at me, and surprised me by saying, "Not the best. How well do you know Sheriff Poole? If rumors around town are to be believed you've had a few dealings with him."

"We've had our ups and downs, but I'm starting to have more faith in his abilities. Why do you ask?"

"Part of the reason my husband and I decided to move back

home to Arvilla to raise our family was that it appeared to be a great place yet to raise a family, but I'm starting to notice an alarming increase of what I believe is meth mouth in many of my patients; surprisingly in many upstanding citizens," she said as she put air quotes around upstanding.

"What is meth mouth?" I asked her.

"I started to notice several of my patients coming in with a lot of problems they shouldn't be having. The changes in their teeth were suspicious to me and when I looked up signs of Methamphetamine use, the symptoms fit. Methamphetamine, or meth as it is more commonly known, is a nasty drug. The research I've done said it can be cheaply made in your own kitchen from many over-the-counter cold medicines. It has to be rather new to the area as some of the first symptoms can be found in the teeth. I think we would have been hearing about other behavior issues as users can become severely anxious, confused, and have hallucinations. With longer use I understand they can become violent and aggressive, but I'm far from an expert on it. In the meantime I'm trying to come to terms with how much trouble I'd be in with my licensing if I alerted the sheriff. If I'm correct, I'd like to think the sheriff could talk to the patients and get a head start on determining who is either supplying and or making the meth before it becomes a bigger problem."

"How do you know it is meth and not bad oral care?" I asked.

"Some of these patients have been coming here for years; the decay in their teeth has been too sudden, things like cavities, sores, and gum disease. I think I need to tell the sheriff."

"I don't disagree, but aren't you subject to HIPAA laws that state you can't reveal patient information?" I asked her.

"HIPAA laws are designed to assure that an individuals' health information is properly protected but they also allow that same health information to be used to provide and promote high quality health care and to protect the public's health and well being. It tries to strikes a balance that permits important uses of information, while protecting the privacy of people who seek care and healing. I want to abide by the law, but I can't stand to think of what meth could do to the people in this community. I've got a call in to other colleagues of mine to get their opinions on what they think would happen to me if I share this information with law enforcement."

"You might want to check with a lawyer too," I suggested.

Judith sighed and said, "I was hoping to avoid that expense but I may have to. Anyway, open wide, let's fix that tooth," and she started to numb the area around the tooth to work on it.

Thirty minutes later, I stumbled out to the front desk to pay. The pain was gone, but it was tough to determine if it was due to the tooth being fixed or all the numbing medication.

"All better?" Faye asked when I was standing at the counter with my debit card.

"I think so, what's the damage?" I started to ask when we heard a shout, a gunshot, and then a crash. Faye and I stared at each other in horror and then we raced down the hall to the room I had just left. Faye got there first. She dropped to her knees and started screaming. I peeked around her and saw Judith lying on her side on the floor with a pool of blood coming out of her back. Faye started crooning, "Oh no, oh no," while my stomach began to roll. At the same time I noticed that Jill and the other two patients from the waiting room had followed us down the hallway.

"Don't come any closer please, somebody call 911, Judith has been shot," I said stopping them. One of the patients grabbed her phone and started dialing while Jill asked if Judith was alive.

"I don't know," I answered stepping in the room, being careful not to disturb anything, and tried both her neck and wrist for a pulse. I shook my head no. As I stood up and moved back in the hallway I saw the back door was ajar. I ran to the door and using my elbow I pushed it open all the way and stepped out trying to see if anyone was running away, knowing it was futile as whoever had done this was more than likely long gone. The alley was empty. I could hear sirens and I walked back inside. Faye was back on her feet being consoled by Jill. I slumped down the wall to the floor as I waited for emergency services to arrive. The EMT's arrived first, and confirmed what I already knew, Judith was dead. I heard them talk amongst themselves and decide to wait until law enforcement got there before they disturbed the body. I put my head down and stared at the floor.

I was jolted out of my stupor when I heard, "You again. Why does every serious crime that happens in this town revolve around you?"

I looked up and saw Sheriff Poole standing next to me. He was a stocky man standing around 5'4" with thinning black hair, the start of a stomach paunch, and was known to have a prickly demeanor at times. As I started to stand up, my phone rang. "Hold that thought," I said and answered the phone by reflex, registering the glare on the sheriff's face too late.

"Kirk, it's kind of a bad time to call. I'll call you back," I said starting to hang up and then stopping when I processed what he had said. "You've got to be kidding, Wizard did what?" Wizard was my brother's Dachshund who was a professional at getting himself and for some reason I had yet to figure out, myself too, into trouble.

"I'm very sorry Carmen, but the International Parcel Delivery (IPD) driver dropped off parts at the shop today. I'd brought Wizard with me to run around while Nick and I worked on the four-wheelers. We were installing the water tanks on them for burning and Wizard got on the truck without the driver or me noticing. The IPD driver just found him and called the shop to say he's heading to Arvilla. He asked if he could drop Wizard off somewhere in town. I was hoping I'd catch you before you left the dentist and ask you to get Wizard from him. The driver said he had a delivery at the new clothing boutique next to the dental office. Could you please get Wizard from him?" Kirk begged. Kirk was my twenty-three year old brother. He got all the height in the family, standing at 6'2" with curly black hair and if the comments on his band's Facebook site could be believed was widely regarded to be very handsome. I envied his slenderness which he inherited from our mom. I resembled our dad, both of us around 5'7", blond hair—although Dad's was now grey—and more sturdily built. I didn't have much hope that at twenty-eight years of age I was going to become slender any time soon. The five year age difference between Kirk and I made me think of him as an annoyance while we were growing up, but I had learned to appreciate him as an adult—although this wasn't one of those times.

I looked up at the sheriff who was staring at me, veins in his neck bulging, "I'll do my best," I said.

Kirk sputtered, "Do your best what does that mean. . ." I could hear him talking as I hung up.

"Sorry," I said feeling sheepish.

"If it's not too much trouble," the sheriff said sarcasm dripping from his voice, "could you tell me what you witnessed?"

"I didn't witness anything. I was with Faye paying my bill when we heard a gunshot and then a crash. We ran down the hallway and found Judith like this. The back door to the alley was open, I ran out and looked but I didn't see anyone."

"Did you touch anything?" Sheriff Poole asked.

"I don't think so. It was obvious Judith was dead, but I did check for a pulse." I gulped and my voice shook as I answered, "I didn't attempt any life saving measures. I might have touched the doorway."

"Did you know her well?" he asked, surprising me with the concern in his voice.

"We weren't close confidants or anything but she was an acquaintance. She was in my friend Jessica's book club and she might have known her better." Suddenly I remembered what Judith told me during my appointment. "You should know she mentioned a possible meth problem in town. She'd been noticing problems with teeth that she suspected was due to meth. She was hoping to talk to you about it—maybe that's why she was shot."

"Did she mention any names?"

"No. She said she was waiting to hear back from a few of her colleagues about possible HIPAA consequences before she came to you."

"Did she give you any indication who she might have been talking about?"

"Only that she was surprised by the so-called 'upstanding' people she was seeing the signs in. I'm not sure who she considered upstanding people—people with positions of authority, people of wealth, or people who acted like they were better than others. Anyway, that's all I know. Can I talk to you later if you have more questions? I'm supposed to be tracking down the IPD driver." The sheriff looked at me like I was crazy. "My brother's dog, Wizard, caught a ride in an IPD truck. I need to rescue him."

Recognizing I was serious, he said, "Okay, Carmen, I'll let you know if I need anything else after I finish interviewing the others. Go ahead."

I made my escape out of the dental office. When I walked out the door my senses were assailed by the sunny day as I struggled to adapt to the contrast of the normalcy of the town bustling around me with the horror I had just witnessed. I heard yelling, turned, and spotted the IPD truck where I feared the yelling was coming from. I ran down the sidewalk and reached the truck just as a harried looking IPD driver was about to drop a white spotted Wizard out of its door. I groaned wondering what Wizard had done, as I recognized the driver's expression as one I had felt on my own face many times when dealing with Wizard.

"I'll take him," I gasped as I panted from running.

"I sure hope so—he's been nothing but a pain in the. . ." his voice trailed off. "I used a piece of twine I happened to have in the truck to tie him up while I made deliveries which worked somewhat even though he drove me crazy with his barking and whining, but this was the last straw."

I peeked in the truck and saw that somehow Wizard had chewed open the corner of a box which contained white Styrofoam beads

someone must have ordered to fill a bean bag chair. They covered
the entire floor of the truck, and with the aid of static were halfway
up the sides of most of the packages.

"I'm going to get fired for this. I should never have been trans-
porting a dog in the first place. How am I going to explain this
damaged package?"

"Who is the package addressed to?" I asked, hoping for a mira-
cle, and it would be someone I knew.

He looked at the box. "It's for a Melanie Wylie. It's my next
delivery," he said as he consulted his hand-held computer.

"We're in luck—her studio is right over there." I pointed across
the street and said, "I know her and will explain. I'll make it right
with her I promise."

He looked at me with questioning eyes, starting to look hopeful.

"I'll meet you there, but first I'll help you clean this up." I stuck
the Styrofoam bead-covered Wizard in my pickup which was
parked nearby and went back to help clean up the delivery truck. It
was a hopeless task as the harder the driver and I tried to corral the
white beads, the more they spread. I hoped Wizard didn't transfer
too many of them to my pickup. I happened to spy Melanie coming
out of her studio and yelled her name. She ambled across the street
towards us in one of her typical vibrant color clashing outfits, fuch-
sia pants with an orange tunic today. She was a short, squat woman
around forty years of age, with a passion for animals and an almost
uncontrollable desire to protect all insects. She operated a meditation studio in Arvilla. I continued to be confounded on how she
could make a living; I had yet to meet anyone who admitted to
utilizing it. To my amazement she had become a good friend the
last seven months. She immediately burst into laughter when she
saw us and I explained what happened.

She giggled again and said, "I've got a vacuum, drive down the
alley behind my studio and park next to the electrical outlet by the
back door. We'll get this taken care of in no time at all."

Twenty minutes later the IPD driver, who's name I'd found out to be Darius, was happily on his way and I was using my phone to place an order for another package of Styrofoam beads. I said goodbye to Melanie after thanking her for her help and walked back to my pickup where an eager Wizard was wagging his tail with enthusiasm, not the least bit bothered by how his latest adventure had once again interrupted my life. Then looking at the little dog covered yet in white beads I found myself laughing. Maybe after the events with Judith, Wizard's adventure was exactly what I needed. I called Kirk to let him know I had Wizard and then told him about Judith. He apologized profusely for bothering me. I interrupted him and said, "It's okay, in fact Wizard's misadventure was a welcome diversion."

I hung up and decided to let my friends know about Judith before the sheriff got back to me and ordered me not to tell anyone. I sent a text to both Jessica and James. I decided to text rather than call as Jessica would be busy at the restaurant and with Karla, James' mother, off on a cruise with my dad I knew James was short-handed and would be busy also. Texting done I called Nick.

"How are you doing?" he greeted me, a hint of panic in his voice.

"How did you know?"

"Faye called. I would have called you earlier, but I knew you were tracking down Wizard and I didn't want to bother you."

Dad and I had hired Nick Banning last summer to be our foreman. He was originally from a small town in Oregon by the Willamette Valley. In addition to being a diesel mechanic he also had experience with irrigation from working on turf grass farms there. He had proven himself to be knowledgeable, dependable, and hard working. He was also thirty-two, 5'10" tall, handsome, with dark brown hair and a lean muscular build. It hadn't taken long for the attraction between the two of us to grow but we were taking it slow, in part because he was closed-mouthed and secretive about his past, but also because I felt he should experience all the seasons northwestern Minnesota had to offer—especially winter. I wanted him to be sure he knew what was involved if he committed to a relationship with me as I wasn't moving anywhere different. This past winter had been a good test as we had record sub-zero cold spells lasting weeks at a time and a lot of snow. He claimed it was no problem, but his outerwear got thicker and more layered as the winter went on and I couldn't help but notice his relief when the snow blower was put away for the year.

"It was horrible, but for a change Wizard was a good distraction," I said and I shared Wizard's adventure with him.

Nick laughed, then sobered and asked, "We can handle the burning this afternoon if you'd rather take the afternoon off?"

Knowing this was a lie as we were short-handed with Dad being gone on his cruise and Nick new to burning, I answered, "I appreciate the offer, but I'll be alright."

"What about Gary Pitterson? I can give him a call and see if he's available," Nick suggested.

Every year we employed a group of four to six people to walk our fields all summer and remove weeds. I don't know what their technical title should be but our farm has always called them roguers, pronounced row-gers. Gary was in charge of the crew and sometimes helped us out when we were short-handed in the spring for burning or in the fall for harvest.

"He won't be today. I asked him yesterday if he was going to available at all this week if we needed him, but one of his kids had something going on today he wanted to watch. He did say any other day would work. Honest, I'm fine. I have to drop Wizard off at home and I'll be there shortly. You and Kirk did get the four-wheelers ready?" I asked, trusting Nick but working with my absent minded brother, Kirk, could interrupt anyone.

"We did. He's filling the last water tank right now, and the propane tanks are filled for the torches."

"I'll be there as quick as I can—we need to take advantage of this wind." I hung up and knowing the sheriff and his deputies would be occupied at the dental office I picked up speed without fear of getting pulled over. As I did, I checked the leaves and noted the wind was blowing southeast. We didn't often get wind from that direction and it was perfect for burning the field by the seed plant. It would keep the smoke from the fire away from the traffic on US Highway 59 and away from a neighbor on the north end of our field. Burning was an integral part of our operation. Just as when fires once swept the plains, our native grass and wildflower fields needed fire to optimize the amount of seed they would produce. It was one of the very few parts of our farming operation I did not enjoy. There was something extremely intimidating about lighting that first match and seeing an eighty acre field start to burn. The heat was intense and while we maintained black-dirt fire breaks around our fields, utilized wet lines, and did a lot of back-burning to be as safe as we could possibly be; anything could happen during a fire. The wind could switch direction in an instant or even worse a sudden wind gust or swirl could carry an ember outside of our firebreaks. I pray daily normally, but during burning season I prayed constantly.

I drove into the yard, Wizard and I got out of the pickup and Tabitha, my calico colored indoor/outdoor cat, took one look at him with the white Styrofoam beads sticking to him and took off running. I put Wizard in the fenced in backyard to do his business while I packed myself a quick dinner. I hadn't done it this morning as my tooth had hurt too much to even think of eating, but Judith's fix had been a success as I tested it by eating a piece of an apple. Thinking of Judith brought a lump to my throat and I grabbed a tissue as a delayed reaction caused tears to flow. I sunk to the floor and cried for Judith, her family, and selfishly I cried for myself—I'd had enough of dead bodies and murders. My tears subsided into gulps until I had myself under control. I looked up and saw Wizard staring at me through the screen door. I got up to let him in noticing that somewhere in the yard he had managed to shed himself of most of the Styrofoam beads. I made sure his food and water dishes were full, gave him a pet, and left, hoping his adventure this morning would keep him out of trouble in the house the rest of the afternoon.

Before I left the yard I called to activate my burning permit. It could be tricky sometimes to get permission to burn. We had an agricultural permit, but even with the amount of snow we experienced this winter, the dryness last summer and fall could make getting the activation approval difficult. However the authorities are familiar with our operation after all these years and know we are responsible and have the proper equipment. That, along with the rain yesterday, allowed for approval today with no problems.

When I arrived at the seed plant, Kirk was already out in the field with the tractor and water tank starting the wet line. Nick was standing next to the four-wheelers waiting for me. He gave me a hug when I walked up to him. "How are you doing?" he asked.

"I'm not going to lie, I had a bit of a break-down when I got home, but I'm better now."

"Are you sure? The burn can wait."

"In fact, it can't, this is the perfect wind. I'll be fine," I said starting to feel like a broken record.

Nick examined my face and must have liked what he saw as he said, "Okay, if you are sure?"

"I am," I said. "Let's get started. I already activated our burning permit and notified the Sheriff's Department."

"By the way, why do you call the Sheriff's Department when you have a burning permit?" Nick asked.

"It's a courtesy. Sometimes when people see the smoke they call 911. If the Sheriff's Department is aware ahead of time where we are burning, it helps them know if they need to notify the fire department or not," I answered him.

We hopped on the four-wheelers and started lighting grass with our torches. Four hours later we were thankful to be finished with an uneventful burn, especially as we were short one person. It was a good start to the burning season.

We gathered around my pickup when were done and Kirk

said, "I'm sorry to hear about Judith. Do you have any idea what happened?"

"I have no clue. She fixed my tooth and I was paying my bill when Faye and I heard the gunshot. Someone must have snuck in the back door, but we didn't see anyone."

Nick looked at me and said, "At least you have no reason to get involved in this investigation."

"I'm thankful I don't. I've had enough of murder. Besides, I think it is drug related." I related to Nick and Kirk what Judith had told me about her suspicions of meth in the community.

"I hope she was wrong, I'd hate to see that stuff getting a toe-hold in around here," Kirk said.

"Me too, but it was kind of troubling that she said she'd seen signs of it in who she called the upstanding citizens. Although I wonder what she meant by that, upstanding like the wealthy or upstanding like ministers and teachers," I mused.

"I can see the wheels turning in your mind," Nick said. "Please don't get involved."

I laughed, "Don't worry I won't. Spring is busy enough without looking into a murder too." My phone rang as I finished talking. It wasn't a number I recognized, and as I answered I stepped away from Nick and Kirk. It was a nice seed sale of blue grama to plant under a solar panel project in southeastern Minnesota. I went over to my pickup to grab my notebook and write down the pertinent information. I walked back to Nick and Kirk and said, "We'll have to spend the morning in the seed plant tomorrow, we have a 650 acre CRP seed mix to blend. The customer will be there by 10:00 a.m. to pick it up and now we also have a shipment of 500 pounds of blue grama to get ready. With any luck the shipping company will be able to pick it up tomorrow on short notice. We'll burn the sideoats grama field in the afternoon. It's supposed to be a north wind which will work perfect."

"I might be late," Kirk said. "The band is practicing tonight. We're recording a new song this weekend to post on YouTube and we have a lot of work to do on it." Kirk and his band had spent the winter touring several locations throughout the Midwest after they had released a record. They hadn't quite reached the big time—but they were on their way. His band consisted of buddies from high school and they specialized in extreme hard rock. I can't make heads or tails of any of their lyrics and after ten minutes of trying I have a throbbing headache. I was happy his music was working for him as he would never be a farmer, for which we were all relieved. His mind was rarely on anything but music and by the time he noticed something was going wrong with equipment it was too late to fix. The responsibility of the band and the touring over the winter had made an enormous improvement in his maturity and I had been pleasantly surprised the last few months by his willingness to help on the farm and even more so by the quality of his help.

"I have a roast in the slow cooker if you have time to eat before you leave for practice?" I asked Kirk. "Nick you're welcome too."

"It sounds good to me," Nick answered. "I think Faye was planning on vegetarian lasagna. I'll take meat any day." Faye was living with Nick while she tried to find a place to live. There was only one apartment building in town, and there were no openings. She was trying to save enough money for a down payment on a house in case an apartment never opened up.

"I won't make it. Kyle is going to pick up pizzas from the bowling alley," Kirk said naming one of his band members. He took off his gloves and walked to his car saying, "I'll swing by home to shower and check on Wizard." Then he got in his car and drove away in typical Kirk style, not registering that the equipment needed to be put away.

I looked at Nick and shrugged, "Every time I think he might be growing up, he proves me wrong." Nick laughed and we spend the next half hour, filling the propane tanks, filling the water tanks, and loading the four-wheelers on the trailer so they'd be ready to transport to the next field tomorrow afternoon. After we had everything put inside, I said to Nick, "I'll meet you at the house.

Faye is welcome too if her vegetarian lasagna doesn't work out—she might want company after a day like today."

"I'll let her know, but I think Frankie was coming over tonight." Frankie Tate had held Faye's job at the dentist office before leaving to open her own mobile pet grooming business. She and Faye had become good friends while Frankie trained her. "I have to stop by my place and shower to get rid of this smoke smell, but I'll be there as soon as I can."

"I need to shower also, so give me at least a half hour before you come over," I said as I got in my pickup and drove away. My phone rang as I turned on to US Hwy 59, it was Jessica. She'd received my message about Judith. Jessica Golding was my best friend. She ran the local restaurant in Arvilla and was known for her delicious old-fashioned home cooking; items such as meatloaf, fried chicken, soups, breakfasts, burgers, and sandwiches—my sole complaint was she was only open Monday through Saturday, 6:00 a.m. – 2:00 p.m. with a brunch buffet from 12:00 p.m. – 2:00 p.m. on Sundays. She was marrying my other best friend, James Harmen. The three of us had been friends since grade school. They were a good match, both twenty-eight, Jessica a petite 5'2" with dark straight hair and James 6'2", broad shouldered with muscles built from wrangling cows and building fences. James and his mother, Karla, had a cattle ranch next door to us. Further entwining the people in my life, Karla, whose husband died 10 years ago, was in a relationship with my dad. It was hard to see Dad with someone other than my mom, but Mom had been gone for six years and though there was a seven year age gap between Dad and Karla, they were enjoying each other's company—explaining the Alaskan cruise they were now on.

"You are going to keep your nose out of this investigation?" Jessica asked after I told her what had happened to Judith and the possible meth connection.

"Don't worry—I want nothing to do with drugs," I assured her.

"I am going to miss Judith," Jessica said with sadness. She had been part of Jessica's book club for many years and Jessica knew her better than I had. We commiserated for a few moments before our talk turned to happier topics like her wedding.

"Did you decide what flavor of cake you're going to have Edna make for the wedding?" I asked knowing her and James had an appointment with Edna yesterday afternoon. Edna Forting was eight years older than Jessica and I and ran a bakery out of the main floor of her house. She was six feet tall, athletic, and her idea of fun was a sand volleyball league in the summer and a basketball league in the winter. Jessica and I, having no interest in sports, didn't do a lot with her socially but she was a good friend. Edna and Jessica were responsible for the delicious food that was offered for breakfasts and dinners when people reserved one of our cabins. Food was offered either fresh daily or the meals for a week's stay could be stocked in the cabin in advance. Most people—after explaining that in northern Minnesota dinner means a noon meal—decided against the daily delivery as they wanted as little disturbance as possible to enjoy the quiet, the plants, and the wildlife of a native prairie. I wasn't sure of their exact arrangement, but between the two of them the food was delivered, it was delicious, and best of all I had nothing to do with it other than to pass on the compliments and make sure to pay them for their efforts.

"We went back and forth between a lemon cake with lemon curd and a blueberry butter-cream frosting and a white chocolate cake with raspberries and a butter-cream frosting. We gave up and decided to have two cakes."

"It sounds delicious, do I get a piece of each or do I have to choose?" I asked laughing.

"As long as you wait until everyone has had a piece, you can have as many of the extras as you want," Jessica answered. "Everything else is falling into place, we found a caterer, a photographer, and we have a florist who's willing to help us decorate the church for the wedding and provide flowers for the reception and dance we're holding at James' place. I'm hoping for a beautiful simple wedding."

"You do know the entire town will be coming," I reminded her.

"I didn't say small, I said simple. Do you have a dress picked out yet?" she asked me.

"I ordered four last night and am hopeful one of them will work as I didn't find anything in Grand Forks, and I don't have time to drive any farther." Jessica didn't care what kind of dress it was as I was both the maid of honor and the only bridesmaid. Her only requirements were that it be full length and mauve.

"I'm sure one of them will be perfect."

"I hope you're right. I'd better end the call, Nick is coming over for supper and I need to get home and shower."

My phone rang the second after I hung up. "Hi Nick, I'm almost home. Will you be there soon?"

"There's been a change of plans. Do you think you could come over to my place? Faye isn't doing well and," he paused, "there's something we both need to tell you."

Taken aback, I answered with hesitance, "Sure. I'll turn around. I should be there in about ten minutes. I haven't made it home to shower though."

"It's okay. I haven't showered yet either, we'll both smell like smoke."

I checked my mirrors and made an illegal a u-turn, another plus of living in a sparsely populated rural area. As I drove, my stomach was in knots wondering what was going on. I hoped the trauma of the day hadn't caused Faye's progress to revert. I also wondered, based on what Nick said, if I was going to hear more about their past. I'd sensed there was more to Nick's story than he'd previously shared and I was both apprehensive and relieved that I might be going to hear more of their history.

I pulled in Nick's driveway and parked next to his pickup. His black cat was stretched out on the front steps. I leaned down to scratch his stomach. He was a unique cat in that he didn't like any-one to pet his head or back—which wasn't so strange for a cat—but he did love to have his stomach scratched. I had decided it was a true show of trust that he accepted me enough to expose his stom-ach to me.

Nick opened the door, I looked at him quizzically and he gave me a hug as he led me in the door. Faye was sitting at his kitchen table looking pale. I grabbed a chair and sat down next to Faye.

"Is Frankie coming?" I asked.

"No, we asked Frankie to stay home." Nick sat down next to me and said, "Faye got a phone call from her old roommate in California who told her Christopher had been released early from jail but hadn't checked in with his parole officer. She thought he might know Faye was here and may be on his way."

"Christopher, her abusive ex-boyfriend?" I asked.

"Yes. He's part of the real reason I came here, and after you hear what I tell you, you may never speak to me again. But before that happens I hope you can put on your amateur detective hat again, because I'm almost positive the sheriff is going to suspect that Christopher and maybe even Faye had something to do with Judith's murder," Nick answered as I looked at him in shock.

CHAPTER TWO

Prairie turnip, also called Indian breadroot,
has an enlarged root that was eaten by Plains Indians.
It has a dense spike of light bluish flowers.

DREADING WHAT I WAS GOING TO hear I turned to stare out the kitchen window. In my dazed state it was difficult to register that the sun was shining and it was a beautiful spring day. The tulips Faye had planted were emerging from the ground and the world was starting to turn a brilliant green in complete contrast to my feelings of darkness. In spite of the heat of the sun shining in the windows I hugged myself trying to get warm. I looked at Faye, then at Nick, and found his eyes looking at me with concern.

I took a deep breath and even though I wasn't sure I wanted to know, sensing whatever Nick was going to say had the potential to change everything, I asked, "Okay you two, what's going on?"

Nick and Faye looked at each other and then Nick said, "I've never been completely honest with you about how I ended up here."

"You saw my advertisement in a farm magazine and applied," I said trying to forestall whatever doom was coming.

"Yes, that is true. But what I didn't tell you was I knew about your farm before that." Seeing I was about to interrupt again Nick said, "Please let me tell you without interruption, this is hard enough and I need to get it out. You already know Faye and I share the same mother but different fathers. What you don't know is our mother was a con artist and in and out of jail often. The men she brought into our lives were content to go along with her scams, including my father and Faye's father. Each of our fathers disappeared when they found out Mom was pregnant, which is why Faye and I share our Mom's last name and not our fathers'. Others would leave when she'd be arrested as none of them wanted to be saddled with two kids that weren't even theirs. Mom had a distant cousin who would reluctantly take us in until mom would be released. The last man she brought home before she died of lung cancer was from Las Vegas and had a nephew by the name of Christopher Charles who came with him. At that time Christopher was twenty-five, Faye was seventeen, and he swept her off her feet. I was gone by then, trying to get as far away as I could. I was happy when I first heard about the two of them. Mom had died and I was glad Faye had some-one—until I came home to visit and saw the bruises." Nick stopped to swallow and looked at Faye who was now weeping in silence with her shoulders shaking. "I tried to make her walk away from him, but by then he had quite a psychological hold on her. Nothing I said could convince her, so I decided to stick around for awhile to see if I could help. I pretended to get along with Christopher and his uncle to make sure I was keeping an eye on what they were up to. I came across an article about the Karlaff farm in a magazine I found in a doctor's waiting room and was interested in your job posting listed next to the article. I brought it home to talk to Faye and try to convince her to come with me. I carelessly left it out and Christopher's uncle saw the article. He saw Chet's name and claimed that was the name of Christopher's father."

"That's ridiculous," I said interrupting him. "My dad would never have cheated on my mom."

"Now that I know Chet I don't think so either, but at the time I believed him. The uncle said his sister worked at a casino in Las Vegas and your dad was attending an agronomy convention. Christopher was the result of an affair during that convention. He and Christopher decided they were going to travel to Arvilla and attempt to get money out of your dad because Christopher was a 'long-lost son.'"

I couldn't help but point out, "Did they really think someone would pay to keep that a secret, or were they expecting Christopher to be welcomed and graced with money?"

"I'm not sure; I only overheard part of their discussion, but I know they felt confident they could get money out of it somehow. Without knowing Chet, the story sounded crazy enough to be true. After all, they had to know DNA would prove or disprove their claim—they must have believed it. I heard Christopher's uncle say something about stolen money also. To be honest, I didn't care what the reason was as long as it would get Christopher away from Faye. Before they could leave, they were both arrested for a real estate scam. I don't know how they did it, but somehow they would pretend to own a piece of property and sell it to wealthy people who were more naïve than wise. Christopher and his uncle would disappear with the down payment long before the supposed buyer would figure out the deed was fake. It was their favorite and most lucrative scam. Faye felt safe with them in jail and didn't want to come to Minnesota so I got her settled in an apartment with a friend of hers in California, in a big city far from Oregon, and I decided to come here and apply for the job after all. I think if I'm being honest I wanted to check out you and your dad, and be here if Christopher and his uncle ever showed up."

"Why didn't you tell me about this when I hired you?" I asked trying to wrap my head around what sounded like a ridiculous story.

"Would you have hired me?" Nick asked.

Realizing I could hardly believe this story after knowing Nick for almost eight months, I had to acknowledge, "No, probably not.

So when nothing happened, why didn't you tell me then? We've been dating for six months, you could have told me."

"I guess I didn't want to rock the boat. Once I got here I found I enjoyed the job and getting to know you is the best thing that has ever happened to me," Nick said as he looked down at his hands on the table.

"That's not all, is it?" I paused looking at Nick and Faye as they both continued to avoid catching my eye. "There is something more isn't there? What is it you aren't telling me? You've avoided telling me about your past since you showed up. What is so bad that you won't tell me?"

Nick gave a big sigh and said, "When Christopher and his uncle got arrested, I was the one who turned them in."

"So," I repeated, "what was so terrible about that?"

"I lied to the cops, I knew what they were doing, but I had never witnessed it first-hand. I claimed I had and then I helped the buyer and the police identify them. I knew where they hid their paperwork and I led the cops to it. When the cops arrested them, Christopher and his uncle knew I was responsible. I'm not proud of lying, but I figured the means justified the end. I didn't want you to know anything about any of this, but it was yet another reason for coming here. If they ever showed up and tried to claimed a part of your farm—either with some sort of real estate scam or because Christopher thought he was Chet's son and deserved it—I wanted to be physically here and available to help if I could."

"I think you were selling me short. None of this sounds so bad that you couldn't have told me."

"I do have a record." Nick stated in a flat tone as he stared at the floor.

"What? That's not possible. I ran a back-ground check on you," I replied reeling.

"The records are sealed as I was a minor." He looked up meeting my eyes and said, "Most mothers would tell their child to get a job when they asked for money. My mom taught us to steal when we needed money."

Faye piped up, "Mom would dress me in rags; then take me to stand on corners begging for money."

Nick continued, "When I was in elementary school she had me go around with fake brochures selling various products for made-up school fundraisers. She'd drop me off in neighborhoods far from where we lived, and would pick me up a couple hours later. When I got too old for that, she had me start delivering packages of money for bookie friends of hers and shoplift. My luck ran out and I was arrested when I was sixteen. I was humiliated and when I got out of the juvenile detention center I left home. I slept on friends' couches until I graduated high school and then left. I wanted to take Faye with me, but she was only eight years old." He hung his head in shame and said, "I hate that I abandoned my sister."

"Again, why didn't you tell me, and better yet—something I've been wondering about for a while—why did you never tell me about having a half-sister?"

"It's kind of hard to tell the woman you're dating, who has a warm, loving relationship with her brother and father; that I come from a mother who never earned an honest penny in her life, taught us to do the same, dragged a multitude of men through Faye and my lives, and I don't even know who my father is. On top of that, I was arrested as a teenager and my half sister, who I abandoned, was involved with a scheming con man and woman beater. And oh, by the way, at some point that same con man may follow me here and involve you in my messed up past. I was considering leaving, even though it would have killed me to leave you, but I was confident Christopher and his uncle would show up one day and you would need my help. As I was considering if you'd be better off without me, Faye called and said Christopher's uncle died in jail and Christopher had been released early. He'd found her and beat her again. That's why last fall I left. Christopher was arrested again, this time for assault, and I tried to convince Faye to come live with me. She initially turned me down, but changed her mind a month later. I believed it was safe to bring her here, because I thought a second offense—in a different state no less—would keep Christopher in jail, but now we know he's out and more than likely heading here."

"Why was your friend so sure he is heading here?" I questioned Faye.

"Her brother was a guard in the facility where Christopher was serving time. Apparently Christopher had made it known he was planning to look for his wealthy father and reconnect with his girlfriend when he was released."

"How does he know you are in Arvilla?" I asked.

"I told him Nick was working here when Christopher found me in California and that Nick wanted me to come live with him." Faye admitted.

"When he beat it out of you," Nick said as he interrupted. "I'm sure he plans some sort of revenge on me."

Faye shrugged her shoulders helplessly and with a trembling voice said, "I shouldn't have told him."

Feeling bad for her I stated, "I guess it doesn't matter, he believes his father is here and would have come regardless."

"But we didn't need to be endangering your family. Knowing Faye and I are here too is most likely angering him even more." Nick insisted sounding upset.

"Do you think he's coming here for Faye, revenge on you Nick, revenge on his father for abandoning him, or for his imaginary inheritance?" I asked.

"I imagine all of the above, but I'm sure money is the primary motive. I do know your dad could never be Christopher's father and I've been trying to figure out who it could have been. Someone must have used Chet's name, as Christopher and his uncle were positive and it could be so easily disproved. I talked to your dad—on a pretext of wondering if he'd ever been to Las Vegas—he couldn't remember the exact year, but about thirty years ago he and your mom had been there for a convention. It was a sponsored trip from the local agronomy company as a thank you for products ordered. He said there were quite a few farmers from here that went on the trip. I came to the conclusion one of them must have used his name. I didn't dare ask your dad any more questions without him getting suspicious. I went to the library and looked through the newspaper archives on the off chance local farmers going to the convention would have been newsworthy enough to have it mentioned in the newspaper. I found a picture of the group before they got on the bus, but no names were listed. I printed a copy of it. Then one evening when I was over at James' house I brought out the picture on the pretense of wanting to get to know the names of some of the locals. I'm sure James suspected something, as who would use a copy of a thirty year old newspaper photo to learn names of people, but he was distracted as Karla was there and started reminiscing when she saw the photo—she and her now deceased husband attended also. After a few discrete questions I found out which of the men pictured were unaccompanied by a spouse or a significant other. I narrowed it down to four men, Al Mitchel, Jed Alman, Cord McCaster and Owen Laterly. They were the only men not accompanied by anyone."

"Why are you so sure it was one of them—someone could have cheated on their spouse whether or not the spouse was with?" I questioned.

"I don't know for sure, but Christopher talked as though his mom spent a lot of time with the man in the short time they were there—I can't imagine a spouse putting up with that."

"True." I nodded. "If they believed my dad was Christopher's father why wasn't his last name Karlaff instead of Charles and why didn't Christopher's mother ever track down the father?" I asked.

"I asked Christopher that same question," Faye said, "and he didn't know. He said his uncle claimed she never told anyone who it was until she was dying, and then only told his uncle on her death bed. His uncle told Christopher she had kept it a secret until then because she was deathly scared of the man. Whoever Christopher's father was, he must have threatened her with something significant as she never even contacted him for help with child support when she found out she was pregnant; and from what she told his uncle she believed the man was wealthy."

"Do you know anything about any of these men?" Nick asked.

"I haven't dared ask any more questions myself."

"Al is a big cattle rancher a couple miles west of our place. I don't know Jed well; he's retired, but did have a pretty big farm. His son-in-law is farming it now. You might know him, Faye. Jill, the dental hygienist, is his daughter." I said and looked at Faye.

"I recognize the name, but only because Jill has mentioned her father. I don't know him." She replied.

I continued sharing what I knew about the men Nick had listed. "Cord never had much success farming, his farmland wasn't prime land and the majority of it was high and dry ridge land. I think he sold or is leasing most of his land to a gravel company. He's making a lot more money now than he ever did farming. I'm not positive who Owen is. The name sounds familiar, I think he owns several buildings in town, but I'm not sure why he'd have been on an agronomy company sponsored trip. Are you planning on talking to them?"

"I'd like to talk to them and warn them about Christopher, but I'm not sure which one it is, and I am finding it difficult to approach a man I don't know and say, hey, thirty years ago did you claim to be someone else and have an affair in Las Vegas? And by the way, you may have a son."

I nodded as I acknowledged the impossibility of doing this. "Al and Cord go to our church. I can introduce you if you'd like, but I don't yet understand why you didn't feel you could tell me any of this?" I asked.

Nick looked down, started to say something, stopped, and looked up at me before finally saying, "I'm not sure you realize how being from a rural area with a not very diverse population skews the thoughts of people."

"What do you mean?" I asked, not understanding where he was going.

"In my almost eight months here I have witnessed many people assume someone's character is the same as the families they come from. If a family has members that are known to be lazy, petty thieves, or have alcohol problems, the whole family is assumed to be the same. I didn't want you to make the same assumptions about me based on my family. Why do you think the sheriff has been so suspicious of me?"

"He knows about your past?" I asked in amazement.

"He found out about my juvenile record when Jessica's brother was killed which is why he wasted time looking at me as a suspect."

"I wouldn't judge you for your past," I insisted shocked that he would think that of me.

Nick wouldn't meet my eyes as he asked, "Are you so sure about that?"

I started to sputter, and then stopped. I thought back to what I thought of certain families in the area and to my chagrin I realized Nick may have a point. "I guess I like to think I'm better than that, but if I'm being honest, perhaps not. But after I got to know you, you should have known that I would have accepted you."

"I know, but by then it felt a little late to tell you my family is pretty messed up and I have an arrest record."

I sighed. "Okay, where do we go from here? Why do you think the sheriff is going to accuse Faye and Christopher of killing Judith?"

"I believe once we tell him about Christopher he's going to assume Christopher shot Judith by mistake in an attempt to get revenge on Faye," Nick said.

"I can't imagine he would think that. . ." and then I stopped realizing Nick could be correct. The sheriff had been known to blindly follow the easiest answer. "That may be, but we do have to tell him about Christopher. He needs to be aware of Christopher and the danger to Faye and you, as I'm assuming he's looking for revenge on you also for your part in putting him in jail. Do you have a picture of Christopher to show the sheriff?"

"I do," Faye said, and she got up and went over to her purse and came back with a picture.

Christopher was a good-looking man—blond, tanned, with an earring. I handed the picture back to her and said, "Maybe Sheriff Poole will surprise us and be helpful."

Nick grimaced and said, "We can hope, but yes, Faye and I plan to talk to him tomorrow. He needs to be aware of what is going on, but we felt you should know everything before the sheriff does, plus I want you to be ultra vigilant. Judith's murder will leave the Sheriff's Department stretched thin, and more than likely any concern about Christopher, if the sheriff does take us seriously, will slip through the cracks. Our primary advantage is people tend to notice strangers, so I'm hopeful Christopher's presence will be noted if he does show up. I wish your dad was home so you weren't in the house by yourself. I know Kirk is around, but he's gone a lot with his band."

"I have Wizard to protect me," I said with a laugh, "besides it's bound to take him some time to get here and Dad will be back soon."

"I'm not so sure about that," Faye said. "Christopher was released a few weeks ago. My friend didn't have my new cell phone number and it took her this long to track me down."

"That isn't good, but I can't imagine I have much to worry about for myself. I'm more worried about you two, if he is here, his first objective will be you."

"I know. After we talk to the sheriff tomorrow, I plan to buy security cameras and install them around our place. I'll drive Faye to work and she's going to ask Frankie if she can stay at her place or help her with her grooming until I'm done with work and can pick her up."

"I hope he is found soon." I stated feeling myself get anxious for them.

"Me too," Nick said. "I'll be at work as soon as I can tomorrow to help with burning after I talk to the sheriff."

"Take your time, there is supposed to be dew in the morning so we won't get started until around noon anyway. I can get the shipment ready and the seed order mixed by myself." I yawned and said, "I'd better get home."

Nick walked me out to my pickup. "Are we okay?" he asked.

I hesitated and then said, "Yes. I can't pretend I'm not hurt that you didn't feel you could trust me, but at the same time I don't like that the picture you painted of myself and my community may have some truth to it. We can be discriminating."

"I'm sorry," Nick said. "If it helps, I know this is a good community and even with a tendency to judge, everyone appears to rally around to help people regardless of what is thought about them."

"I know, but you've given me something to think about." I kissed Nick goodnight, got in my pickup and drove for home. The visit with Nick and Faye had made me anxious so it was nice to see Kirk's vehicle home and the lights on. When I walked in the house I could hear music coming from Kirks' room and a muffled bark from Wizard.

Kirk poked his head out of his room. "Did you have a good practice?" I asked not wanting to get into Nick's story tonight.

"Yep, I put away the stuff you had in the slow cooker. It didn't look like you ate, but I assumed you and Nick must have gone out to eat." He studied me, and then asked, "Are you okay, or as okay as you can be after Judith's murder?"

"It's been a long day," I said; realizing Judith's murder now felt like it had happened weeks ago. "I'm heading to bed."

"I'll see you in the morning. I let Tabitha out when I got home." He closed his bedroom door.

Before heading upstairs I peeked out the door to see if Tabitha was waiting to be let in. She wasn't, so I locked the door, turned off the lights and went upstairs hoping for a good night's rest knowing it was unlikely.

CHAPTER THREE

Bracted spiderwort is a plant up to three feet in height with small clusters of inch-wide, medium purple flowers at the top of the stem. Perhaps gets its name as it was once considered a cure for spider bites.

I WAS JOLTED AWAKE FRIDAY MORNING WITH the sudden realization that not only had I slept surprisingly well, but one of the next cabin guests was arriving today at 3:00 p.m. and the other tomorrow. The one cabin that had been rented the previous week had checked out early Wednesday night due to an emergency in their family. I had cleaned the cabin after they left, but in the frenzy of yesterday I had completely forgotten about the other cabin. I had planned to put fresh sheets on the beds and do a quick spruce up cleaning yesterday after the burning was finished. I checked the time; it was 6:00 a.m. With any luck I should have plenty of time to stop by the cabins before I had to be at the seed plant to mix the seed order and have it ready by ten. The semi from the shipping company would be there at eleven to pick up the blue grama which would give me enough time to get that order together after the seed mix was done. I threw on clothes, raced down the stairs, and amazed myself by managing to not trip on a dog toy Wizard left on the stairway. Kirk wasn't awake yet. I opened his door as quiet as I could to let Wizard out to take care of his business while I ate. Tabitha came running in when I opened the door. I was thankfully alert enough to cover the dead mouse she had left on the porch with my slipper before Wizard grabbed it. I knew if he had swallowed it, I'd have been cleaning up puke in the house sometime later today. I fed Tabitha while my bread toasted and the coffee finished. By the time I ate my toast and peanut butter, Tabitha had finished eating and went back outside when I let Wizard in. I could see Clyde, our old tom cat, peeking out of the cat door in the garage. Clyde had a distrust of the house and I've never been able to get him inside. He didn't suffer as he had a heated garage with food and water that Tabitha would share with him when she wasn't inside. We also had one other outdoor, rarely seen cat which had a separate spot with food and a heat lamp in another little shed. He was feral for the most part, and must have been dropped off by someone as he showed up here about a year ago already neutered. He thanks us for the room and board by being the best mouser of the bunch. I stuck Wizard back in Kirk's room giving him less chance for getting into mischief until Kirk woke up. I grabbed my insulated coffee mug, filled it, and head out the door. I loved spring mornings, sun just coming up, no bugs yet, warm—but not hot temperatures and the sound of robins singing. I raced to the cabin site thankful I had put the sheets in my pickup yesterday morning and that I'd had the foresight to put them in an airtight bag so they weren't dirty from riding around in my pickup all day. A doe and her fawn were startled and ran off when I drove up to the cabins. We only had two of the cabins rented for the week. The first occupant, Hugh Murkins, a cousin of the local banker, was arriving today, and the Erickson's, who were a couple from Maple Grove, Minnesota, were coming tomorrow. I opened the windows, made sure the screens were intact and put sheets on the bed. I did a quick dusting, swept, and made sure the supplies like facial tissues and toilet paper were well stocked. I decided to leave the windows open and looked at the time. It was only eight, plenty of time to get to the seed plant and do the seed mix. One hour and forty-five minutes later, I was dusting off my clothes, and starving. I had finished the seed mix and had the blue grama order shrink-wrapped and waiting on a pallet for the semi-truck. The driver knew our operation, having been here many times and would load the seed himself. I walked over to the break room to check if there was anything there to snack on. As I opened the door, Nick drove in.

"I didn't expect to see you so soon." I said to him as he got out of his pickup. "It must have gone alright at the Sheriff's Department."

"I'm beginning to understand your difficulties with the sheriff," Nick stated looking frustrated.

"I don't mind him as much anymore. He was even helpful with the last fiasco I was involved in."

"Maybe so, but he didn't have too much time for Faye and I today. He told us to let him know when Christopher showed up, as he didn't have the time to worry about someone who wasn't even here."

"I'm sorry. But I'm sure Judith's murder has him rattled. Look on the bright side, at least he didn't tie Faye and Christopher to Judith's murder like you feared he would."

"True, but I didn't appreciate his lackadaisical attitude. Christopher is not someone to think is harmless."

"Where is Faye now?"

"I left her at the dental office."

"I'm surprised it's open."

"Jill debated about closing, but decided the best way to honor Judith was to keep her clinic open until Judith's husband, Dan, decides what to do. They are continuing, but only with teeth cleanings for now. Did you get the seed order mixed and the shipment ready?"

"I just finished and was heading over here to see if there was anything to snack on."

"I think you're out of luck, I finished off the last bag of chips yesterday and I don't remember seeing anything else in there. I do need to go to the four-wheeler dealership to pick up a part. If you're free you can ride along and we'll grab something to eat on the way."

"I can't, the seed customer should be here in a few minutes." As I finished saying this, a pickup and trailer pulled off the highway and drove up to us.

"Is this where I pick up my CRP seed?" he asked when I walked up to his pickup window.

"It is. If you could drive over to the overhead door I'll load your trailer with the forklift."

He drove towards the door, and I said to Nick, "If you can wait, this shouldn't take but ten minutes and I'll come with you." I started to walk away and then remembered, "While you're waiting could you call Gary and see if he could help with the burning this afternoon? I have a cabin guest arriving and will have to be gone for a short time if Gary could fill in for me."

"I'll give him a call," Nick answered as I walked away.

Ten minutes later I had the customer loaded, paperwork filled out and a check in my pocket. Nick drove up and I got in his pickup. "Can Gary help?"

"Yep, he'll be here at one. Kirk is going to help also I hope?"

"He better be here."

"Do you need to call and remind him?"

"I'm not planning to. This record business and touring has forced Kirk to grow up. He's been surprising Dad and I with his new-found responsibility the last couple of months." My brother Kirk is a wonderful person, but in the past he has not been known to be particularly helpful when it came to the farm. It was nice to have an extra body around, but to be honest his lack of skills weren't missed much when he was unable to be here.

"I thought so too, but wasn't sure I should say anything in case I was becoming delusional."

I laughed, "Talking about Kirk reminds me that I need to get to the high school to visit with April Hewsy. Kirk let me know that their touring dates will have him gone most of the summer, so I have to find help for the rogueing crew."

"Who's April Hewsy?" Nick asked.

"She's the guidance counselor at the school. Jessica suggested I visit with her to get a few names of reliable kids who are graduating this spring and would be the necessary eighteen years of age for any handling of herbicides. I keep forgetting to call and make an appointment with her. Anyway, so where do you want to grab something to eat? It has to be someplace quick."

"Would you rather go to the Dairy Queen or swing by the convenience store?" Nick asked.

"We better try the convenience store, it's close to noon and the Dairy Queen drive-through will be packed. Too bad we didn't think ahead we could have ordered from Jessica's restaurant. Her meatloaf and mashed potatoes would have really hit the spot," I responded making myself even hungrier thinking about it.

"The convenience store works for me, I like their individual pizzas," Nick said as he pulled in the parking lot. He grabbed a pepperoni pizza and I picked out chicken strips. We found a bag of chips to share and then were on our way to the Kentz's four-wheeler dealership. When we drove in I whistled.

"I haven't been here for at least six months. Either you or Kirk has picked up parts. Their business must be booming; the expansion is impressive." Since I had last been here they had added on to their shop, almost doubling the size of it, added a show room for new four-wheelers and ATV's, and had paved their parking lot.

"I was talking to Tony Kentz the last time I was here. His son, Cory moved back home. Cory made a lot of money flipping houses and invested it back in his dad's dealership. Now with the two of them working they're gaining a lot of new business, even getting customers from North Dakota and Canada," Nick said.

"That's great. I don't remember his son that well, he was four or five years older than me, but if my memory is correct, he was quite wild and Tony was worried about him. It doesn't look like he needed to be. Tony has been fixing our four-wheelers and ATV's for years and does a great job. I'm glad the business is going well for him." Nick and I got out of the pickup. I stood by the door and looked around at the improvements while Nick walked in to pick up the part.

"It looks good doesn't it?" A voice behind me said startling me.

I turned around, "Hi Tony, yes it does. It's obvious I haven't been here in a while as I missed all this."

"My son, Cory, is responsible for a lot of it. It's good to have him home. We had our problems while he was growing up and to be honest I never thought I'd see him back here. But not only is he back, he invested in this place."

"He must have done well for himself. What did he do?" I asked, my nosiness as usual coming to the forefront.

"He and a buddy spent five years fixing up houses and selling them in the Sioux Falls, South Dakota, area. They had a lot of success," Tony said with pride.

"I'm happy for you that he moved home." Nick walked up to us holding a bag. "We'd better get moving; we have to burn this afternoon."

"Be safe," Tony told us as we got in the pickup.

"Now that's one proud father," I said as we drove away.

"I think he has reason to be," Nick agreed.

I looked at the time on my phone, "We should be back in plenty of time to get things ready for the burn before Gary and Kirk show up. I'll have to leave by 2:30 p.m. to check my cabin guest in. It's a forty acre field so there shouldn't be much left when I leave other than to watch it burn. I'll stink like smoke, but it can't be helped." When we got back to the seed plant I checked to make sure the shipment had been picked up. The pallets were gone. I grabbed the signed paperwork and took it over to the break room. I then hooked up to the trailer with the four-wheelers while Nick got on the tractor with the water tank behind it. We drove the short half mile drive to the field where I was surprised to find Kirk already waiting. Gary drove in behind us. I called to activate my burning permit and I also called the Sheriff's Department while the guys unloaded and then we took a few minutes to strategize. Kirk took off on the tractor putting in a wet line ahead of us while Nick and I started lighting a back burn behind him. Gary was lookout and took off on a four-wheeler with a water tank on the back of it to keep watch in case the fire jumped anywhere. It was hard for the people lighting the fire to know what was going on as the smoke made it difficult, if not impossible, to see anywhere but in front them. The wind was perfect and the field was merely smoldering in a few spots when it was time for me to leave. I grabbed Kirk's car knowing he'd catch a ride back with Nick or Gary and drove back to the break room where my pickup was. I took a few minutes to use the restroom and wash my face and hands. I then blasted down the highway to the cabin site, beating Hugh there. I wanted to check the inside of the cabin to make sure either Edna or Jessica had delivered the food before he showed up but I didn't dare, knowing the smoke smell from my clothes would transfer in to the cabin. I didn't wait long, a blue SUV pulled in and parked next to my pickup. A tall, heavyset man with dark hair who appeared to be in his early 40's got out and walked towards me.

I held out my hand, "Hugh Murkins?" I asked. When he nodded I went on to say, "I'm Carmen Karlaff. It's nice to meet you. I understand you have ties to the community."

"Yes. My cousin, Peter Inver, works in the bank in town."

"I know him well; he's been my family's banker for about fifteen years now. Welcome to our humble cabins. Do you need help with anything?"

"No, I should be good. I packed light; all I intend on doing is connecting with Peter as I haven't seen him for a few years and also enjoying the peace and quiet."

"We can provide that. Here are the keys and if you could do me a favor before I leave you to your solitude could you open the cabin and make sure the food is there and see if you are missing something you think you might need. I'd do it myself, but I'm fresh from a fire and I think the smoke smell would transfer to the cabin if I went in."

"I can. I chose the food to be pre-delivered, would that be in the freezer or refrigerator?"

"A little bit of both. I would imagine today's and tomorrow's food would be in your refrigerator and the rest in your freezer. Snacks and beverages are on your own should you need them but there tends to be more than enough."

"I'm sure there will be," he said and disappeared inside the cabin, coming out after about five minutes. "Everything looks more than adequate. The refrigerator and the freezer on top are packed. It doesn't look like I'll even need to find an evening meal."

I laughed, "You may be right. You have a great time and if you need anything my cell phone number is in the paperwork sitting on the table. Please don't hesitate to call."

I turned to leave and he said, "What do you mean you were in a fire? I hope nothing serious?"

"Not at all, my family's primary business is a native grass and wildflower seed farm. Our crops need fire to maximize their seed production. Spring tends to be busy with burning, spreading fertilizer, selling seed and mixing seed orders."

"And you are doing cabin rentals also? Do you have a big family to help?"

"My father helps on occasion, but he is retired. I have a brother who also helps when he can, but he is pursuing a music career. I do have excellent hired help."

"I hope so. How long does it take you to burn all your fields?"

"If we get the right winds, around ten days takes care of it. We started this week and have about another seven days left. You don't have anything to worry about though, we don't burn anything close to the cabins—you won't get smoked out," I said with a smile. "But I do need to get back. Again, if you need anything don't hesitate to call."

"I won't."

I walked to my pickup, got in, and drove away as Hugh started hauling a couple of bags inside the cabin. I got back to the break room as the guys drove up.

"Thanks for your help today Gary. Will you be able to help tomorrow also? I have another cabin guest arriving."

"That won't be a problem. What time do you want me here?"

"There isn't supposed to be any dew tomorrow, so we can start burning earlier. Can you make it by ten?"

"I'll see you then," Gary replied as he got in his car and drove away.

"That was a successful burn," Nick commented as he worked on loosening the chains to unload the four-wheelers so Kirk could take them over to the outdoor spigot where we filled the water tanks.

As I started to help him and I asked, "Do you have any plans for tonight?"

"Not yet," Nick replied with a suggestive look at me.

I laughed. "Back down. I was wondering if you and Faye would like to go out to eat for supper? I thought it would be good for her to get out of the house and take her mind off Judith's murder and Christopher, plus there will be safety in numbers."

"I'm sure she'd appreciate it. I'll call her right now." Nick stepped away to make the phone call as Kirk came back for the last four-wheeler.

"Are you and Nick busy tonight?" he asked me.

"We're working on planning something with Faye right now. Did you want to come with? No, that's right; the band has a performance tonight doesn't it?"

"Yes, we do. I wanted to make sure you weren't home alone tonight, I know you're getting used to finding dead people," he nudged me, his smile letting me know he was teasing, "but Judith getting shot practically in front of you has to be bothering you."

My brother was concerned for me, he was growing up. "Thanks, but I'm doing okay. Judith was a friend, not a close one, but yes it was shocking," I admitted.

"You aren't going to get involved in the sheriff's investigation are you?" he asked.

"I have no plans to get involved. The sheriff hasn't falsely accused anyone I know is innocent," I answered smiling.

"Yet, anyway," Kirk said.

"Don't even think that," I said to him as Nick joined us.

"Faye is ready to go out, but she was wondering if Frankie and George could join us. I told her yes, as I knew you wouldn't mind. Frankie and George will meet the three of us at Wally's at six," Nick said naming the new steakhouse that had opened two weeks ago.

"That's great!" I looked at my phone and saw it was 5:30 p.m. "I need to get home and take a shower."

Nick said, "I'll pick you up at your place."

"Thanks," I said.

As I looked around, Kirk said, "I'll finish up here, you guys go ahead. I don't need to meet up with the band until eight so I have plenty of time."

"Thanks," both Nick and I said as we raced for our vehicles.

I drove home, mentally reviewing my closet trying to figure out what to wear knowing time was limited and I wouldn't be able to try on multiple outfits as I was prone to do. I parked and as I walked to the house I noticed Tabitha and Clyde sleeping together on a lawn chair cushion. I let Wizard out in the fenced-in backyard while I showered and dressed. I decided on casual, yet dressy, which for me meant a simple light-weight dress with white sneakers. I hadn't been to Wally's yet, but I couldn't imagine a steakhouse in Arvilla would have a dress code. I let Wizard in, took a quick look around to make sure I hadn't left anything out he could destroy and was walking out the door when Nick and Faye drove up. Faye got out so I could sit next to Nick.

"You didn't have to do that," I said to her as I got in.

"Yes, I did. I can't be responsible for my brother's girlfriend not sitting next to him."

I smiled; her words making me feel a bit shy. Nick and I had been dating for quite a few months now, but it was new enough that it felt strange when someone called me Nick's girlfriend. "How are you doing Faye? Did work go okay today?"

"It was busy, so that was good, but it was also bad as everyone wanted to ask about what happened to Judith and theorize who might have killed her. I could have done without that."

"What did you say to them?"

"I said nothing. I would nod and say, 'that's interesting', but not offer anything further. That shut most people up, but there are always a few that don't take a hint."

"Did anybody have any interesting theories?" I asked recognizing too late my nosiness was making me one of those people. "Sorry," I said. "This is supposed to be a night away from thinking about it."

She laughed, "I know you can't help yourself. Nick may have mentioned a few times how you tend to stick your nose into murder investigations. There were plenty of strange theories, none of which had any basis in reality in my opinion. And because I know you'll try very hard not to ask about it in an effort to prove Nick wrong, I'll go ahead and tell you. A few people thought it was the new principal at the high school."

"Why him?"

"A couple people think Judith and he were having an affair as they were seen together several times. The theory was when she wouldn't leave her husband, Dan, for him he shot her."

I laughed, "That is a quite a leap. It's kind of hard in a town this size to not be seen with a person that isn't your spouse."

"Not only that, but everyone knows Judith and Dan were devoted. Yet, it is strange that Judith and the principal were seen together anywhere as they didn't have any kids in the high school. Another person thought the new veterinarian might have killed her, as Judith was seen with her also. Another theory was a drug deal gone wrong with people assuming Judith was dealing drugs out of the office as there had been rumors about meth being available from someone in town. I know that's false, as Judith is the one who was concerned about meth. I have to say the most unsettling thing to me was how often the "new" person was suspected. What does it take to not be considered "new" in this town? I understand the high school principal has been here over two years and people continue to call him new?" Faye asked exasperated.

"You're correct, I never thought about it before, but I've been guilty too. It's something to consider, I guess a person should just refer to them by their name," I said acknowledging the truth of Faye's words. Unable to stifle my curiousness, as it coincided with what Judith had told me, I asked, "Who said meth was available from somebody in town?"

"Melanie Wylie," she answered. "But the most disturbing thought someone voiced is that it was a stranger who killed Judith."

"Why would that be disturbing? I think that answer would be the best—it was a stranger who then disappeared."

"But what if it was Christopher; and Judith got shot by mistake and he was after me like we thought the sheriff might believe?" Faye asked, her voice starting to shake.

Trying to reassure her I replied, "I don't think you have to worry about that theory, someone would have noticed a stranger in town. Also, if it was Christopher, he would have had to ask where you work—and someone would have remembered that and told the sheriff." While I was talking, Nick had parked in Wally's parking lot. We got out of the pickup; I hugged Faye and asked them both, "Do you want to go out to eat, we can go home instead?"

"No I want to do this. I need something to distract me," Faye answered. She squared her shoulders and started walking towards the front door.

Nick and I looked at each other, shrugged and hurried after her. Frankie and George were waiting for us in the entry, holding hands. Frankie Tate was barely five feet tall with vivid red hair. George Munson was a small, shy, unassuming man with a balding head. He was Jessica's right-hand man at her restaurant.

"Hi guys. It will be a ten minute wait," Frankie said as we sat down next to them.

"How is your mobile pet grooming business going?" I asked her.

"Great! I've been pleasantly surprised by how busy I've been. I wasn't sure there was enough population here to support the business, but I've been booked for at least five hours of every day and I am paying my bills with a little extra to spare. I have been amazed that I haven't had a visit from Wizard yet," she said with a grin. Wizard's reputation was well known.

I laughed, "So far, knock on wood, I haven't needed your services yet. But don't worry; it's only a matter of time before Wizard finds something foul to roll in." We spent the wait time for our table visiting about various things until the hostess came to seat us. I was impressed with the restaurant. The décor was grays and blacks with elegant tables and booths to choose from. The music was quiet and the carpeting further muted noise which allowed the conversation at our table to flow naturally, allowing everyone to hear. The menu was vast making it difficult to choose an entree. It was fortunate they were only open in the evenings or they might steal some of Jessica's business. At one point Jill Farris came over to say hello. She and her husband were out for supper also.

After she greeted us I asked her, "Judith mentioned a problem with meth during my appointment and I would expect the sheriff would lean towards that being a reason for her murder. You clean teeth, did you ever notice anyone with bad teeth or can't you name anyone either?"

Jill surprised me by answering, "I'll tell you what I told the sheriff, I don't care about my license, if it helps catch whoever killed Judith. It's hard to say for sure if a person's teeth problems are a result of meth, bad eating habits or bad oral hygiene, but I can say

Al Mitchel, Cory Kentz, Nolan Richland, Sally Stewart, and Owen Laterly have been repeat patients as of late. I also gave the sheriff the names of a few teenagers, but I don't feel comfortable repeating any minor's names."

"Who are Sally Steward and Nolan Richland?" I asked as I wasn't familiar with those names.

"Nolan is the new high school principal and Sally is the new veterinarian," Jill answered.

I caught Faye's eye and we smiled at each other, thinking of our earlier conversation about how long someone had to live here to lose the "new" designation.

After Jill left I asked Faye, "Do you think there is any basis for what she said about any of those people?"

"I wouldn't put too much stock in anything she says. To be honest, she's not a nice person. I don't know anything about Cory, but Sally told me bad teeth were hereditary in her family, Al and Owen are older men, and Jill doesn't like the principal as her son got in trouble at school and he suspended him for a week. I get along with her, because I have to, but I don't like her."

Frankie chimed in, "I never liked Jill either. She never has anything good to say about anyone other than her dad and her kids. I have never even heard her say anything good about her own husband."

The waiter brought our food to the table and the conversation stopped while we dug into our meals. I whispered to Nick after we had taken a few bites, "It was interesting Jill mentioned cattle rancher Al and Owen who owns buildings in town. They were on your list as possible fathers for Christopher. Do you think there could be any connection between Christopher, Al, Owen, or Judith?"

Nick thought for a moment while he chewed. After he swallowed he whispered back, "I don't see how."

I didn't think so either, but I filed it away in the back of mind as something to remember. The rest of the evening we avoided all talk of Judith's murder. It was nice to see Faye relax and enjoy herself.

George surprised me by how his relationship with Frankie had taken him out of his shell. He and Nick carried on a conversation about car engines while Frankie, Faye, and I talked about a variety of things from the happenings around town to Jessica and James' upcoming wedding. The time flew and before we knew it, it was nine and time to leave. We left a big tip to make up for keeping the table for so long, but I had been watching and there were always a few open tables. I didn't think we had caused any problems.

"Does anyone want to go somewhere else; it's Friday night and early yet?" Frankie asked when we walked out the door.

"I'm game," Faye answered.

"Not me, we have to burn tomorrow and I have more guests checking in a cabin. I don't want to ruin the fun; if someone can run me home, you folks can continue with the night."

"I imagine you're not too anxious to stay out any later either?" Faye asked Nick.

"We can bring Faye home," George offered.

"That works for me," Nick said. "I'm bushed."

He looked at Faye, again waiting for her confirmation that it was okay if he left, no doubt thinking about Christopher. She nodded okay. We waved goodbye to them as we got in Nick's pickup.

"That was a fun night," Nick said. "Frankie and George make a good couple."

"They do. Do you think we do too?" I asked attempting to flirt and taking hold of Nick's hand. He did me one better, leaning over and kissing me.

He started the pickup and we drove towards my house. "You said you had more guests coming tomorrow? Is the cabin venture going well?"

"It is. I don't have all three cabins rented every week this spring, but starting in June all three are reserved through the fall and I continue to get calls. I'm hoping when I review the income from them at the end of the year I'll be able to afford someone to handle the check-ins and cleaning. I hadn't planned for check-ins to take up as much time as they do. If I could force everyone to arrive at the same time it would help, but that isn't realistic. I've also been looking for someone to clean them all winter with no luck."

"It may be for the best that you are there when they check-in. I'm sure they appreciate the owner greeting them and it doesn't appear to take too much of your time."

"No, I guess it doesn't. But it is a pain to be running back and forth." I stopped myself and said, "But I shouldn't be complaining. It was my dream to get these cabins up and running."

"Careful what you wish for," Nick said smiling at me.

"That's for sure, after all I wished for a man in my life and I ended up with you," I said teasing him.

"Ouch," Nick said. "Are you okay with what Faye and I told you about our past?"

I considered for a few moments and then said, "It was hard to realize you had a huge part of your history that you were uncomfortable telling me about, but I have to admit you had some basis for your worry. As much as it pains me to admit, I might have viewed you differently if I had known about everything before getting to know you, and I'm sorry."

"I know," Nick answered. "I'm thankful things worked out. They did, didn't they?"

"You know they did. I don't know if you are aware of this yet, but I am crazy about you," I answered him as I blushed.

"I feel the same about you," he responded while squeezing my hand.

"Faye appeared okay once we got to the restaurant," I stated trying to change the subject as I wasn't very good at mushy things.

"Yeah, she does better around people. She's more social than I am. I hope she doesn't find small town life too confining. I'm enjoying having her here."

"She's appears happy."

"So far, but I wonder what Christopher will do, if he will follow her here or not?"

"It is kind of hard for a stranger to not stand out around here," I offered.

"I doubt he'll make his presence obvious. It wouldn't take much to fly in here quick, ask a few questions, locate her, and cause problems before anyone connects the dots."

"We'll protect her," I said trying to sound confident.

"I know. Thanks."

We drove in the yard and parked. "Did you want to come in?" I asked not looking forward to walking in an empty house after talking about Christopher. I knew Kirk would be home late.

Something in my voice must have sounded off as Nick looked at me intently before answering, "I'd love to come in if you're sure?"

"I have some butter pecan ice cream." I replied avoiding a direct answer as I wasn't sure myself if the invitation was prompted by my not wanting to walk into an empty house or if I truly wanted Nick's company.

"How can I refuse—it's my favorite kind," Nick said, his eyes looking at me with tenderness.

My heart warmed as the answer to my internal question was answered—I wanted Nick's company. Wizard greeted us at the door when we walked in the kitchen. Nick let him outside while I got the ice cream out of the freezer. As I started to scoop the ice cream into two bowls Nick came over to stand next to me and put his arm around me. I turned to face him and we kissed—which was an inadequate word to describe the turn to mush feelings that it produced in me.

We eventually sat down at the table next to each other and ate in silence for a few minutes until Nick said, "I've never felt this way about someone before."

"Neither have I," I responded not being able to stop a big smile from spreading across my face.

It shouldn't have, but our mutual declarations of affection appeared to make us both feel shy as neither one of us had anything else to say. Nick finally got up and put our empty bowls in the sink. I stood up and walked over to him. He gave me a hug and said, "Much as I hate to leave, it's late and I'd better get going."

I walked him to the door and we exchanged another toe curling kiss. "I'll see you tomorrow," I said as Nick walked down the steps and Tabitha and Wizard rushed in the door. I put food and water in their dishes, gave Wizard a head scratch, and floated up the stairs to my bed.

CHAPTER FOUR

*Showy goldenrod has densely clustered small yellow flowers,
¼ inch wide and can grow three to four feet tall. It tends
to like dryer soils in full sunlight or partial shade.*

I WOKE UP SATURDAY MORNING WITH AN unsettled feeling. It took me a few seconds to remember Judith and my worry over Faye's ex-boyfriend, Christopher. I couldn't do anything about either situation, other than be observant and helpful if I could, but knowing that didn't help shake my feelings of unease. I dressed and went down the stairs to make coffee. Kirk's bedroom door was closed and the house was silent. I missed Dad. He and Karla wouldn't be home from their cruise for another six days. Dad was almost always up before me, had the coffee ready, and most days had a delicious breakfast waiting. I might as well get used to it though; it was time for me to find my own place to live. I had moved in with Dad after Mom died to help alleviate his loneliness. Karla had helped fill the hole Mom's death had left, and Dad didn't need me living here anymore. It was now time for me to get out on my own. Dad was only sixty-three and deserved the privacy of his own house without his daughter living in it. Even Kirk planned to move in with a band member after the summer. It was hard to consider leaving as I would miss being here, the roominess of the house, the pets, the yard, and the closeness to the farm. It was hard to find rural housing around Arvilla and I had no desire to live in town. Nick had lucked into his place, but it had been uninhabited before he moved in and he had to do a lot of work to fix it up. I didn't have the time or skills to tackle a project like that and building a new place was out of my price range. I'd have to keep my eyes open and hope something would come on the market. On occasion an older couple would downsize and move to town, but again those places were typically large houses with outbuildings and out of my price range. I cooked myself a couple of eggs to go with my toast. After I finished eating I made sure to grab another set of clothes so I wouldn't have to check guests in today with smoke filled clothes again. As I was packing a dinner, Kirk and Wizard shuffled out of their room, Kirk yawning and Wizard looking disappointed that his food dish was empty.

"Good morning, there's coffee ready," I told him.

"Thanks. Am I late?" he asked when he noticed I was getting ready to leave.

"No, I have two guests checking in later this afternoon and I'm stopping by their cabin on the way to make sure it's ready. I'll see you later." I walked out the door, stopped, and went back in to say, "Make sure Wizard can't get into anything."

"Will do," Kirk answered with a salute.

I felt my tensions from the last couple of days start to lessen as the beauty of the morning overtook me. It was a glorious spring day. The sun was shining, there was a slight breeze, and the temperature was 68 degrees Fahrenheit. It would be warmer this afternoon, but the high was only supposed to be 72 degrees. The lone drawback to the day was the slight breeze. The wind would need to be stronger for the burn to be successful, but the weather station I used predicted the winds would pick up within the hour. In fact, as I turned off the highway onto the gravel road leading to the cabins I could see the tree leaves moving more than they had when I left our yard. Hugh's vehicle was parked by his cabin. It looked dustier than when he had arrived so he must have gotten out and about to see the countryside yesterday afternoon or evening. It looked quiet now; probably sleeping in. I could see a blanket on the rocker in front of the cabin so I hoped he had taken time to sit outside last night and enjoy the evening. We had built the cabins and the paths to each one far away enough from the other, to minimize the disturbance of a vehicle driving by. I arrived at the next cabin and was puzzled by the scratch marks on the door, almost like someone had tried to pick the lock which made no sense. Perhaps a raccoon tried to get in. I unlocked the door and checked the refrigerator and freezer. Once again Edna and Jessica had things under control. The food was stocked in abundance. I was amazed by the amount of people that requested all the food upfront instead of fresh daily. Everything looked in order and the knotty pine smell along with the window I had opened yesterday had the cabin smelling fresh. I closed the window, locked up again, and drove towards the break room. On the way, I decided I had plenty of time to swing by the convenience store and pick up a treat for the crew. I debated between donuts and jelly-filled rolls and decided on both. A snack when we were done burning was good too. When I got back, Gary, Nick, and Kirk were waiting with the loaded four-wheelers. I passed the treats around and put what was left in the break room. I hopped in with Nick and we drove to the prairie cordgrass field we planned to burn. This would be a hot fire as prairie cordgrass isn't a crop we combine low to the ground. About two feet of stock remained from harvest. It would burn fast and hot. Once again we resumed our jobs, Nick and I on the four-wheelers, Kirk on the tractor pulling the water tank, and Gary acting as lookout. We finished the back-burning and had lit the main fire which had been burning for twenty minutes when I got a phone call. Normally I don't answer the phone during a burn, but when I saw it was Gary I answered at once, scared the fire had gotten away from us somewhere.

"Is something wrong Gary?"

"You could say that," he answered sounding frantic.

"What's wrong?" I asked, my heart pumping, as I fought the panic I was feeling.

"There's a body over here, in the fire, I don't know who it is. I put out the surrounding flames, but I didn't dare move it. I called the sheriff first; he said he would be here in about ten minutes."

I couldn't even wrap my mind around what he was saying. All I could say was, "Thanks, I'll be right there." I put my head down, feeling faint.

Kirk must have noticed my reaction, and drove up on the tractor. "What's wrong?" he asked.

"Why does this keep happening? I'm tired of being around dead bodies," I mumbled.

Kirk got off the tractor and knelt down next to me, "What are you mumbling?"

"Another body. . ."

Kirk looked around, clearly confused. "What did you say?" he asked again as Nick drove up on the four-wheeler, got off, and walked up to us.

"Gary called. He found a body on fire in the field," I said again.

"Somebody was in the field and got caught in the fire?" Nick asked in disbelief.

"I don't know. Gary said he found a body, put the fire out by it, and called the sheriff. I need to get over to him; the sheriff will be here soon." I got up, but then said, "I don't want to. I don't want to deal with this." I couldn't help sounding like a petulant child.

Nick gave me a quick hug. "You can do this. Kirk and I will get the fire extinguished and then join you."

I started to walk towards my four-wheeler; then went back for one more hug. After the reassuring hug, I ran to the four-wheeler and drove to the northeast corner of the field where we had first started burning. Gary was pacing back and forth when I drove up to him. I could see a body lying amongst the smoldering grass clumps on the field.

"How did you even see it?" I asked him as I heard the sound of sirens. "Never mind, that's the sheriff; you can wait and tell your story once."

Gary nodded at me, then finally stopped pacing and sat down on my four-wheeler seat. I stood in awkwardness next to him waiting for Sheriff Poole. It was fortunate this corner of the field was next to the field road enabling the sheriff to drive right up to us.

He got out of his vehicle. "Is finding dead bodies becoming a weekly event for you?" he asked glaring at me.

"Yes, I wake up every morning and figure out who the heck can be killed in my proximity today," I exasperatedly retorted.

He took a step back as it was evident my response was a tad over the top. "I was joking Carmen."

I sighed. "I know, but really, what in the world is going on in my life? Though Gary is the actual person who found the body this time."

"Do you know who it is?" he asked us both.

Gary answered, "No."

"I haven't even looked," I said.

The sheriff walked over, took some photographs and motioned for me to come closer.

In reluctance I walked his way. I took a peek expecting to see a charred body, but to my surprise it wasn't as horrible as I thought it might be. Gary must have found the body at almost the same time the fire reached it. I took a closer look and said, "I think it may be Christopher."

"Who's Christopher?" Sheriff Poole asked as Gary looked at me in surprise.

"He's Faye's abusive ex-boyfriend. We had heard he was on his way here to find Faye. Remember Nick and Faye told you about him?" I reminded the sheriff, knowing he hadn't taken them at all serious.

"She was very scared of him," he stated and I could practically see his mind start churning.

"Don't even think it," I said as Nick and Kirk walked up to us.

"Think what?" Nick asked.

"I think that is Christopher, based on the picture you showed me," I said and pointed at the body.

Nick looked at me in amazement and then walked over to the body. "It's him," he said after a brief look and walked back to us.

"The sheriff thinks Faye had something to do with it," I stated flatly knowing that was where Sheriff Poole's mind was going.

Nick looked at the sheriff, "Is that true?"

"You or her; it would make sense, you're the only two people who would want him dead."

"We are not doing this again," I interrupted the sheriff. "Neither Nick nor Faye is a murderer. This man was a criminal and an abuser. Anyone could have followed him here knowing his death would be blamed on Nick and Faye."

The sheriff snorted. "Not likely. I'll be calling all of you in for questioning, but right now I need to secure the scene and call for the forensic people from Bemidji again. You know the drill Carmen."

"We'll wait in the break room for you back at the seed plant," I answered as I motioned for the guys to follow me.

"Is the fire out?" I asked Nick and Kirk as we walked away.

"It is," Nick assured me.

"Let's load everything and go back to the break room and wait for the idiot." We loaded the four-wheelers on the trailer and drove to the break room, Kirk following on the tractor pulling the water tank. On our way, we met another deputy's vehicle with sirens blaring heading our way, no doubt to wait with the body for the forensic people while the sheriff talked to us. I must have been correct as we had only been in the break room for a few minutes when the sheriff joined us.

"How did you happen to notice the body?" he asked Gary.

"I saw a mound in the field and I thought it looked strange. Sometimes the grass is bunched up, but this looked different. I got out my binoculars to take a closer look and was sure I could see a shirt. The main fire had skipped most of that area as it is a wet spot, so I put out the little that was burning as I drove closer. When I was sure it was a body, I put out the flames by it, called you, and then Carmen." He looked at me and then trying to inject some levity said, "I think I'm going to have to resign, this is the second body I've found in fields on your farm. I can't take too much more of this." His voice broke as he finished talking.

"You and me both," I mumbled.

"Did the fire kill him?" Kirk asked.

"The back of his head looked crushed. The coroner will have a better idea what might have caused it, but I do know the fire didn't produce that kind of damage. It looked to me like he was dead and dumped here. I didn't see any blood but the fire might have affected that. The killer must have assumed the fire would burn up the body," Sheriff Poole answered looking at Nick.

"Don't look at Nick," I said. "He's not that stupid. Our fires burn hot but the grass burns fast, there is no way a body would be completely consumed. I think somebody put him here to implicate Nick or Faye."

"No one else knows him but those two. When I get a better idea of time of death I'll be contacting the two of you for your alibis."

"I went out to eat last night with Faye, Frankie, George and Carmen," Nick stated.

"That's nice, but the body might have been put out here days ago," Sheriff Poole retorted.

"Coyotes, wolves, or even eagles would have gotten to the body if it had been days ago. From what I saw, other than the fire, the body didn't have much damage to it like animals would have done if he had laid out here for days," I said.

The sheriff raised his eyebrows at me and said, "Let's wait for the coroner before we start making things up. In the meantime, neither yourself, Nick, or Faye, better leave the area; and Carmen, stay out of this."

I snorted, and then taking a deep breath said, "In case you've forgotten, Judith was murdered also. Somehow I can't believe two murders in this town aren't related. And we both know there is no way Faye killed Judith."

"Thanks for reminding me Carmen, perhaps Christopher was back in town to get Faye and shot Judith by accident. That would make sense; Faye knew she had to kill Christopher to be safe."

My stomach rolled as I listened to the sheriff repeat exactly what Nick and Faye had feared he might think. Faye was scared, would she have . . . I shook my head, there is no way she was capable of something like that, and neither was Nick.

"You're wrong sheriff," I insisted.

"I hope I am Carmen," he said, his voice softening. "We've had our differences, but I wouldn't be doing my job if I ignored the most obvious suspects." He nodded and walked out the door leaving Nick, Kirk, Gary, and I sitting in silence.

Kirk cleared his throat and said, "Carmen, normally I would caution you to stay out of this, and I think Nick would agree; but I know you aren't the type of person to leave this alone and I don't think you should."

"She won't. She's Nancy Drew at heart." At the sound of Nick's voice and his confidence in me, my world became a little warmer.

CHAPTER FIVE

Large-flowered beardtongue (a type of penstemon)
has sharp capsule tips when ready to harvest.
Be sure to wear gloves if hand harvesting its seed.

KIRK LEFT FOR PRACTICE WITH HIS band and Gary went home to take his kids to their softball practice. Nick and I sat in stunned silence for a few minutes, before he said, "I'd better call Faye and let her know what is going on."

"Why don't you go over and talk to her in person. We're done here for the day." I looked at my phone. "It's almost two; I need to check-in my cabin guests anyway. Do you and Faye want to come for supper tonight? We should talk."

"I think that's a good idea. Do you want me to bring anything?"

"You could bring milk if you have any. I'm running short and I would rather not stop anywhere."

"I do have an almost full gallon. I'll bring it, anything else?"

"No, I should be good. I'm not sure what I'll make, but I'll find something."

"There is nothing wrong with a frozen pizza," Nick suggested.

"I think I can come up with something better than that. I'll see you guys around six."

"See you then," Nick said as he gave me a hug before walking out.

I sat in silence for a few minutes contemplating the latest mess I appeared to have found myself in. At last I got up, retrieved the clean clothes from my pickup, changed, washed my face, and combed my hair. My hair reeked like smoke, but it couldn't be helped. I gave another big sigh, and got into my pickup. As I drove to the cabin site I tried to get myself in the mindset of a cheerful host. The Erickson's were waiting when I drove up to the cabin.

"I'm so sorry I'm late. Have you been waiting long?"

"We just arrived and were contemplating which cabin we were going to be in. Do we have a choice?"

"I'm afraid not, cabin A is occupied and your food has already been put in cabin C, which is the one in the far corner. Cabin B is unoccupied this week and I thought I'd put you folks in the cabin that was the farthest from the occupied one."

"That sounds perfect; it is exactly what we were hoping for," Alex Erickson replied.

"You should come up with different names for your cabins," Marge Erickson said. "They are too charming to be referred to as A, B, & C."

I smiled at her hoping it wasn't a grimace and said, "I'll keep that in mind. Maybe you can come up with possible names for me while you are here this week."

"I might do that. We're looking forward to the solitude and hoping to see a moose."

"A moose might be difficult, but deer, elk, coyotes, and wolves are a common sight."

"I thought northern Minnesota was known for moose?" Marge asked sounding surprised.

"Northeast Minnesota has a fair amount. On occasion one passes through here, but our moose population is almost non-existent anymore."

"Why is that?" Alex asked.

"I don't think the researchers have quite settled on any one answer other than brainworms being a major factor. But as far as I know no one has come up with a reason why they are getting the worms. You may luck out, we did have a cow moose go through one of our game cameras a month ago, but we haven't seen her again."

"It will be something to look forward to," Marge said looking determined.

"Here are your keys and my cell phone number is on a piece of paper in the cabin. Please don't hesitate to call if you need anything at all. Would you like help with your bags?" I asked as I handed them the keys.

"No, we packed light," Marge answered.

"Enjoy your stay, and again please call if you need something." I walked to my pickup and watched as they drove over to cabin C to make sure they got in. When I was sure they were okay, I left for home. As I drove home I considered if I was ethically obligated to tell them about the murders. I felt guilty for not sharing, but I finally concluded that as the sheriff hadn't issued any kind of public warning I didn't need to feel obligated to mention it. Suddenly my body was overwhelmed with tiredness and I was regretting inviting Nick and Faye over for supper. But recognizing that going home to an empty house wasn't appealing either I started going through the pantry in my mind trying to come up with an idea of what I might cook. By the time I drove in our driveway I had settled on fried potatoes and hamburger steaks. I knew I had mushrooms in the refrigerator and if I fried them with garlic and olive oil they would be delicious on the hamburger steaks. I threw a couple pounds of ground beef in the microwave to thaw while I took a shower. Feeling better after my shower I started cutting up potatoes and onions to fry when I realized there was an absence of animals. Where was Wizard? I then noticed a note on the counter from Kirk. He had taken Wizard with him to band practice. I peeked out the window to see if I could spot Tabitha. She was in her usual spot behind an oak tree hoping Wizard's squirrel friend would be stupid enough to come down the tree and not notice her. I smiled to myself knowing this game had been getting played over and over for years and the squirrel remained alive. Of course it could be a new squirrel, I would have no way of knowing if it was the same one. But Tabitha and Clyde like to present their kills to us for praise and a squirrel body had never been one of them. I had the potatoes and onions about done, mushrooms ready to cook, and the ground beef patted into steaks when Nick and Faye drove in. I turned on the burner under the mushrooms and put the steaks on the grill.

Faye was the first in the door, somehow looking both relieved and worried at the same time. "Can you believe Christopher is dead and I don't have to worry about him ever again hurting me? Of course even in his death, he's managed to mess with my life. Nick told me the sheriff suspects us of killing Christopher." She collapsed on a kitchen chair.

"Hello," I said to her as I leaned over and gave her a hug.

"Do you have one of those for me?" Nick asked when he walked in the door carrying the milk which he set on the table.

"Always," I answered. "Even better I have a kiss for you."

"Get a room you two," Faye said wanly smiling at the two of us. She stood up, "What can I help you with?"

"You can set the table and Nick, if you don't mind, would you check on the steaks?"

"Steaks, that sounds good," Nick said as he started for the back porch where the grill was.

"Don't get too excited. They're hamburger steaks."

"That is way better than a frozen pizza," was his reply as he walked out the door.

Faye set the table and then said, "I forgot I made cookies today. I left them in the pickup, I'll go grab them."

While she was gone I got the condiments on the table. She came in with a Tupperware container and set it on the counter.

I opened the lid and peeked to see what kind. "Yummy, peanut butter, my favorite," not being able to stop myself I grabbed one to eat as I turned off the burners under the mushrooms and potatoes and looked for serving bowls. "These are delicious cookies!"

"Thanks. I like baking and for some unknown reason Nick had three jars of peanut butter in the cupboard. I decided to make use of it."

"I'm glad you did." I had everything on the table when Nick poked his head in the door to ask for a plate for the steaks. For a last minute meal, it turned out well. We were all full, especially after stuffing many peanut butter cookies in our stomachs.

"Thanks a lot Carmen," Nick said as he started to pick up the dishes.

Faye stopped him, "You guys sit down while I clean up. You both worked today, while I had the day off. All I accomplished was the cookies."

"And we're glad you did," I said as I settled back in my chair. "I hate to ruin the evening, but we do have talk about the elephant in the room. What are we going to do about the sheriff thinking the two of you murdered Christopher?"

"What can we do?" Faye asked as she loaded the dishwasher.

"Somebody murdered him. So let's think, who else might have a reason?"

"I think someone followed him from Oregon and took advantage of him not realizing he was being followed and grabbed their opportunity. He was always scamming someone, I bet they got revenge," Faye offered.

"I don't think so," Nick said. "If they followed him here, why not kill him somewhere along the way in a place where nobody would know him."

"What about his father?" I suggested.

"What do you mean?" Nick asked.

"You told me he believed his father was from here."

"He thought it was your dad."

"Did you ever correct him?" I asked.

"I didn't," Nick answered.

"I did," Faye said. "When Christopher found me in California I had mentioned to him that you didn't think Carmen's dad was his father and you were sure it was someone else. I don't think he believed me though."

"Is it possible he figured out who it was?" I asked.

"Christopher was an awful person, but he wasn't stupid. I'm sure he could access the convention picture on-line like I did," Nick said. "Maybe he found something in his mother's stuff that told him who it was."

"She's the one who told his uncle it was Chet," Faye said, "but I do know Christopher had a small box of her possessions he kept."

"Do you know what was in it? Could there have been a picture?" I asked getting excited.

"He never let me look in it. I suppose it's possible. If he did have a picture it could be that when I told him Nick didn't think Chet was his father he started comparing the picture to who was at the convention," Faye said.

"If he did figure out who his real father was, what would he do?"

"What do you mean, what would he do?" Faye asked.

"Would he be looking for a touching reunion or would he try to get money out of it for himself?" I asked.

"He would be looking for money," Nick said, starting to see where I was going.

"We don't know for sure how long Christopher was in Arvilla before his body was found. We're assuming someone would have noticed him, but if he had figured out his father wasn't my dad and he knew who it truly was, he may have approached them immediately when he arrived and wanted his share of their finances?" I asked.

"But no one has to give him anything. It's not like every kid is due their share. All they had to do was say no," Nick pointed out.

"But what if Christopher was going to cause problems for them? Whoever it was did impersonate my dad and that wouldn't be very well received in the community," I explained.

Faye spoke up, "Christopher was very good at playing the injured party too. What if he threatened to go around town telling everyone how his awful father wouldn't acknowledge him?"

"Reputation does carry a lot of weight around here. If whoever it was valued their position in the community, Christopher could cause problems and I know at least three of those men are considered paragons in the community," I said.

"But how would Christopher have identified the person? Even if he had a picture, he would have had to ask someone who it was. The newspaper didn't name any of the people in the picture. It took me a few months along with talking to James and Karla to figure out who each person was," Nick said sounding frustrated.

"It would depend on who he talked to when he got here. As no one has commented on a stranger in town he may have gotten lucky right away and asked the right person who directed him to his father," I said.

"That easy enough to find out, we'll just ask them," Faye offered.

"If someone killed Christopher to keep it quiet after all these years, I doubt they'll admit to talking to him," Nick said.

"It is however a better motive and a better suspect for the sheriff than both of you," I insisted.

"He's never going to believe this theory," Faye stated sounding discouraged as she sat back down.

"It's worth a try," I said, starting to get disheartened myself. "I know you both tried talking to the sheriff before about Christopher. I'm going to talk to him also; maybe he'll listen to me."

"Good luck," Nick said. "I'd like to go with you if you'll have me."

"I'd love it. Tomorrow's Sunday, but maybe after church we could swing by the Sheriff's Department, with two unsolved murders he might be there."

"It sounds like a plan. What about burning? Do you want to try any tomorrow?"

"No, we aren't behind enough that we need to work on Sunday. Plus there isn't supposed to be any wind tomorrow," I said and at the same time we heard a dog barking. "Kirk must be home." I peeked out the window and saw Kirk walking Wizard around making sure he did his business before coming in for the night.

"Did you have any supper?" I asked him when he walked in.

"Yeah, we picked up a couple of pizzas from the bowling alley. How are you guys doing? Pretty crappy day wasn't it?"

"It was. How did practice go?"

"We've got two new original songs I think are ready. We're planning to introduce them during the tour when we leave next week," Kirk said sounding excited. "You're sure you'll be okay to finish the burning when I'm gone?"

"It shouldn't be a problem. Gary is going to fill in, and Dad will be back too," I answered.

"I heard something interesting tonight," Kirk said.

"What did you hear?" Nick asked.

"It was about Judith's murder. Someone was saying they saw her talking to Darius a couple of days ago."

"Who is Darius?" Faye asked.

"He is the IPD driver that services this area. Maybe she was asking about a package." I suggested.

"It could be, but they said she was taking notes after he drove away."

"An IPD driver would be good cover for dropping off drugs," I mused. "He was in the vicinity when Judith was killed."

"But he had Wizard," Kirk reminded me.

"True—but maybe that is why Wizard had so much time to chew up that package." I reconsidered, "Although it does only take Wizard a blink to get himself in trouble. Who told you this?"

"Our drummer, Kyle, mentioned it when we were taking a break and of course Judith's murder came up."

"Would he be willing to tell the sheriff this?" I asked.

"I already took care of it. He's going to call him on Monday."

"Thanks Kirk, and also thanks for taking Wizard with you tonight. It was nice to not have him underfoot while I cooked."

"It might not happen again," Kirk said as he looked down at the floor.

"What did Wizard do?"

"He got out of the garage at Kyle's place and before we noticed he was gone he had dug up all the flowers Kyle's girlfriend had planted this morning. I had to pay her $170 for the flowers he ruined."

We all laughed at Kirk's sheepish expression. Wizard must have sensed he was being talked about as he barked and squirmed around Kirk's legs.

"Any chance you can take him with you when you go on tour?" I asked knowing it was a futile question and I would be stuck with Wizard. At least Dad would be home by then to help. I would never admit it to Kirk but Wizard, for all his troublemaking, had wormed his way into my heart. You couldn't help but love the little guy. They do say there is a fine line between love and hate, perhaps explaining why even though you love him, you'd like to give him away some days.

"I'd love to. I miss him when I'm gone, but we both know he wouldn't travel well."

"I know, but I can hope." I laughed at his expression and relented, "It's okay; he's grown on me a little bit." Wizard chose that moment to bark as if agreeing. That broke up the evening and I walked out with Nick and Faye. Faye got in the pickup leaving Nick and I alone for a few seconds to say goodnight.

After a satisfying kiss, Nick said, "I'll see you tomorrow. I don't know that I'll make it to church, but I will meet you at the Sheriff's Department around noon. Maybe we can catch a bite to eat after?"

"That would be great. Do you mind if I invite Jessica and James? I haven't seen them for a few days and Jessica and I were going to try to get together tomorrow."

"It's fine with me," Nick answered looking a little disappointed. I felt bad as Nick and I didn't get a lot of time alone together, but Jessica and I had arranged this a couple of weeks ago. "Is Faye going to be okay?" I asked him. "I think so, she's tough. The situation isn't ideal of course, but it has to be a relief too, knowing Christopher can never hurt her again. On that note, I'd better get going." He gave me hug and walked to his pickup.

Before going back in the house I sat down on the front steps and took in the stillness of the night. I could hear frogs croaking and the rustle of tree leaves. I pondered my life and wondered what was going on. I was running a business I had a passion for, lived in a community I adored, family and friends I loved and treasured, a special man in my life and yet I continued to find myself involved in murders. I had enough on my plate. Why did I think it was my responsibility to solve murders even if people close to me were suspects? It wasn't my job. I shook my head, knowing I had no answers. As if sensing my turmoil both Tabitha and Clyde came over to rub against my legs. I smiled. Animals are truly special. Tabitha was a typical stand-offish cat and it wasn't normal for Clyde to seek out human touch, yet here they were. I stayed outside lavishing them with attention and brushing them. We had an old curry comb we left on the steps that we used to brush the cats, and they loved it. By the time I decided to go in I had a nice covering of fur on my clothes. I held the door for Tabitha but she wasn't interested in coming inside for the night. Kirk and Wizard had gone to bed and after dropping my fur covered pants and shirt in the laundry room I went to my bedroom also.

CHAPTER SIX

*Prairie smoke possibly gets its name from its large stands of flowers
that create a gauzy effect which resembles hovering smoke.*

I WOKE UP LATE ON SUNDAY MORNING and took a moment to
enjoy the pleasure of not being jolted awake by an alarm clock
blaring. There were no bin fans to check, no burning to get ready
for, no harvest, no seed mixing, just a relaxing day off. Then I
remembered the murders and the trip to the sheriff's office I would
be doing later today, and all of the sudden the day wasn't so serene.
I scrambled out of bed, put on my bathrobe and slippers, and plod-
ded down the steps. I could hear Wizard making noise by Kirk's
bedroom door. I opened it and let him out. He went right to the
back door obviously needing to do his business. His squirrel friend
was in the tree and chattered at him when he ran out of the house.
I started the coffee, made two slices of toast, poured myself a glass
of orange juice, and sat down to read the news on my phone while I
ate, which almost never happened. Kirk hadn't stirred by the time I
finished, cleaned up the kitchen, and went back upstairs to change
for church. I came back downstairs, let Wizard back in Kirk's bedroom, and walked out of the house.

Jessica and James had left room in the church pew for me. We had a few minutes to talk before the service started and we arranged for Nick and me to meet them at her restaurant after we talked to the sheriff. Jessica's restaurant didn't offer menu options on Sundays, but it did offer a delicious buffet. This gave her the ability to take Sundays off, except for early morning when she went in and helped her staff get everything ready. I don't think she even did that too often anymore as George was taking on more and more responsibilities. As the church service went on, my attention wandered, and as I looked around the church I realized both Al Mitchel and Cord McCaster, possible Christopher father suspects, were in church today. I wondered if there was any possible way I could casually talk to them without it being odd—other than nodding and smiling I couldn't remember the last time I had spoken to either of them, if ever. I thought for a moment and realized I had a perfect reason to at least talk to Cord. When the service was over I slipped out of the pew trying to catch Cord before he left. Jessica and James looked at me strange when I dashed out, but I would explain later when we met at the restaurant.

I was in luck; Cord was standing in the church entryway looking at his phone. "Hi Cord, do you have a minute?" I asked him.

He put his phone in his pocket, "Sure Carmen, what can I do for you?"

"I need gravel for the seed plant. The driveway by the corner of our building, where the semi-trucks turn, is rutted up and I heard a new company was leasing your gravel pits. Do you have a contact number for who I could get a load of Class 5 gravel from?"

"I do, but it isn't a new company, they only acquired another company and changed their name." He scrolled through his contacts, "Jeff is his name, I don't have his last name, but here's his number."

I entered it into my contact list as he read it off to me. "Thanks a lot. By the way have you seen any new people around town?"

"No, why do you ask?" Cord inquired.

I lied and answered, "James had mentioned there was a guy in his early thirties who had stopped him in town one day looking for work. I need roguers for the summer and I was hoping to track him down."

"No one approached me, but maybe he's the one that was found in your burned field," Cord answered looking at me as if he knew exactly what I was up to.

I swallowed and said, "You could be right. I guess he won't be available for rogueing." Never knowing when to quit, I continued, "I was cleaning last week and I came across a box of Dad's stuff. In it was a picture of my parents from 1993 when a large group went to some sort of convention in Las Vegas. I think I recognized you in the picture. I never realized Dad had ever been there," I said feeling proud of how well I had come up with yet another lie—then briefly wondered if I should be proud of that.

Cord smiled, "I had forgotten all about that trip. I didn't know too many people from here at the time and I enjoyed getting to know everyone."

"I heard a rumor that the dead man was looking for a father he never knew," I blurted, embarrassed by my ineffective questioning.

"It's interesting the rumors that people come up with," he commented and stared at me.

"Did you win any money gambling?" I asked trying to feel him out if he had been in the casino. If so he might have run into Christopher's mother. I recognized it was perhaps a futile question as I'm sure everyone spent time in the casino, but you never know.

"I spent a little time there, but like farming was going for me at the time, I had no luck gambling either. If my memory is any good, I don't think any of us had any good fortune at the tables. Although Al and Owen might have, they didn't stick with the group as much as the rest of us. I better get going, thanks Carmen; it's always fun to reminisce about the old days, back when it didn't hurt to get out of bed." He laughed and went out the door.

I stood there for a moment, barely registering the church emptying around me, as I pondered if my babbling questions had resulted in my first real clue as to who Christopher's father might be, Al or Owen. I checked the time and realized I was going to be late to meet Nick at the Sheriff's Department.

Nick was standing beside his pickup which was parked next to a Sheriff's Department vehicle when I pulled up. "Good morning, or is it good afternoon?" I called to him.

"We'll go with good afternoon," he said greeting me with a kiss when I joined him.

"Now that's a nice start to the afternoon, but the buffet at Jessica's restaurant will be even better," I replied with a smile.

"That's a low blow," he said. "True, but hurtful. Are you ready for this?" he asked as he gestured towards the building.

"I think so. By the way, I talked to Cord after church today. I don't know how much stock we can put in this, but he alluded to the fact that Al and Owen didn't spend a lot of time with the rest of the group on the trip."

"And how did that happen to come up in conversation?" Nick asked shaking his head.

"I have my ways," I said as I pantomimed a seductress. "But I'm not sure we should tell the sheriff about it, I hesitate to implicate anyone yet."

"I agree, we'll tell him about Christopher, the trip, the four men we suspect are his father, and the sheriff can pursue whichever direction he thinks is right." Nick looked at me and said, "We both know the sheriff is going to focus on Faye, so—although I can't believe I'm saying this—you are going to continue investigating this, right?"

"You know I will, but I agree we don't single out Owen and Al. The sheriff can question all four of them easier than we can."

We walked up the steps to the Sheriff's Department, stopped at the dispatcher's desk, and asked if the sheriff was in. She said yes but walked back to his office to make sure he wanted to talk to us before waving at us to follow her.

The sheriff was eating a sandwich, and motioned for us to sit down. He took a drink of water and wiped his face with a napkin. "What can I do for you folks today?"

I looked at Nick indicating he should start as it was his story to tell. Nick then told him about the agronomy company sponsored trip, how someone impersonated my dad, and how Christopher had believed my dad was his father.

When Nick finished talking, the sheriff said, "This is interesting, but I'm not sure what you are getting at?"

"We think Christopher not only came here for revenge on Nick and Faye but was also planning to confront his father, whom I know wasn't my dad. When looking at a picture Nick found in an old newspaper he discovered the following men were solo on the trip, Al Mitchel, Jed Alman, Cord McCaster and Owen Laterly. We think one of them impersonated my dad. I'm not familiar with them personally, but I believe most of them are wealthy, upstanding members of the community. Perhaps Christopher approached one of them insinuating that they should pay him off for his silence or even demanded his share of what they would be giving their kids," I said thinking if it sounded nuts to me, I could only imagine what the sheriff was thinking.

"Except by your own admission, he thought Chet was your father, so how would he have even known to approach any of those men?" the sheriff asked leaning back in his chair and crossing his arms.

"I think he may have found a picture in his mother's belongings and realized it wasn't Chet. Faye mentioned she had told Christopher that Nick didn't believe my dad could be his father; maybe that caused him to start snooping. If you ask around maybe you can find someone who remembers meeting and talking with Christopher," I stated recognizing I wasn't making a convincing argument.

The sheriff considered for a few minutes and surprised me by saying, "You may have something. I've been looking into Christopher's record and everything Nick told me about him checks out. He was an unsavory person. I'll do what I can. I'm not sure how strong of a motive it is as all any of them had to do was say no to Christopher. None of them would be under any legal obligation to give him anything, so I'm not convinced murdering Christopher would be their only solution."

"They are all about the same age as my dad and I know how much his reputation means to him—maybe they're the same. Maybe that was enough of a motive," I suggested.

The sheriff annoyed me by raising his eyebrows and saying, "Doubtful. I'm sorry, but you, Nick, and Faye have the strongest motive for killing him, and I'd be a fool to ignore it, whether I believe it or not. I don't honestly think either one of you would murder anyone. But," he stood up, "fear for your life is a powerful motivator and Faye was afraid of Christopher—and Nick, as her brother, you can't help but be protective of her."

"Do you know what Christopher was hit with?" Nick asked.

"Only that it was something wide and heavy, best guess at this time is a shovel. Thanks for coming in with this information. I will check in to it."

Nick and I stood up also. As Nick walked out of Sheriff Poole's office, I remained and asked, "How is the investigation of Judith's murder going?"

The sheriff sat back down, "Not much progress I'm afraid. Her husband Dan confirmed she was concerned about a meth problem and was trying to figure out what she could legally do about it in regards to her license. He let us look through the files she had at home, but there was nothing in them. Tomorrow we're going through the dental office files. We had to have a warrant for that as patient files are confidential and it only came through late Friday. If I'm being honest I don't put much credence in the idea she was shot by Christopher mistaking her for Faye, but I do have to consider it." The sheriff stood up again and said, "I'll walk you out," clearly signaling our time was over.

"Thank you for your time." I told the sheriff when we joined Nick who was waiting for me by the front door. The sheriff opened the door and held it for us as we walked outside.

"Is it okay if I leave my pickup here and jump in with you?" I asked Nick.

"Sure. Are you ready to head to Jessica's restaurant?" Nick asked.

"I am, as long as you are. Jessica and James will be waiting for us."

Nick sighed and said, "I'm not going to let the sheriff get to me, I know Faye and I have nothing to do with Christopher or Judith's murder." He shrugged. "Let's go, I'm looking forward to the mashed potatoes and baked chicken on her buffet."

"I'm kind of partial to the breakfast part of the buffet. I love her waffles and scrambled eggs, and now I'm starving. Could you drive any faster please?" I said trying to lighten the mood.

Nick chuckled, but I did notice he increased his speed from twenty-five miles per hour to thirty miles per hour, the legal speed in town.

"Why didn't you mention the IPD driver?" Nick asked while we were driving.

"Kirk said Kyle will tell him tomorrow," I answered. "I don't think the sheriff needs any more theories from me. Maybe he'll take it more seriously from someone else and to be honest I kind of bonded with Darius over the whole Wizard and Styrofoam beads incident. He appeared to be a genuine, nice guy who was panicked at the thought of losing his job. I don't think he'd risk his job by delivering drugs."

"Maybe he was panicked as he wouldn't be able to deliver drugs if he lost his job," Nick responded looking at my reasoning with the exact opposite interpretation.

"I guess that's possible. Either way, I think it is better someone else brings Darius to the sheriff's attention." We arrived at the restaurant to find the street parking was full, so Nick pulled into the alley and found a spot to squeeze in; making me thankful I didn't drive my pickup too. Jessica and James were waiting in my favorite booth. My favorite as it was strategically located closest to the buffet so you didn't have to walk past so many people for your third or fourth trip to the buffet. Her buffet was well known throughout the community; it was huge, featuring a large variety of breakfast, dinner, and dessert items along with an amply stocked salad bar.

Jessica spotted us, and jumped up to give me a hug. "You've had quite a week, why didn't you call me about the body that was found in your field?"

"To be honest, things have been crazy, plus your wedding is coming in two weeks. You should be focused on nothing but happy thoughts," I answered her trying to cover my lapse in not taking the time to call her. She sat back down, and Nick and I slid in the other side of the booth.

"Enough chit chat," James said. "I'm starving and sitting here smelling everything while waiting for you guys has been cruel and unusual punishment."

We agreed, got up, and each grabbed a plate and started working our way down the buffet. By the time we made it back to the booth our plates were filled with our favorite things, items like chicken, mashed potatoes, dressing, waffles, sausages, scrambled eggs and pork roast. "This is awesome," I told Jessica. "How can you afford to provide all these choices?"

"It's surprising but the Sunday buffets are my most profitable days. Word has gotten around, and it's rare I have leftovers to throw away. If there is a significant amount of anything left I drop it off at the nursing home," Jessica answered.

"What is the scoop on the body that was found in your field? And as I say that, what's with your fields being dumping grounds for bodies?" James asked with an apologetic look at Jessica as the last body that was found in one of our fields was her long lost brother.

We spent the next half hour alternating between stuffing our faces and discussing Christopher and Judith, until Jessica said,

"Enough, let's talk about happier things. The wedding is thirteen days from today. Did one of the dresses you ordered work?"

Not daring to tell her they had arrived via the postal service on Friday and I hadn't yet tried them on, I answered, "I'm debating between two of them."

She hadn't been my best friend forever without knowing me. "You haven't even opened the packages have you?" she asked shaking her head.

"No, but I will today," I promised.

We discussed the wedding while the guys talked about cattle and equipment. It always amazed me how Nick could talk intelligently about cows with James, considering he had never worked with cattle in his life. I was even more thankful Nick and James genuinely liked each other, not just accommodating the partner of their significant other. It would have been awkward for Jessica and me if they didn't get along.

"It sounds like everything is coming together," I said smiling at a glowing Jessica. I'd never seen her happier and I was thrilled my two best friends were getting married.

"What are you going to do with your house?" I asked Jessica knowing she'd be moving in James's house. He was currently living in his own small house while Karla lived next to him in the main house James had grown up in. Karla had surprised Jessica and James with an early wedding gift telling them it was ridiculous for her to be rambling around in a big house and she was going to switch houses with them.

"I decided to rent it out. I'm not ready to sell it—I'll get there, but not yet," Jessica answered. "It is the only home I've ever known."

"Maybe I should rent it," I surprised myself by saying.

They all looked at me in surprise. "I've been thinking it's time to get out of Dad's house, but I haven't figured out where to go," I said by way of explanation. "Twenty-eight is too old to be living with Daddy yet."

"I wish you had said something before," Jessica said. "I already rented it to April Hewsy."

"That's funny; Nick and I were just talking about her."

"Why?" Jessica asked.

"Do you remember you told me to get ahold of her for help finding people for the rogueing crew?"

"That's right, you'll like her. She's very friendly," Jessica said.

"I don't recognize the last name, is she from here?" James asked.

"No, she moved here about three or four years ago. She is originally from Minneapolis, and was working in one of the school districts down there, but got tired of the traffic, the overcrowding of the school system, and was looking for a change."

"She certainly got that." I laughed. "I'm hoping I'll get a chance to meet with her this week."

"You'd better hurry up; most kids looking for summer jobs have already found them by now," Jessica cautioned me.

"I know, I know, life has been busy the last couple of weeks—but it's no excuse."

"I've got her cell phone number, how about I text her right now and ask if she can meet with you tomorrow?" Jessica asked fingers ready to type on her phone.

"I hate to bother her on a Sunday," I protested.

"Trust me, she won't care." Jessica started texting. She was putting her phone down when it dinged announcing an incoming text.

She looked at her phone, "Does tomorrow at noon work for you?"

"Sure, I'll meet her at the school," I said surprised by how quick this was happening.

Jessica text some more, then put down her phone. "Done, Jessica to the rescue, you can thank me by picking out a dress for the wedding—today."

"I will," I said as I started eating again.

"Has the food been going over well with the cabin guests?" she asked after we finished eating.

"Your lasagna has been a big hit along with Edna's caramel rolls. I've only received compliments, no complaints, and they know they can text or call me with any problems. I haven't heard anything negative yet. I do my best to stay away; people come here for peace and quiet, although I do make an effort to stop by at least once during their stay. By the way do either of you know Owen Laterly?"

"Only that he owns a couple of buildings in town that he rents to people. He's also very active in the hospital association, trying to make sure we keep the clinic running in town. I'm not positive, but I believe he has a ministry background as he fills in for several churches in the area when they are missing a minister," James answered.

"That's why the name is familiar. I think he was at our church a couple of times, when our minister was laid up from a leg surgery. Does he have any family?" I asked.

"I think he has one daughter, but I can't remember for sure. His wife died around ten years ago. Why the sudden interest in him?" James asked.

I looked at Nick, and he subtly shook his head. For some reason he didn't want to share our theories with Jessica and James so I honored his unspoken request and said, "No reason, his name came up the other day when I was in the grocery store and I was trying to figure out why I knew the name." I'm not sure it was a good thing lying was becoming easier for me. In the past I was known to be a terrible liar as I broke out in a sweat. I did notice Jessica looking at me with a puzzled look. As I said before, she knew me too well.

Nick stretched and said, "I'd better get home and check on Faye. Are you ready to go Carmen?"

"I am. I've got a dirty house and a stack of laundry I better get through before the start of the week."

"And dresses to try on," Jessica said glaring at me.

"That too," I agreed. "It was so nice getting together with you guys." I stood up and put money on the table.

"No, no, you aren't paying for your meals," Jessica said.

"She's right, you aren't," Nick said. "I am."

"Neither one of you is correct," I said and walked away leaving the money on the table.

I heard James snickering as he said to Nick, "I wouldn't argue with her if I were you. I've known her a long time and stubborn is her middle name." By intention his voice got louder the farther away I moved to ensure I would hear him. I turned around and glared at him, then opened the door, walked out, and ran right into retired farmer Jed Alman who was standing on the sidewalk. He was my height with thinning hair and a barrel-chest.

"Is the restaurant still open?" he asked me.

"No, sorry, it closed at two."

"That's stupid," he harrumphed and started to walk away.

Not wanting to miss my fortuitous opportunity to talk to him, I asked, "Is Jill okay?"

He turned and snarled, "Why do you ask?"

Taken aback by his tone I answered, "She was present when Judith was shot."

"Oh, that—yes, she's fine," he responded tersely.

"Did you hear about the body that was found in our field when we were burning?"

"Yes. What about it?"

"He was a stranger who was supposedly looking for his father. His mother told him he was a result of an affair she'd had with someone from Arvilla who had been to Las Vegas for an agronomy convention," I answered hoping to shock a reaction of some type from him. "Did you happen to notice a stranger in town?"

"No, I didn't," he answered.

"I think you were with on that trip. Would you have any idea who might have been his father?" I asked him probing.

"That was a long time ago, and no, I don't have any idea," he answered then abruptly turned and walked away.

Nick joined me. "It looked like you were sleuthing, so I waited to join you. How did it go?"

"I'm not sure—he wasn't too communicative—but I don't know

the man and my questions weren't exactly prepared," I answered and shrugged.

"Thanks for paying for the meal," Nick said as we walked to his pickup.

"It was my pleasure."

"I have to admit my masculinity has a hard time with you paying for me," Nick commented.

"Too bad, you'll have to deal with it," I replied, giving him a kiss to let him know I wasn't too serious. We got in his pickup and drove to the Sheriff's Department where we'd left mine.

"Why didn't you want me to say anything about Owen Laterly?" I asked when we parked.

"I thought the least amount of people who know about this the better. After all we are accusing someone of cheating on their wife and worst case scenario possibly killing someone."

"Jessica and James wouldn't tell anyone," I assured him.

"I'm sure they wouldn't, but you never know who might be eavesdropping in a busy restaurant," Nick stated.

I immediately felt foolish, "You're right. I feel sort of stupid right now."

"You are far from stupid. I'll concede you may have a slight problem in that when you get on the trail of a mystery there is no stopping you," Nick said.

"I'm sorry. I can't help myself from trying to figure things out," I apologized.

"You have nothing to be sorry for. Faye and I asked you to look into this, besides I'm falling in love with you exactly the way you are and I wouldn't change a thing about you."

I was momentarily stunned. "You're falling in love with me?"

"You didn't know that?" Nick asked looking surprised.

"I hoped, but neither of us has said it yet," I answered.

"Are you going to leave me hanging?" I must have looked confused as he clarified, "Is there any chance you are falling in love with me too?"

"Oh yes! There is no doubt, a definite wonderful yes!" I was so happy I barely registered kissing Nick goodbye, getting out of his pickup, my drive home, getting out of my pickup, and walking in the house. And that's where I was snapped back to reality at the sight of shredded toilet paper covering the kitchen floor and well into the living room, where I found Wizard zonked out in a big pile of fluffy paper.

CHAPTER SEVEN

Consider a native grass and wildflower seed mix
to transform wet areas in your yard such as septic systems.
Native species root systems not only help prevent
soil erosion but they absorb excess moisture.

"WIZARD!" I SCREECHED. HE JUMPED TO his feet, recognized bloody murder in my eyes and took off as fast as his little legs would carry him. How does it always happen he does these things when nobody but me is home to clean it up? I guess I should be thankful it was an easy enough mess to pick up, he'd gotten into worse things before; flour came to mind. I spent a few minutes picking up the paper, checked to see if our toilet paper stash was in need of replenishment, all the while pondering how to approach the remaining men on the list. Cord didn't strike me as a particularly good suspect—other than his comment about Christopher's body, and Owen sounded like a saint. Although after a moment of consideration, he might have the most to lose with respect to his reputation if an illegitimate child showed up. But who would be so bothered by an illegitimate child that they would resort to murder? Maybe I was thinking about this all wrong. I knew Nick and Faye didn't kill Christopher and I doubted anyone followed him here and happened to place a body in a location that would point to Nick or Faye. It had to be someone local, someone who knew we burned our fields and put the body there hoping it would be destroyed in the fire. I wondered if there was a way they knew about Christopher's connection to Faye, but I couldn't see how. Maybe I could use James as a connection for talking to Al Mitchel. There weren't that many cattle ranchers and they must at least know of each other. Dad might have a connection to Jed. He was retired so I was sure Dad would have run in to him somewhere. The retired farmers tended to gather together at Jessica's restaurant in the morning. I had deliberately not bothered Dad on his cruise. He deserved to have a vacation without his daughter checking in. I debated for a short time and then decided I could make a quick phone call.

"Is something wrong Carmen?" Dad asked when he picked up.

"Why would you think something is wrong?"

"I don't think you'd interrupt our vacation for a simple hello," Dad answered wise as usual.

I took a few minutes to explain what was going on, deliberately not telling him about the murders, only about Faye's connection to Christopher and how Christopher was the son of someone who impersonated him on the Las Vegas trip. Dad was shocked by that, and then I explained our concern for Faye's safety as a reason for my phone call and questions. I told him about Al, Cord, Owen and Jed. When finished I asked, "Do you have any insight into any of them, in particular Jed?"

"I do. You wouldn't remember—it was long before you were involved in the farm—but Jed and I used to share a plow."

"How do you share a plow?" I asked.

"We rarely needed one so Jed and I agreed to split the cost when he was buying a new one. I paid twenty-five percent and he paid seventy-five as he would use it the most."

"How did that work out?" I inquired.

Dad laughed, "Not well. Every time I needed to use it, Jed did too. We tried for two years until we gave up and he bought out my share. He's retired now. I believe Jed's son-in-law took over his farm after Jed's wife died a couple of years ago."

"That's Jill's husband, correct? She works with Faye in the dental office," I said.

"I don't remember her name, but he only had one daughter so I assume so," Dad agreed.

"Do you think he could have been Christopher's father?"

There was a pause; I assumed Dad was thinking, and then he said, "It's possible, he and his wife had several bad years. I have to admit he isn't my favorite person, he's abrupt, even rude at times, but I can't envision him impersonating me."

"I'll keep him on my list anyway," I said. "What about the rest of them?"

"I haven't kept in touch with Owen, mostly because he is a good buddy of Al's and I try to avoid him. Al is a little too full of himself. Cord is a nice guy, I was happy for him when the gravel company leased his land. He tried hard to farm that marginal land without success, I was glad he found a way to make money, but visiting with him in church is the extent of our social interaction anymore. But back to your original question, I can't see any of them impersonating me. At least it's not a murder this time, how do you keep getting involved in these things anyway?" he asked.

"I wish I knew," I answered feeling guilty about keeping Judith and Christopher's deaths from him, but not wanting to ruin his vacation as he would worry about me. "Are you and Karla having fun?"

"We are. In fact we have a surprise for you when we get home." Knowing me well, before I could question him he said, "Don't bother to ask me what it is. You'll find out soon enough. I sense you are keeping something from me too, just promise me you'll be careful. When you get involved in rooting around into people's pasts you have a habit of ending up in danger," Dad cautioned me.

"I will," I said hoping I wasn't promising something I couldn't deliver.

"Remember I do need you alive and well to ensure the farm continues to operate at a profit so I can afford more vacations."

I laughed and said, "I love you Dad, see you Thursday."

After hanging up, I spent a few minutes trying to figure out what the surprise might be before giving up and deciding I might as well try and catch James and see if he could help with a reason to visit Al.

"Good afternoon Carmen. We did say goodbye no more than an hour ago?" James asked when he answered his phone.

I chuckled, "We did, but I was wondering if you had any thoughts on how I might go about questioning Al? I'm hoping because you both have cattle you might know him."

"Why do you need to question Al?" James inquired.

"Nick didn't want me to talk about it at the restaurant in case someone overheard us but we think he may have been the father of Christopher, Faye's ex-boyfriend," I said and explained the situation to him.

"Al has a huge ranch, with a lot of hired men. My operation is small potatoes compared to his. I'm not exactly on a come on over and visit basis with him. Sorry, I'm not much help," James said.

"Thanks anyway," I started to hang up.

"Just a minute Carmen," I heard him say.

"Did you think of something?" I asked.

"What are you doing the rest of the day?"

"Nothing—other than trying on dresses, why?"

"I do need a new bull, and I know Al has one for sale. I wasn't going to look at it, because he's asking way too much money for it, but he doesn't know that. I could call and see if I could check it out today. If I can, you could ride with," James suggested.

"That would be great, I'll be right over," I said getting excited.

"Let me get ahold of him first, and don't get too eager, I'm sure one of his hired men will be dealing with it, not him," James cautioned.

"It is Sunday, so maybe not. Let me know what you find out," I said hoping it would work.

"I will," James said sounding resigned. Throughout Jessica, James, and I's friendship he had always been the reluctant voice of reason when getting involved in our schemes.

Thinking of Jessica I asked, "How come Jessica isn't with you?"

"She stayed at the restaurant to clean up so George could leave early. He's been covering for her a lot the last month and will be again when we leave on our honeymoon so she's trying to give him as much time off as possible."

"That makes sense," I said and tried to hang up again.

I stopped when James said, "By the way Carmen, if Al isn't available you have to come with me regardless. The only reason I'm doing this is for you, so even if it's a hired man instead of Al himself, you're coming."

"Okay, okay," I said laughing. I hung up, ran upstairs, changed out my church clothes, and wondered what a person wore to look at a bull. I decided my normal work clothes would suffice. By the time I tracked down Wizard who was hiding behind the couch, and stuck him in Kirks' room to keep him out of trouble, James had text that someone would be available to show him the bull. I grabbed my keys and ran out the door.

James was waiting for me by his pickup when I got there. "You lucked out; Al himself will be meeting us at his place."

"Great," I said as I jumped in his pickup.

"You owe me big time for this. You do know how awkward it's going to be when I don't buy this animal now," James said.

"Maybe there will be something wrong with it," I answered starting to feel guilty for putting James in this situation.

"The only thing wrong will be the price, Al's a good cattleman; it will be a high quality animal," James replied.

"So where did you decide to go on your honeymoon?" I asked trying to change the topic as we drove to Al's.

"I'm not telling you. I'm planning to surprise Jessica and I know you can't keep a secret from her," he answered.

"That's not true, I knew you were going to propose and I didn't tell her."

"Only because you were chasing a killer and too preoccupied," James reminded me.

I considered and then conceded, "Probably true. Can you at least tell me if it's tropical or not?"

"My lips are sealed. Don't even try to get it out of me," James said staring straight ahead.

I gave up and said, "I can hardly believe in less than two weeks my two best friends are going to be married!"

"I can't wait. I think I've loved Jessica since elementary school," James said with a big smile.

"How did you ever keep it to yourself? Although you shouldn't have, she dated several real losers; you could have saved her some trouble."

James laughed, "I'm confident that would have backfired. She did not think of me that way at all. If I had said something too soon it would have been very awkward between us."

"I guess, but all's well that ends well," I said as we pulled into the farmstead. I whistled. "This is a fancy place."

"Like I said, his operation is huge with no lack of money," James agreed.

The three barns were enormous, each one easily 200 feet by 60 feet. The house was huge—more like an old manor house—and the landscaping was immaculate. "How do you even know where to go?"

"The barn by the man waving his hand over there would be my first guess," James said mocking me.

I rolled my eyes at him. We parked next to the massive bear-like man who turned out to be Al himself.

"Good afternoon James." He reached out to shakes James' hand.

"This is my good friend Carmen Karlaff; she was at loose ends today and decided to ride with," James said explaining my presence.

"It's nice to meet you," I responded feeling awed by the opulence of this place.

"I've seen you at church. Aren't you Chet's daughter?" he asked putting out his hand for a handshake.

"I am," I answered shaking his hand.

"I heard Chet retired and you took over. When Chet first started dabbling in that native stuff I thought he was crazy, even more so when I see some of your equipment. But I guess it turned into a nice little farm for you," he said looking at me almost like it was a question.

"Yes it has turned out well for us," I answered bristling at his attitude.

Perhaps picking up on my animosity he went on to say, "I've always wanted to stop by one day and check out your place. Anytime I've heard anyone talk about it in town, they make it sound like a big mystery."

"I believe less of a mystery than unfamiliarity," I answered.

"You may be right," he said with a smile of acknowledgement. "If you are successful, sometimes the less people that know what you are doing the better."

"I agree. Did you build this farm yourself or inherit it?" I asked.

"Some of both—my father left it to me, his only child, but my wife and I have grown it to its present size. My two sons are taking it over now."

"If you don't mind my asking, do you have that all legally taken care of? I ask because my dad and I have been discussing how to best get our farm transferred to my name," I explained. I was lying as our paperwork had been completed years ago but I was making a lame attempt to find out if there would be any reason an unknown child could mess anything up.

"My wife and I made of point of putting aside plenty of money for retirement so when it was time to turn things over to my sons, there would be no problems. Everything is legally in their names. I haven't always been the best father and I wouldn't want an illegitimate child showing up stealing their inheritance," he said as he roared with laughter.

While I didn't like Al, I didn't think he was that good of an actor. I didn't believe he'd be laughing about an illegitimate child if he had been approached by Christopher. I put Al at the bottom of my mental suspect list, but not being able to help myself I asked, "I hear the man we found in the field we were burning was in town looking for a father he never knew—is there any danger of that being you?"

He doubled over with laughter again at the question, "Nope the missus would've killed me had I ever strayed and trust me I never had eyes for anyone but my wife."

"That's sweet," I said, meaning it and giving him a few points for that—but so far that was the only thing I could say I liked about him.

"But talking about me isn't why you came, walk this way James. I think you're going to find this bull will greatly increase the quality of genetics in your herd." James and he walked in the barn while I followed them.

Twenty minutes later after learning way more about bulls, semen, genetics, and what the right bull could add to a herd, James was the proud owner of a new bull. We got in the pickup with James looking stunned. "You owe me so bad," he said after sitting in silence for a few minutes. "I had zero intentions of buying that bull."

"He did reduce the price for you," I said in an attempt to make him feel better.

"He did, and he was quite the salesman, but. . ." his voice trailed off.

"Would it help if I said I was sorry?" I offered.

"It helps, but you owe me," James said with a big sigh.

"What can I do for you?" I asked expecting him to say nothing.

He thought for a moment and said, "Jessica and I are using my pickup to leave for the honeymoon after the wedding. There's a lot of cow manure on it."

"You want me to wash your pickup?"

"I do," he stated emphatically.

I knew when I was beaten. "I agree," I said and we shook hands.

Kirk was in the kitchen when I got home. "What is that smell?" he asked.

"Me, I had to wash James' pickup for him." I looked at my clothes wondering if they were worth washing or if I should throw them away.

"Why did you wash his pickup?" Kirk asked.

"It's a long story—suffice it to say I owed him. You cooked?" I asked happy to smell something beside myself. "Wow what's the occasion?"

"I saw the paper in the garbage. I figured I owed you for the Wizard mess," Kirk answered and shrugged.

I looked in the kettle, "yum, you made vegetable beef soup. I'll take a quick shower and I'll be right back." I ran upstairs and as I was dressing after my shower I noticed the unopened packages containing the maid of honor dress options. After supper, I promised myself I would try them on, and then I hurried back downstairs.

"I haven't had much chance to talk to you the last few days; you've been busy with the band. Are things going well?" I asked when we were sitting down to eat.

"They are, but I feel bad I'm leaving you in the lurch this summer," Kirk answered.

"You don't have to feel bad. Dad and I have always known that your heart isn't here. We never planned for you to spend your life on the farm. By the way, the soup is great. I think you should have been cooking more often over the years. I didn't even know you could."

"I'm not stupid," he grinned. "You would have expected more meals from me."

I smiled and acknowledged the truth of the statement. "I'll wash the dishes as a thank you for cooking. I have to clean and do a few loads of laundry anyway."

"Thanks, I'll take Wizard out for a walk. He's been cooped up all day."

"I don't feel too sorry for him—he did find his own entertainment." We both looked at Wizard who was wagging his tail not at all upset by the mention of his latest misdeed. I cleared the table and Kirk and Wizard went outside. Before starting on the kitchen, I gathered up the dirty clothes, sorted them, and threw a load in. It was too late in the day for a thorough house cleaning, but I ran a vacuum over the floors, picked up the miscellaneous garbage that always miraculously multiplied and accumulated, and did a quick cleaning of the two bathrooms. Kirk and Wizard came in as I started on the kitchen. Kirk swept while I washed the dishes and put another load of clothes in the washing machine.

"I'm going to my bedroom. I have a few lyrics going through my head that I want to try and write down," Kirk said when he finished sweeping.

"Have fun. You are going to be able to help burn tomorrow I hope? The wind won't pick up until after dinner, so I won't need you until one or two in the afternoon."

"That will work. I'll be there," Kirk answered and went to his bedroom with Wizard following.

I went upstairs and not being able to avoid it any longer, I opened the packages. Two of the dresses were hideous and could be returned, but the other two were promising. I spent the next forty minutes going back and forth trying them on. I settled on the dress I had matching shoes for which would save me the trouble of shoe shopping. I sent Jessica a text letting her know I picked a dress and did one last load of laundry.

CHAPTER EIGHT

*The flowers of sweet joe pye weed have a faint
vanilla scent that is an attractant for butterflies.*

I WOKE UP AT 6:30 A.M. MONDAY morning to the sound of my phone ringing. It was the Erickson's. "Good morning Marge. Is something wrong?"

"Yes and no," she responded.

Puzzled, I asked, "What does that mean?"

"There is a bear outside our cabin," she said, almost whispering now.

"That's kind of exciting. You wanted to see wildlife didn't you?" I questioned wondering what the problem was.

"I agree. It is thrilling, but the problem is, we were sitting outside last night having an impromptu picnic and not thinking, we left our garbage outside without putting it in the garbage receptacle you provided. The bear appears to be quite content going through everything and I don't think he's leaving anytime soon," she said.

"I'll be right there." I threw on cloths, skipped breakfast, figuring I'd be back soon and drove to the cabins hoping I wouldn't disturb Hugh Murkins. When I got close to cabin C there was what looked to be a 300 pound bear tearing at the garbage. Not wanting to honk the horn and wake up Hugh, I drove as close to the cabin as I could. The bear looked up and started to amble off. I continued to drive behind him, not chasing him, but letting him know I was serious. He eventually ambled off into the woods about a half mile from the cabin and disappeared. I drove back to the Erickson's, got out of the pickup, and knocked on the door. "He's gone, but he may be back now that he knows food is here," I told them feeling a little exasperated.

"We are so sorry, we know better than to leave food around," Alex said apologizing.

"I'll clean it up for you. I don't think you have anything to worry about. It was a black bear and they're more scared of you than you need to be of them, unless there are cubs present. I believe that was a boar, which is good, but be alert and make sure you clean up the food."

"Why did you call it a boar?" Marge asked.

"A male bear is called a boar, which is why I said it was good—if it was a sow, a female bear—she might have had cubs with her and could potentially be more dangerous if she felt she needed to protect them."

"Thank you Carmen, and again we're so sorry," Alex repeated.

"Can you get me a garbage bag from the cabin?" I asked.

They pitched in and helped me pick up the garbage. I checked to make sure the bear hadn't damaged the critter-proof garbage receptacle I had provided for the cabins and then put the bag of garbage in the back of my pickup. I said goodbye and head back home hoping this wouldn't continue to be a problem.

I was hungry and starting to get a headache from missing breakfast and my morning caffeine. It was going to be a long day. Kirk was in his bedroom and I could hear him on his keyboard, but he had made coffee. I poured myself a cup while I scrambled two eggs and made toast. As I sat at the kitchen table eating my breakfast I wondered not for the first time if I had made a wise decision to dabble in the tourism business. But then I reminded myself of what my latest spreadsheet had shown; the profits from the cabins were making the loan payment, paying Jessica and Edna for their food, and leaving me a small profit each month. It would be even better if I decided to open them up for the winter months. I know snow-shoer's and cross country skiers would love it, but I had yet to work out the logistics of keeping a road plowed for food delivery and the cost to heat the cabins. Although the heat wouldn't be that much extra as I already had to keep them heated to ensure the pipes wouldn't freeze. However, we had a tough time keeping up with the snow removal we already did; I couldn't imagine adding the cabin road. Oh well, a problem to be dealt with another day. My thoughts turned to Judith's death. When she had talked to me I remember thinking I hoped she was overreacting and meth wasn't that big of a problem around here, but I guess it was everywhere else, why not here? If it wasn't being brought here, then someone was making it locally. I started thinking of possible people who might be involved and came up blank. I sighed, it was a good thing Judith's murder was the sheriff's problem. My only concern was Christopher's death—I didn't want Nick or Faye to be blamed for it. They were new to the area and as much as I hated to admit Nick was right, we did tend to view outsiders with some skepticism. If Christopher's murder remained unsolved, people would always think it was one or both of them, and I did not want either one of them to move away. I finished my breakfast and saw it was time to head to the farm. I had to meet with the school guidance couselor, April, at noon today, and burning was this afternoon, but with a chance of rain in the forecast for tomorrow, fertilizer had to be spread on the fields that were already burned. Nick had been thinking the same; he had the fertilizer spreader hooked up to the tractor when I drove in.

"Good morning. I see great minds think alike," I said nodding at the equipment.

"I may be new here, but I'm getting things figured out. Pretty soon I'll be anticipating your every desire," he said with a mock leer.

I laughed and asked, "What are you going to do while I spread the fertilizer?"

"I'm going to get the parts we picked up the other day installed on the four-wheeler."

"I have to meet with April Hewsy at noon about finding a few summer roguers. If I'm not done spreading fertilizer can you take over for me?"

"I can, call me when you have to leave and I'll bring your pickup out to the field and switch places with you."

"Thanks." I had three fields to cover. I decided to start with the one farthest away. I pulled out on the highway after making sure all my hazard lights were working. Driving on the main highway was nerve wracking. The traveling public often didn't recognize how much slower farm equipment was. I was thankful the trip was uneventful and I arrived safe at our fields. It wasn't going to be a smooth ride, the gophers loved prairie cordgrass and there were a lot of gopher mounds to bump over. I made a mental note to give Gary a call and let him know. One of his kids trapped gophers for us. I was on the last field when I checked the time and realized Nick was going to have to fill in for me. I was just about finished, but I knew April had a set dinner period, and I couldn't be late. I called Nick and he was there in five minutes. I jumped in my pickup and sped towards the school taking a peek in the rear view mirror to make sure I hadn't managed to get dirt or grease on my face. All was good. I parked on the street in front of the school. I graduated a long time ago and hadn't had any reason to be on the school grounds until now, so it felt awkward walking in the building. I stopped in the administrative office first as the resource officer indicated I needed to sign in. They told me where April's office was and I hustled to it, thankful classes were in session and the hallways weren't full of teenagers. April's door was open and

I poked my head in as I rapped on the open door. I started to walk in, but hesitated as I was sure I saw Hugh Murkins going around a corner. I shook my head, I must have been mistaken. I couldn't imagine why he'd be on the school grounds.

I was jerked back to reality when April asked, "Are you Carmen?"

"Yes I am. I'm sorry. I was distracted, I thought I saw someone I knew, but I must have been mistaken. Thank you for taking the time to meet with me."

"It's my pleasure. I understand you're looking for recommendations for a responsible eighteen year old that might be interested in a summer job."

We spent the next fifteen minutes discussing the details of the job, the pay, and what would be required.

"Well, that lets out a few of my recommendations. Two were looking for evening work as they had prior commitments for the morning, but I think I know two who would work well for you. I can't of course give you their contact information, but if you could leave me yours I'll let them know and they can call you if they are interested."

"I appreciate this; it's kind of out the scope of your job to be lining up summer employment."

"I don't mind. The two I'm thinking of are good kids, both intelligent and have been accepted to the University of North Dakota for the fall semester and could use the money. Knowing their home lives it's best to keep them busy with a job so they don't get into trouble. Heaven knows there are enough temptations to derail kids."

"Besides home situations causing problems, out of curiosity, have you noticed any drug problems here in the school?"

"Of course, doesn't every school deal with that?" April answered.

"I'm finding out I'm very naïve. I had assumed, or maybe hoped we were immune to it way up here in the boonies."

She laughed. "That is naïve."

"You heard about Judith Lansing's murder I'm sure?" I probed.

"I did. What a tragedy. I didn't know her personally. She did fill a cavity for me once, but that was my only interaction with her. Did what happened to her have something to do with drugs?"

"I think so. I was getting a tooth fixed the same day she was killed, and she told me she was seeing a lot of meth mouth in people. I think she had suspicions about the source or at least who was involved." As I answered I watched to see if she had any sort of suspicious reaction.

"She didn't tell you who?" she asked.

"No, she was checking with colleagues about the possible effect on her license if she told the sheriff."

"It sounds like someone got to her before she could spill. That's too bad. There have been several kids who have been a heart break to their parents by letting drugs ruin their lives. We do what we can, but I don't think anything helps anymore. Drugs are everywhere," she said, her voice sounding defeated. "It's a shame she didn't get a chance to tell anyone what she knew."

"I agree, but I've taken up enough of your time. You have my cell phone number to pass on to the kids?"

"I do and I will. I hope at least one of them works out for you."

"Thank you. Do you want your door shut?" I asked as I walked out the door.

"Please," she answered.

I shut the door, and started to walk away when I remembered I should have told her I wasn't opposed to hiring more than one person. I went to knock on the door and I heard her voice say in anger, "that was very risky, but I think you lucked out. Don't ever pull anything like that again." Her voice sounded so at odds with the demeanor I had just witnessed from her that I felt uncomfortable talking to her again. She was sure to know I had overheard her. I decided to walk away feeling sorry for whatever poor kid had done something wrong. I signed out of the school in the administrative office, walked out to my pickup, and checked the time. I didn't realize how late in the afternoon it was. After calling to authorize my burning permit, I drove to the convenience store and grabbed a deli sandwich for dinner and ate it as I drove to the seed plant hoping Nick and Kirk would have everything ready for burning.

I didn't need to worry. They were waiting for me with the equipment ready. I did one last check of the wind, it was going to switch direction in about two hours but we should have plenty of time to finish the field before that happened. It would be a long day of burning as the direction the wind was switching to would be favorable for the next field which was our largest acreage crop, big bluestem. Six hours later we were smoky smelling, ashy, and exhausted. Kirk asked if he could leave as the band was practicing tonight and he was already late. We told him to go ahead, and Nick and I put the equipment away.

"What do you have planned for supper?" Nick asked.

"Nothing."

"Why don't you come over to my place, Faye tried a slow cooker barley soup recipe this morning and it should be ready."

"That sounds good. I'll swing by home to take a shower first and I'll be right over," I answered thankful I wouldn't have to find something to cook for supper.

By the time I arrived home Kirk had already been and gone, taking Wizard with him. I hoped for Kyle's sake Kirk would keep better track of Wizard this time. I didn't see Tabitha, but Clyde and the feral cat were lounging on the patio chair cushions. I looked around and finally spotted her sleeping in a sunny spot at the base of a tree. I took a quick shower, put on shorts, a t-shirt, and grabbed a box of frozen garlic toast from the freezer to go with the soup.

Faye and Nick were setting the table when I got there. Nick's huge black cat was sitting in the entryway looking skittish. "When did he move in the house?" I asked.

"When Faye moved in; she felt bad about him being outside so she's been letting him in the house," Nick answered not sounding at all upset by it.

"He's not quite sure about it though," Faye said. "He only comes as far as the entryway and is nervous the entire time. But I'm making progress. He started out by panicking when the door shut behind him and jumping at the door. Now he watches us and sometimes takes a short nap on the cushion I have sitting by the door. I'm hopeful by the time fall is here he'll feel comfortable enough to stay in the house for the winter."

"It's not like he had it rough, he had a heated water dish and an insulated heated house to stay in," Nick commented.

"Yes, but he didn't get much attention," Faye said. "I'm envisioning you reading a book or watching television with a cat on your lap. It'll be company for you if I ever do find my own place to live."

"It looks like whether you like it or not you're going to have a house cat," I teased Nick knowing he didn't mind one bit, as he loved cats.

I put the garlic bread in the toaster oven and when it was done I placed it next to the slow cooker Faye had set on the table. We ate in comfortable silence.

Faye was putting away the leftovers when she said, "I forgot to tell you what I found in Judith's files today."

CHAPTER NINE

Native plants are a perfect choice for rain gardens.
A rain garden, which is a shallow, bowl-shaped area,
collects water runoff from impervious surfaces such as
downspouts, roofs, and paved areas.A rain garden creates
a holding area for the water that often comes too fast
for the soil to absorb.

"YOU FOUND SOMETHING IN HER FILES?" I repeated.

"Yes, the sheriff brought a warrant and I was helping him go through files today."

"What did you find?" I asked eagerly.

"Judith had a notebook tucked in the back of her bottom desk drawer. I almost missed it as she had stuck it in a magazine."

"What was in it?" I asked; my nosiness at peak attention.

"She scribbled the names of six different people with notations next to each name," Faye answered as she sat back down.

"How come you're only saying something now?" Nick asked.

"How could you have not been bursting at the seams to tell us this right away?" I chimed in leaning in excitement towards her.

Faye laughed. "I wanted to be able to enjoy the expressions on your faces."

"So whose names were in it?" Nick asked.

"The sheriff took it from me," Faye answered leaning back in her chair.

"Oh, crud," I said disappointed.

"But not before I snapped a quick picture with my phone," Faye said grinning at us. "I printed it out when I got home. Here it is."

I grabbed it and started mumbling the names, "Nolan Richland, the new principal—with scribbles about the high school, Darius, the IPD driver, Sally Steward; I think she's the new veterinarian, and April Hewsy. She's got arrows going back and forth between the principal, the veterinarian office, the Kentz's four-wheeler place, and Peter Inver, the banker." I stopped and then said in a shocked voice, "I know most of these people. None of them would be involved in drugs." My voice trailed off.

Nick put his hand on my shoulder while he took the piece of paper from me. "I kind of wish you guys hadn't seen this."

"Why?" Faye asked.

"Because messing with drugs and finding out who murdered Judith is the sheriff's job; and none of the names you listed have anything to do with Christopher."

I shook my head and admitted, "You're right, I don't want anybody to mistakenly think we're trying to find out who killed Judith and who was selling meth."

"Besides we need to be concentrating on who killed Christopher," Faye said. "The sheriff was polite to me today, but I could tell he didn't trust me."

"Maybe he was right not to," Nick said as he held up the piece of paper.

Faye looked sheepish and replied, "I couldn't help it. Judith was my boss and friend, plus you heard the sheriff, he thinks one possible theory for Judith's murder may have something to do with

Christopher's; which means in his opinion we might be involved in both murders."

"She's not wrong," I said to Nick.

"I know," Nick grunted, sitting down again looking discouraged. "But we know the two murders aren't tied together, so we need to concentrate on Christopher. I'm sure it's one of the men I suspect of being his father."

"I did talk to Al Mitchel, Cord McCaster, and Jed Alman. None of them gave me any indication they had been approached by anyone. In fact Al told me his sons are already in charge of his farm so I can't imagine a long-lost son showing up would cause any undue hardship. Cord appeared blasé when I brought anything up. Jed didn't even react when I suggested Christopher was in town looking for his father plus Dad told me Jed's wife is dead and his son-in-law took over his farm. I don't think an illegitimate son showing up would be a big deal to him either. I don't know Owen Laterly, so I haven't thought of way to talk to him yet. Did the sheriff give you any indication today if he took our theory serious enough to talk to any of the men?" I asked Faye.

"He didn't say anything one way or the other," she answered shrugging.

"I'll have to come up with a reason to talk to Owen," I said.

"James said Owen owns several buildings in town. Maybe Jessica rents from him?" Nick asked.

"No, she owns her building, but I bet Melanie does. Jessica and I were planning on going out to eat with her and Marcy tomorrow night. I can ask her if she knows him. I doubt Marcy would as she owns her house and unless Owen is a reader she wouldn't have run into him at her workplace, the library."

"What's the plan for work tomorrow? It's supposed to rain. What would you like me to do?" Nick asked.

"The rain isn't supposed to start until mid-morning so I'm hoping you can get the fertilizer spread on the fields we burnt this afternoon. I've got a 1000 acre CRP seed mixture I'll be working on. I don't have enough of the same seed lots for the entire mix so I have work to do on the computer to figure out a seed tag that shows all the different lots, plus I haven't entered the new lot of prairie blazing star I had to buy in due to the moth larvae eating a quarter of our crop before I got it sprayed—that's expensive seed to replace—I'd better be more diligent this year. I'll do that while you spread the fertilizer. We should be done about the same time and then if you could help me mix it that would be great. The custom seeder is picking it up around noon."

I turned to Faye, "What are you going to do about a job? I assume Judith's husband, Dan, is closing the clinic."

"He's not. He told us he would keep paying us while he advertises for another dentist to come in. Well, at least for six months. We have plenty of cleanings to do and a dentist from Parkville is willing to fill in one day a week for emergencies. If he hasn't found a dentist to take over the practice in six months then he'll have to close," Faye answered.

"That's nice of him. I hope he finds someone, it's handy to have a dentist in town."

"I was surprised he was willing to keep it open. He's devastated by Judith's death of course, but he's thinking of us. That tells you what kind of a guy he is," Faye stated.

"Has Dan said anything about when the funeral is?"

"It doesn't sound like there will be one. He said Judith hated funerals and wanted to be cremated with only a small ceremony for immediate family. I guess they both had talked about end of life decisions." Faye wiped her eyes.

"They were young to have discussed those types of decisions; wise though," I pondered.

"Is Kirk leaving at the end of the week?" Nick asked switching the topic, no doubt knowing I was starting to get suspicious of Dan.

"Yes, on Friday. He and his band are going on a three week tour through upper Michigan and Wisconsin that their agent lined up."

"He's missing the wedding?" Faye asked.

"He's going to make an all-night drive after their performance on the Friday night before the wedding. He's hoping to catch some sleep after the Saturday wedding and then drive back and meet up with the band on Sunday. They didn't schedule a performance the night of the wedding, so other than lacking sleep his plan should work. The only problem is I'll be on Wizard duty for a few weeks," I said shaking my head ruefully.

Nick laughed and said, "Better you than me."

"Thanks. On that note, it's almost nine and I'm exhausted. I better get home. I'll see you tomorrow."

"I'll walk you out," Nick said and got up startling his cat that had fallen asleep on the cushion by the door. He blasted outside when Nick opened the door. "I don't think he'll be back in tonight," Nick said to Faye.

"You're may be right; but I am making progress." Faye smiled.

"Thanks for supper Faye, it was delicious."

"Anytime, I'm glad you liked it."

Nick and I walked out to my pickup, and before getting in we hugged and held on to each other enjoying the closeness. After a few minutes, Nick broke away and kissed the top of my head. I tilted my face up and we shared a gentle kiss.

"That was nice," I said.

"Yes it was. We somehow need to find the time for more of that," Nick said as I rested my head on his shoulder.

"I agree," I concurred enjoying the earthy scent of him.

"Perhaps if dead bodies would quit showing up there would be more time for us," Nick said holding me away from him and looking in my eyes.

"Does it bother you that I keep getting involved in murders?" I asked him, a little concerned what his answer would be.

"Bother, no, especially as this time it is due to my family, but I'd be lying if I didn't admit that I'm worried. Not just one, but two dead bodies and drugs too."

"But I'm only investigating the one murder," I said trying to make him feel better.

Nick smiled at me, and then pulled me close again, "Somehow I can't help but believe you're going to be involved in it all."

We said goodnight again and as I drove home, I thought about the piece of paper Faye had shown us. I tried to reconcile the thought of any of those people being involved with meth. It made me sick to think that people associated with the school might be making and selling meth. It wasn't much better that people I knew and respected, like the Kentz's or Peter Inver were listed also. I wondered if Judith had any basis for her doodles or if she was only thinking. I couldn't help but remember Nick saying I would end up getting involved in it all. I smiled to myself—he really did know me. Every day I appreciated Nick more, not only did I enjoy his company—my friends and family liked him too. He gave every indication he was content and happy with my farm and lifestyle and most of all he let me be me. I'd come to the conclusion I wasn't worried about his past—I knew the type of man he was. I was only sorry I hadn't been the type of person he felt he could share his past with earlier. My thoughts were interrupted by my phone ringing. Caller id showed Jessica's phone number.

"Hi Jessica, what's up?"

"I was wondering if you'd have any time tomorrow to pay a condolence visit to Dan?" she asked.

Her words hit me in the gut, upset with myself for not thinking of doing something before. "Of course, I'll make time—let me know when."

"I should be done at the restaurant tomorrow by 3:30 p.m. Does that work for you?" she asked.

"That will be fine, it's supposed to be raining tomorrow afternoon."

"Great, I'm going to make a hotdish and bring it over to them for supper," Jessica said.

"I'll make cookies tonight to take with too." We spent a little time discussing wedding plans; we hadn't yet found anyone to do our hair and makeup. Personally I thought we could make do without, but Jessica was insisting. She tried to get out of me what I had planned for her bachelorette party. It wasn't hard to keep from telling her any details as other than picking the date and inviting everyone, I hadn't gotten much farther with any plans. We finished talking and I hung up the same time I turned in our driveway. I was surprised to see Kirk's car parked in front of the garage. I thought he was going to be late tonight. I opened the door to the muffled sound of Wizard's barks, then discordant chords of music.

I knocked on Kirks' door, and he said, "Come in."

I opened the door and burst into laughter. Wizard was dressed in a doggy version of a black leather jacket sitting next to Kirk who was on his keyboard.

"Listen to this," Kirk said looking at me smiling. He started playing one of his more popular songs and when it was time for the refrain, he pointed at Wizard who enthusiastically barked along. When the refrain was over, he pointed again, and Wizard stopped, wagging his tail waiting for more. "What do you think?" Kirk asked.

"It's amazing; I didn't think Wizard had it in him to be trained to do anything?"

"There's nothing saying he'll do it again, but right now he's enjoying it," Kirk said smiling with pride.

"True. I thought you were going to be practicing until late tonight?" I asked.

"I thought I was, but Squirt couldn't make it." Squirt was the nickname of their bass guitar player who was a short, muscled blonde with full sleeve tattoos. I always wondered where the nickname Squirt came from, and yet wasn't sure I wanted to know either. "Do you have a minute to talk?"

"Sure, what's up?" I asked knowing something serious was coming my way as Kirk wasn't in the habit of asking to talk with me.

"I think something is wrong with Squirt," he surprised me by saying.

"What do you mean?" I asked.

"He's missed a couple of practices, and when he does show up, he's not himself. He's very agitated and short tempered. The other guys are talking about kicking him out of the band. I can't do that—he's been my friend since third grade. But the band is starting to enjoy a bit of success, and we can't rely on him anymore."

"Have you talked to him?"

"I tried, he brushed me off. I think he might be taking drugs. What am I supposed to do?" Kirk asked, clearly hoping I would have something wise to suggest.

I sat in stunned silence for a few moments. Drugs were popping up everywhere around me lately. "Are you sure?"

"I haven't witnessed him taking anything, but the signs are all there. I don't know how to help him."

"Have you talked to his family?"

"I tried to talk to his sister, but she didn't want to hear it. She said I was crazy and told me to stay away from their parents as they had enough to deal with. Squirt's father is recovering from a hip replacement and his mother is in her final treatments for breast cancer."

"Couldn't Squirt be distracted because he's worried about them?"

"That's what convinced me something more serious is going on. When I asked him about his parents, he looked at me with a blank expression and told me he hadn't been to see them for about a month. His family has to know what's going on, but must not have the energy to deal with it."

"That's understandable given all they are going through. Could you and the band hold an intervention?"

"I suggested that too, but the other guys didn't want to get involved."

"I don't know what to tell you, other than to keep in touch with him and be there for him." I knew I wasn't helping Kirk a whole lot, but I honestly didn't know what else to say.

"I will, but if I have to kick him out of the band, I doubt he's going to want to continue to be my friend."

"You're in a tough spot. You're not going to like this suggestion, but I think you should talk to the sheriff. It appears Judith's death is related to drugs and he might want to interview Squirt. Maybe whoever he's buying them from will know something about her murder."

"That will endear me to Squirt, turning him over to law enforcement. He most likely won't tell the sheriff anything beneficial and he'll hate me too."

I nodded acknowledging the truth of his words, "I don't know what else to say."

Kirk hung his head as he absently scratched Wizard. "I know, thanks for listening anyway."

I gave him a hug and said, "I'd better get to bed, good luck." I stood up and suddenly remembered the cookies I had told Jessica I'd make for Judith's family. "Oh, no, I forgot."

"What's the matter?" Kirk asked.

"Jessica and I are going over to Dan Lansing's tomorrow. She's going to bring a hotdish, and I was supposed to make cookies tonight."

"I can do it," Kirk offered.

I looked at him in surprise, "You can make cookies?"

"Yes I can, I'm not a complete imbecile," he replied smiling at my astonishment. "After all, I'm the one who distracted you and I don't have anything going on tomorrow morning." Noticing my hesitation he said again, "I can do it. Don't worry."

"Are you sure?" I asked.

"I'm positive."

"Okay. Thanks a lot Kirk."

I shut his door and walked up the steps to my bedroom thinking about what Kirk had told me. What a waste of a life, I said a silent prayer that Squirt would come to his senses. Tabitha was lying on my bed. She stretched and jumped down when I walked in. She walked out the door, sat down in the hallway and meowed at me. "I guess your royal highness wants to go out for the night," I told her as I followed her down the steps and let her outside. As long as I was downstairs, I helped myself to a glass of orange juice and then walked back upstairs to get ready for bed.

CHAPTER TEN

Establishing a native landscape in your yard will require less mowing and fewer pesticides than traditional lawns, but patience is needed as it may take a couple of years.

ON THE WAY TO THE SEED plant Tuesday morning I thought about Kirk's situation with Squirt. I was happy when Kirk informed me this morning that he planned to talk to the sheriff. Hopefully the seriousness of the sheriff talking to him would at least scare Squirt enough that he would get the help he needs. I only hoped Squirt would understand Kirk's role in this someday. He and Kirk had been friends for many years and I would hate for this to ruin it. When I asked Kirk what made him decide to talk to the sheriff he told me he kept thinking that if something ever happened to Dad or me, he would want the sheriff to know about anyone who might know something.

When I arrived I could see Nick's pickup parked by the shop and the fertilizer spreader was gone. Nick was busy and it was time for me to get productive too. I head to the office, entered the prairie blazing star seed lot in the computer and started calculating a seed mix using up various small seed lots that had been left over. It was a time consuming process as I had to make sure the seed tests were current, along with checking that the seed percentages required for the mix were correct. I also had to periodically run over to the seed plant to check the inventory of each lot. We did our best to keep track, but when you got down to the last few pounds of grass seed and ounces of wildflowers left in inventory—what the computer said we had didn't always match what was on the shelf. After several tries I completed the seed mix. The list of seed lots on the seed tag was longer than I liked as there were several different lots of the same type of seed, but it couldn't be helped. I went over to the seed plant and started pulling seed bags off the shelves to get them ready for mixing. Nick joined me after I had been working for about thirty minutes.

"What can I help with?" he asked after greeting me with a kiss that made me forget what I was even doing.

I shook my head trying to ground myself. "I need thirty bags of big bluestem, Lot 1887, and ten bags of sideoats grama—there is only one lot left of that."

Nick took the forklift and started getting the sideoats off the top shelf. We worked for around two hours, accumulating the seed lots and putting it all in our seed mixer. We finished as the custom seeder was pulling up with the cleaned out horse trailer he used to haul seed around. We loaded his trailer, had him sign a bill of lading, and he was on his way, hoping to get some seeding done before the rain.

Nick looked at the weather on his phone and said, "It looks like the rain is a couple hours away yet—do you want to chance burning one of the smaller wildflower fields?"

"No. I should, but to be honest I'm hungry and by the time we got all the equipment moved it would be too late. Jessica and I are paying a condolence call on the Lansing's this afternoon so I need enough time to get home, shower, and check on the cookies Kirk was going to make for me."

Nick looked at me in amazement, "Did I hear what you said accurately?"

I laughed, "You did." And I explained to him how Kirk ended up making cookies for me. "Do you want to head to town to eat at Jessica's restaurant or did you pack a dinner?" I asked him.

"I did, but it was only a peanut butter and jelly sandwich, Jessica's food sounds a lot better," Nick said.

My phone rang, I didn't recognize the number and I stepped away from Nick to answer it. When I finished I walked back to Nick with a spring in my step.

"You look happy, good news?" Nick asked me.

"That was the two teenagers April Hewsy, the guidance counselor, recommended for rogueing. They want the job, and being good friends they each were on the line wondering if it was possible they could both work for me. I was more than happy to hire them. Our rogueing crew should be set for the summer." I was excited that I had one less thing to worry about. "Are you ready to go to town for dinner? We'll have to drive separate though, as I need to go home right after we eat." Before Nick could answer me, my phone rang again. "Hi Kirk, did you get the cookies baked? He did, Oh no. I'll meet you there."

Alerted by the sense of urgency in my voice, Nick stepped closer to me and asked, "What's wrong?"

"Somehow Wizard got a hold of a bag of chocolate chips and ate them all. Kirk is on the way to the veterinarian's office right now. I'm going to meet him there."

"I'll take you." We ran for Nick's pickup, and he ignored the speed limit as we raced to the veterinarian's office which was located about four miles out of town on a twenty acre wooded piece of property, with a decrepit old house on the opposite end of the acreage. It was a good location guaranteeing there were no complaints from neighbors concerning smells or barking dogs.

"I can't believe how worried I am about that dog, I've always thought of him as a giant pest," I said as we pulled in the veterinarian's parking lot. Before Nick had even brought the pickup to a full stop, I unbuckled my seatbelt, let myself out, and raced in to the veterinary office where Kirk was pacing back and forth. Nick joined us a few seconds later.

"How is he?" I asked Kirk.

"I don't know. They took him back and are trying to induce vomiting. If that doesn't work, they'll have to pump his stomach."

I took Kirk by the arm and led him over to a chair, "How did he get a bag of chocolate chips?" I asked him when we were both sitting. Nick stood next to us.

"I finished a batch of cookies after you left this morning and then I thought I would go talk to the sheriff about Squirt. Before I left I decided to take out the ingredients to make another batch of cookies when I got back to share with the band. When I got home, the floor was a mess of butter wrappers, chocolate chips, and empty chocolate chip bags. Wizard was laying there panting. I can't believe I was so stupid, I know dogs can't have chocolate. I left them on the table and one of the chairs wasn't pushed in, he must have climbed up somehow on the table. I should have put everything on the counter."

"Don't feel bad, Wizard has a way of getting into things no matter what we do. I'm sure he'll be okay." As I finished talking the veterinarian came out to talk to us. She was a short, strong looking woman with black curly hair. She walked with a pronounced limp.

"He's going to be fine," she said. "We got him to vomit, but he needs to stay here overnight so we can keep an eye on him."

"Can I see him?" Kirk asked.

"Give us a few minutes until we get him in a kennel. One of the technicians will come get you." She started to hobble away, then turned and limped back to us. "Are you Carmen Karlaff?"

"Yes, have we met?" I asked knowing I was sure we hadn't. The previous veterinarian had retired and I remember James lamenting the new veterinarian didn't treat large animals. He had to use one that was over forty minutes away.

"No, we haven't, my name is Sally Stewart. I've heard rumors you're the person to talk to about Judith's murder."

"I think the sheriff would be better than me," I answered surprised. Nick looked at her in puzzlement, but walked away giving us privacy.

"I tried talking to him. He didn't act like anything I told him was worth considering—I wasn't impressed." She continued, "Judith was a good friend of mine. We went to the same college. She was instrumental in my coming here. I know something serious was bothering her the last few weeks."

"The symptoms of meth she was noticing in her patients," I answered, then noticing her expression I continued, "at least that's what she told me about when she was fixing my tooth."

"I have no doubt she was concerned about the meth, but I think there was something more, I think she knew who was responsible. Judith kept tablets she used as journals; she wrote in them every day, if she revealed her suspicions anywhere, it would be in her journals. If I'm right, Judith would have hid them from Dan—he didn't want her pursuing it and could be vindictive when she didn't obey him. Judith said she was scared of what he might do to her. I don't think they got along very well anymore. Your boyfriend's sister works in Judith's dental office; will you please have her keep an eye open for the tablets?"

"I'll let her know. Thanks for helping Wizard."

"My pleasure, he's a cute dog. But don't be fooled by Dan, he's not the nice guy he portrays himself to be, and I don't believe Judith didn't want a funeral." She turned and limped away.

I sat there stunned until Kirk walked out of the back room looking a lot happier than he had five short minutes ago. Nick had been perusing magazines and came over also.

"How is he?" I asked Kirk.

"He's pretty out of it, but he did lick my hand. I'm so relieved he's going to be okay," Kirk said as he sunk into the chair next to me.

"I am too." Wizard may drive me crazy, but I loved him. "Is it okay if Nick and I leave? We need to eat before I pick up your cookies and meet with Jessica to stop by Dan's house."

"Yes, thanks for coming. I'll be leaving in a little bit too. They said Wizard will sleep the rest of the day and I can pick him up early tomorrow morning."

"I'll see you later, and thanks for making the cookies for me." I gave him a hug and Nick and I walked out to his pickup.

"Did I hear the vet correct—she almost sounded like she was accusing Dan of killing Judith because she was investigating the meth problem?" Nick asked in amazement.

"I'm not sure she went that far, but she sure made it sound like Judith was scared of Dan. She claimed Judith was a close friend of hers and that Dan and Judith weren't getting along. She also claimed Judith would have wanted a funeral. I don't think I believe a word she said. I didn't know Judith well, but I never got any impression she didn't have a happy marriage. Jessica knew Judith better than I did, maybe she'll know for sure."

"What purpose would the vet have for lying?" Nick asked.

"No idea, maybe she wasn't lying, only interpreting things incorrectly," I offered. "She did say Judith kept journals, which would be helpful if they were found. I'm looking forward to visiting with Jessica about Judith though, and it should be an interesting visit with Dan. I would hope we'd be able to tell something from his demeanor, after all if he killed his wife, he'd have to be acting at least a little strange, wouldn't he?" I asked Nick.

"I wouldn't count on it, people deal with grief differently and if their marriage wasn't going well he could be feeling a lot of guilt over that, without having had anything to do with her murder," Nick cautioned.

"True." I looked at the time and reluctantly said, "I better skip eating at the restaurant and grab a bite to eat when I go home to pick up the cookies."

"I understand," Nick said and he drove me back to the seed plant where my pickup was parked.

"Thanks so much for driving Nick." I leaned across the seat, gave him a kiss and started to get out of the pickup.

I stopped when Nick said, "Give me a call tonight and let me know how it goes, will you?"

"I will." I smiled at him and walked to my pickup. I drove home, made my favorite quick meal—two over-easy eggs with toast-showered, dressed, grabbed the cookies, and left to meet up with Jessica at her restaurant.

I pulled in the back alley of the restaurant with seconds to spare. Jessica was standing next to her car waiting for me. I rolled down my window and asked, "Do you want to take my vehicle?"

"I already have my hotdish in my backseat, why don't you jump in with me," she answered.

"Okay." I parked, grabbed the cookies and climbed in her car. As it was a short drive to Dan and Judith's house, I jumped right in and told Jessica about Wizard's trip to the veterinarian and what Sally told me about Judith and Dan.

"There is no way that lady knows what she's talking about," Jessica said indignantly. "First of all, Dan is the nicest man, he loved Judith and I very much doubt there was any trouble in their marriage. I also know for a fact that they had talked about funerals plans—I remember because she brought it up once when we were discussing a book that dealt with the death of a spouse. Now granted, one can't ever know for sure what is going on in another person's life, but she has never in the five years of being in a book club together, not to mention many get-togethers, ever mentioned Dan in anything but glowing terms."

"She also claimed Judith was an avid journal writer, is that true?"

"That is true. Judith told me she'd been writing in journals since she was ten years old."

"The vet, Sally, said if we can find Judith's latest journal, it will prove Dan and Judith were having marital troubles and maybe even name whomever Judith thought was selling meth. I'm going to let Faye know to look for it at the office, but it wouldn't hurt to take a peek while we are at Dan's." We pulled into the Lansing's driveway as I finished talking. We grabbed our food and walked to the door.

CHAPTER ELEVEN

Swamp milkweed is a native perennial flower that prefers wet, clay soil and full sun. It produces a milky juice when broken and attracts monarch butterflies for pollination and egg laying.

WE KNOCKED ON THE FRONT DOOR and Dan answered looking exhausted. His clothes were rumpled, eyes bloodshot, and it was obvious he had been crying. "Hello Jessica, hello Carmen. Come in." He held the door open for us and we awkwardly tromped in carrying our food.

"Can we put this in the kitchen?" Jessica asked. "It's a turkey noodle hotdish and Carmen brought chocolate chip cookies."

"Thank you, I appreciate it, but my refrigerator is overflowing at the moment. Everyone has been so kind."

"We'll put it in your freezer if that's okay? You can thaw and reheat it whenever it's convenient." Jessica walked down the hallway towards the kitchen with the food leaving me standing with Dan.

I asked, "Is there something else we can help you with?"

Dan rubbed his head and said, "I don't know, everything is a blur. This has been such a shock. To be frank—I'm not coping well at all. It's fortunate the parents of my kids' friends have been taking them places and keeping them entertained, but then I end up feeling even worse that I'm not being there for my own kids." He sat down with a sigh, dislodging several dishes and books that had been sitting precariously on the couch.

Jessica joined us again as I asked, "I understand there won't be a funeral?"

"No," he answered with a haunted look. "Judith's parent's and her only sibling passed away within two years of each other. It was hard on her, both with the planning and the actual services themselves. She made sure we discussed our wishes, and she was adamant she didn't want a funeral or ceremony of any type. I'm trying to honor her wishes, but I think the kids need closure, so when things calm down our immediate family will do something in honor of her."

Jessica gave him a hug while I looked around. I asked, "Can we help by cleaning for you?"

Dan looked up with a spark of hope in his eyes. "If you wouldn't mind that would be great. I've been keeping up with the laundry but that's about it."

"We'd be happy to help," Jessica said giving me a look letting me know she knew precisely what I was up to.

"The cleaning supplies are in the closet under the upstairs stairway. If you don't mind I'm going to sit in the backyard," he said as he stood up and shuffled outside leaving us alone in the house.

"You only want to find her latest journal," Jessica hissed.

"I do, but honest I want to help too. It can't be good for the kids to come home to this," I whispered back.

"You're right," Jessica agreed, "but if you do find it, we leave it here."

"I wasn't planning on stealing it," I insisted but then acknowledging my nosiness said, "but I will take pictures. I'll start here in the living room if you want to tackle the kitchen."

"Okay," Jessica said. "I'm sure a lot of food should be thrown out depending on when people brought stuff, and I did notice a lot of dirty dishes when I was in the kitchen." She turned and walked back down the hallway.

I found a garbage bag and started filling it while stacking any important looking papers and books on one of the end tables. I followed up with shaking couch and chair cushions, then dusting and vacuuming, keeping my eyes open for anything that looked like a tablet or a journal. When I finished the living room, I moved to the bathrooms. I debated about the bedrooms before deciding that would be too much of an invasion of their privacy. I couldn't help myself from at least checking out the master bedroom, looking in the nightstands and under the bed. No luck. I could hear Jessica working in the kitchen so I decided I had time to search the den. I repeated the same pattern as the living room, sorting garbage out of the papers and books, and then dusting. One chair appeared to be a favorite reading spot, I assumed it to be Judith's, and when I picked up the cushion to shake it; there was a tablet. My heart started pounding, and before opening it, I peeked out the window to make sure Dan had remained outside. He was sitting on an Adirondack chair in the backyard, staring into space. I opened the tablet, paged through it, then took my phone out of my pocket and snapped pictures, going back thirty days. Hearing a door slam I pushed the tablet back under the cushion and resumed dusting. Dan walked in a couple of minutes later.

"Well the kitchen is all tidy," Jessica said as she joined us in the den.

"It looks great in the house. Thank you both so much," Dan said looking somewhat better.

"I'm glad we could help." I dusted the last knick-knack and then pushing my luck I asked, "I didn't know the new veterinarian in town was a good friend of Judith's."

Dan looked at me in surprise, "Is that what Sally told you?"

"She told me she and Judith were friends in college and that Judith is the reason she settled here in Arvilla," I answered.

"Well she's partially right, Judith is the reason Sally is here, but they weren't close friends, at least not anymore. They got along well enough in college, but when Judith and I got married, Sally got weird. When we had our first kid she really freaked out. I think she was jealous. Judith tolerated her, but she didn't go out of her way to get together with her. We were both shocked when she moved here." Dan shook his head in sadness.

"I didn't know," I replied wondering whose story was correct, maybe a mixture of both. It could be as simple as knowing that Dan didn't like Sally, Judith kept it to herself when she and Sally got together. "Anyway, she said she's missing Judith."

"A lot of people are," Dan said looking at me with a funny expression on his face.

"I only have to vacuum in here and then I'll be done as well," I said. Fifteen minutes later Jessica and I were saying our goodbyes to Dan and letting him know that if he needed any help to not hesitate to ask.

"Did you find what you were looking for," Jessica asked as we drove away, her wipers scraping the windshield. The rain was here, five hours later than forecast.

"I did. I didn't get a chance to read anything, but I snapped a bunch of pictures. I hope they turn out okay; I didn't take the time to check. I snapped pictures and turned pages. It's a good thing too, if I hadn't hurried, Dan would have caught me. I don't think I could have explained what I was doing reading his wife's journal."

Jessica laughed. "Marcy sent a text while I was in the kitchen wondering if it was okay to meet her and Melanie at the Dairy Queen. I didn't think you'd mind so I told her yes."

"It's fine with me. I'm looking forward to seeing them. I'm sure they'll want to know how the wedding planning is going and they'll help remind me if I'm forgetting to do something the maid of honor is supposed to be doing."

"Are you sure about this, we could cancel—after all, you have those pictures to look at?" Jessica asked me with a grin.

"I think I can hold my curiosity in check for a few hours," I answered, although I silently wondered if that was true.

Marcy and Melanie had already ordered and were waiting for us in a booth when we walked in. We each ordered chicken strip baskets and sat down with them.

"Do you rent your building from Owen Laterly?" I asked Melanie while we waited for our food.

"No. But I did buy it from him," she responded.

"Do you have an opinion of him?" I asked her knowing Melanie had a good instinct for people.

"He's what I think of as an orange person," she answered distractedly as she was watching a grasshopper that was sitting on the outside window ledge. Then she looked at me noticing my confused look and smiled.

"What does that mean?" I asked.

"A person without much individual character—they like to become and act like those around them, kind of like a chameleon. Except unlike a chameleon who blends with everyone and I call a green person, an orange person only blends with people they perceive to be in a higher social class. An orange has very little time for someone they think less of. It was obvious from his brusqueness with me I was not thought to be in a higher class than him."

"Is this color thing something you've studied?" Jessica asked.

"No, only another quirk of mine," she answered with a grin.

This led to an interesting discussion until Marcy changed the subject and asked, "Has anyone heard from Chloe? Is she enjoying her cruise?"

Jessica replied, "I haven't heard from her other than one text saying she was having the time of her life." She looked at me, giggled and said, "I find it hilarious that she, your dad, and James' mom are all on the same Alaskan cruise. Chloe told me before she left that she was going to be chaperoning the two of them making sure they stayed in their respective cabins and that there was no hanky-panky going on."

Jessica and I had come a long way in our relationship with Chloe Johnson. It was hard to believe only five months ago, Chloe had a reputation for chasing unavailable men—men who were either married or involved with someone, Jessica and she were enemies, and I thought Chloe was a murderer. We had subsequently found out Chloe, who owned the grocery store in town, was simply lonely; and now she had become a good friend of ours. Our order numbers were called, we picked up our food and spent the rest of the evening discussing the wedding and getting everyone's input to ensure nothing was missed. By the time we wound down the only duty I had left to take care of was to nail down the details of the bachelorette party. I didn't admit that I kept forgetting and I pretended it was a surprise. As I drove home I pondered if my avoidance of planning the party was my subconscious not wanting Jessica to get married. I was thrilled for her, but there was a part of me that knew things were going to change in our relationship when she and James were married. They both wanted children and things wouldn't be the same. Tonight was a perfect example; it would be tough to plan these spontaneous nights out when she had a family. Yet Jessica and James were my best friends and I couldn't be more excited for them. Kirk was in the kitchen when I got home.

"No practice tonight?" I asked him.

"No, my mind wasn't in it, worried about Wizard I guess."

"It does feel strange to not have him here. Did you see Tabitha anywhere?"

"She was busy hunting. I left the garden shed open for her. I saw a mouse in it as I was taking the lawnmower out when I got home this afternoon."

"Why did you need the lawnmower? The lawn doesn't need mowing yet."

"No, but I thought I'd get the blades off and sharpen them. They took a beating the last time I mowed." He looked down and mumbled, "Too lazy to pick up the sticks in the yard and I mowed over them."

Will wonders never cease, once again it was affirmed Kirk was becoming an adult. "Thanks, I appreciate it. Did you get the blades sharpened?"

"I tried, but they were shot, I ordered a new set. They'll call when they come in. How was Dan?"

"Not good. I can't imagine losing your spouse like that. We had an awful time dealing with grief when mom died, but at least we had warning. She was sick, so we had time to come to an acceptance; a murder is so sudden and abrupt."

"I don't know; death is death, no matter the cause. I don't think anyone is prepared when it happens," Kirk said.

"You're right, that was insensitive of me," I told Kirk acknowledging the truth of his words. "I'm going to bed." I peeked out the window. "It looks like the rain stopped." I checked the weather forecast on my phone. "Yes, it's done. But the grass will be wet—we won't be able to start burning until later in the morning. You're planning to help, right?" I asked Kirk.

"Yeah, I'll be there, but I have to leave at six," Kirk answered.

"That won't be a problem, if you could be at the seed plant by ten that would be great."

"I'll be there. The veterinarian is open at 7:30 a.m., so I'll have plenty of time to pick up Wizard and get him home and settled in before then. Goodnight," Kirk said as he yawned and stretched.

I ran up the stairs realizing although I was tired, I couldn't wait to get alone and check out the pictures I took of Judith's journal. I opened the picture gallery on my phone. The print was way too small, so I sent them to the printer in the office and went back downstairs to get them. Kirk was in his bedroom and I could hear music playing. The ink was out of course and only five pages had printed, I loaded a black cartridge and the rest of the pages spit out of the printer. I grabbed them and went back upstairs. I arranged the pages by date from oldest to newest and started to read. After the first three pages I got up and found a piece of paper and pen. I gathered there was some strain in her marriage, but nothing she had written indicated it was anything more than the usual ups and downs of a long lasting marriage. Her interest in meth started about three weeks ago, and Dan was not in favor of her pursuing it. She wanted to report several people, including Sally, Nolan Richland, the new principal, and Tony's son, Cory, along with several other people she didn't put a name to but if I had the time maybe I could figure out who they were. Dan was against her reporting anyone, arguing that she'd lose her dental license and it would be for nothing as she had no proof, only suspicions. I gathered she may have done something despite his wishes, as she wrote about planning to talk to an old high school friend who she'd thought had gone into law enforcement. Her entry on the last page of the journal was five days before she was killed and she had been trying to locate him. I wished I had more time in her house, perhaps I would have found the next journal. At least I assumed there was another one as I couldn't imagine she would have written in a journal every day and then quit for five days. I considered letting the sheriff know about the journals as he could get a search warrant to look through the rest of her house, but then I'd have to explain to both the sheriff and Dan what I had been doing in Dan's house and how I had invaded his privacy. I decided to hold off on that, but only for a couple of days, in the meantime I started taking notes on whatever facts I could glean from the pages I had. I must have drifted off as I woke up, my head on the bed where I'd been reading the pictures of the pages and drool on the piece of paper I was taking notes on. Recognizing I had to be fresh for burning tomorrow I put everything away, changed into my pajamas, and crawled in bed.

CHAPTER TWELVE

White prairie clover is a perennial, native legume. It is common in dry prairies and is an important browse species for antelope, deer and upland game birds, particularly sharp-tail grouse.

I WOKE UP WEDNESDAY MORNING TO A beautiful sunny day with a breeze out of the northwest. Which was perfect, not only was it good for drying the grass but it was the perfect direction for the fields we were burning today. I decided I'd better drive by the cabins and check to make sure everything was going well this morning. There was a fine line between honoring people's right to peace and quiet, yet making sure their visit was going well. Other than the bear incident I hadn't heard from the guests in either cabin, which wasn't necessarily a good thing. Some people wouldn't dream of calling me with a complaint, yet they could be displeased with something and leave a bad review on-line. I hoped eight-thirty in the morning wouldn't be too early to drive through, and see if there was any indication of anyone being awake. If not, I'd make a point to check back while we were moving between fields. Kirk was already gone, no doubt in a hurry to pick up Wizard. I realized Dad and Karla would be home tomorrow, which led to me wondering what their surprise might be. I couldn't remember the exact time their plane would be landing and would have to ask Kirk or look it up if he didn't know. It had surprised me when Karla agreed to take a cruise so close to the wedding, or maybe it shouldn't have, she would be determined to not step on Jessica or James' toes and let them plan the wedding they wanted without her input. On second thought I realized she was wise, as while Karla was a lovely person, she had a strong personality and I'm sure she knew it would be better if she were absent so she wouldn't assert her opinions on the happy couple. While my eggs cooked, I packed a quick dinner, and most important made coffee. With my coffee mug and packed dinner in hand I let myself out the door appreciating the fresh smell in the air leftover from the rain. Tabitha was sitting with Clyde on the steps basking in the morning sun. I gave them both a couple of quick pets and then drove to the cabins. It looked like Hugh must be out and about as there was no vehicle by his cabin but Alex and Marge were sitting on the small porch attached to the front of theirs.

"Good morning." I greeted them after I parked next to their vehicle.

"Good morning to you. It's a beautiful day isn't it?" Marge replied.

"It is. I didn't mean to interrupt, but I wanted to make sure everything is going well."

"We are doing wonderful. It's been so peaceful; we haven't moved much, other than a few walks. I don't think our neighbor could say the same," Marge said.

"What do you mean?" I asked her.

"He has been back and forth many times a day. Other than sleeping, I don't think he's spent much time here at all."

"He does have a cousin that lives in town. I'm sure he's visiting him."

"Do you know if he and his cousin are on good terms?" Marge inquired.

"I have no idea. I assume so, why are you wondering?" I asked Marge, beginning to think she enjoyed gossip.

"He looks so serious. We've waved a few times and he never even acknowledges us, does he Alex?" Marge said looking at her husband for backup. He simply nodded.

Not knowing how to answer her—pointing out Hugh was under no obligation to be congenial to her may not be the wisest choice—I finally said, "Perhaps their family is dealing with something serious."

"Oh, do you suppose he's related to the woman that was killed a couple of days ago? We heard about it when we went to town to buy ice cream we had a craving for. Wouldn't that be terrible?" Marge asked looking just the opposite of thinking it would be terrible. Her excited response alleviated some of my guilt at not telling them about the murders when they checked in.

"I don't believe he's related to the woman who was killed. I know his cousin and there is no connection I'm aware of," I answered. Then I wished I hadn't said anything as maybe if she thought Hugh was in the midst of a family tragedy it would stop her from being curious about his reluctance to acknowledge them. Then again, if I hadn't said anything Marge may have head over to Hugh's cabin to offer their condolences. But I did have to agree, if only to myself; it was strange to rent a rustic cabin in the middle of nowhere and then spend no time there. A hotel room in town would have been much cheaper. Yet, it was none of my business.

"Do you know if they've caught anyone? Are we in any danger?" Marge asked sounding like she was trying to act nervous but looking animated.

"To my knowledge they don't have anyone in custody, but the sheriff has made no indication the public at large is in any danger," I answered trying to reassure her.

"That's a relief," Alex said breaking his silence.

"If you don't need anything, we have a couple burns scheduled for the day so I'd better get going. My crew is probably wondering where I am," I said attempting to make my escape.

"What are you burning?" Alex asked.

I took a few minutes to explain how native grass and wildflowers needed fire to prompt them to produce large quantities of seed. They didn't have too many questions and I was on my way after a few short minutes.

I had time before I met with Kirk, Gary, and Nick at the seed plant so I decided to drive to town and pick up doughnuts from Edna's bakery. I was surprised to see my cabin guest, Hugh, and Melanie sitting at a table together when I walked in. Melanie saw me and motioned for me to come over.

"Hugh took advantage of one of my brochures you put in your cabins and came in for meditation early this morning," Melanie said. "We've been busy visiting ever since."

Hugh must have appealed to her as Melanie was practically glowing. As she finished talking her eyes focused on something by the door and she got up and rushed over to it. I turned to look and saw her carefully grab a butterfly that had flown in and put it back outside. I looked at Hugh to see how he was dealing with Melanie's behavior.

He looked at me and said, "Don't ever tell her I collected bugs for many years when I was in 4-H." Then he winked.

I snorted realizing a bug collector meant bugs were dried and pinned to a board, definitely not something Melanie would approve of. I excused myself before Melanie got back to the table and could further delay me. I hurried over to Edna to place my order of assorted doughnuts.

"What do you think about those two?" I asked Edna as she put my selection in a box.

"I think it's great," she said. "Although I'm starting to worry about my charms, or lack thereof, if even Melanie has found a man and I continue to be single."

I laughed, paid, and left for the seed plant where Kirk, Gary, and Nick were waiting for me when I drove in. I hopped out of my pickup, grabbed the box of doughnuts, my mask, and gloves and rushed over to them.

"Did you get Wizard home?" I asked Kirk handing him the box.

"Yes, and he was so glad to see me. I felt bad leaving him again," Kirk said as he grabbed a doughnut and passed the box to the others.

"I hope he's not mad at you for leaving, and decides to destroy something," I said.

"I doubt it, he was extremely red-eyed. Contrary to what the veterinarian's office said, I don't think he slept very much there last night. He piled into his bed when we got home."

"Thanks for helping again, Gary," I said to him.

"It's not a problem, it's nice to get a few extra hours in before we start walking in the fields. Thanks for the doughnuts."

"Is everything ready to go?" I asked.

"It is," Nick answered. "We were only waiting for you. Did you call in the burning permit?"

"Thanks for reminding me." I went back to my pickup to get the permit number and called it in while they ate. "We are all set, I'll call the Sheriff's Department on the way," I said when I walked back to them. I got in Nick's pickup which was pulling the four-wheelers. Kirk followed with the tractor pulling the water tank and Gary drove the truck carrying our extra 500 gallon water tank.

"What was going on that you were late this morning?" Nick asked.

I explained how I stopped by the cabins and what the Erickson's had to say about their neighbor Hugh. "Do you think it's strange he isn't spending much time at his cabin?" I asked Nick.

"I think both you and the Erickson's have too much curiosity. As long as he paid and doesn't trash the place what does it matter what he does with his time?" Nick answered in his typical laid back manner.

"That is true," I conceded. I debated with myself for a few seconds and then I said, "Jessica and I stopped by Dan's yesterday."

"You said you were going to. How did it go?"

"Dan is devastated of course, but Jessica and I helped clean his house and I found Judith's journal."

Nick looked at me and asked, "You didn't steal it did you?"

"Of course not, why is that everyone's first thought? I did take pictures of the last few pages though."

Nick laughed. "Did you find out anything interesting?"

"I'm not sure, but she did have people she suspected. She named a few, but others she only described. I think I can figure out who they are, but it's tough to figure out the difference between whom she was suspecting and who she was only writing about." Nick looked at me and I continued, "For instance, I believe Faye is talked about as Judith mentions an employee of hers who was becoming a lot more proficient and had become a valuable asset. She mentioned how they had introduced a new texting notification system, but never said a name. I'm sure that was Faye. Judith did a lot of writing about things happening in her life, after all, it was her journal. I fell asleep while I was taking notes trying to figure out who were suspects and who were only people she was journaling about. I'm hoping to look at it more tonight."

"Any chance you're going to share this information with the sheriff?" Nick asked.

"I will, but not yet. First I have to come up with a good reason for how I ended up with pictures of the journal pages. Maybe if I can figure out whom the primary people she suspected of selling meth were it will be less damaging when I tell him."

Nick rolled his eyes, "Good luck with that." He continued, "I'm not sure I'd be much help, as I'm not familiar with all the local people yet, but I could come over tonight and try."

"That's not a bad idea. Do you think Faye would be available also? She may have some insight as she worked with Judith. Most of the pages had something to do with the dental office."

"I'll ask her," Nick answered accepting my inadvertent ruining of another possible chance at a night alone for the two of us.

"If you don't mind I think I'll invite Jessica and James over too," I said.

"Sounds like fun," Nick responded, trying to look like he wasn't disappointed.

"I'll cook something for supper if we get done burning early enough," I said as I started typing a text to both of them. "If we don't, I'll grab a few pizzas from the bowling alley," Nick offered as we arrived at the blue grama field. We got out of the pickup and my phone pinged, it was James answering my text. He looked forward to coming over. I didn't expect to hear from Jessica at this time of the day as she'd be busy at the restaurant but I was confident if James was coming, she'd be there too. But it was time to focus on burning. You didn't want your mind on anything but the task at hand when burning. The first burn of the day would be a relatively easy one, we had firebreaks around the field and other than the chance of it jumping into the abandoned gravel pit on the east side, the other sides were surrounded by a gravel road on the south and two conventional crop fields on the north and west which were currently black unplanted fields. I sent Gary with the tractor and water to watch the gravel pit side while Kirk took off with a wet line ahead of Nick and me. We waited until he was done with the east side before starting the back burn. I saw Kirk jump off the tractor and rescue a couple baby bunnies and then the fire took off and we were busy for the next two hours. We finished up around one, and while we waited for a few of the smoldering clumps to die down, we ate our packed dinners. When we finished eating Nick and I took off on the four wheelers and sprayed down the smoldering clumps making sure the fire was out when we left. I would come back later today and again tonight to ensure nothing ignited again after we left. I realized I wasn't going to have time to check in with Hugh this afternoon so I sent a text to him asking if everything was satisfactory and if he needed anything. There was no answer by the time we got to the little bluestem field. This burn would be a lot more complicated as a neighbor's home was nearby, and we had a CRP field to deal with. The wind was the right direction to keep the smoke away from their house, but we would be burning this field slow and careful with a lot of back-burning. It was a long afternoon, and it wasn't helped by unseasonable warm temperatures. Eighty-three degree air temperature during a fire made for an unpleasant afternoon and I was regretting inviting people over for supper by the time the day was over. We finished up around six. Supper would be late but I was sure James, Jessica and Nick wouldn't care. I could find something quick to whip up. As I was trying to figure out what that might be, my phone pinged. It was Jessica offering to bring leftovers from the restaurant for supper. I happily accepted, told Nick no pizzas were needed and I'd see him later. I invited Kirk but he declined as he had practice with the band tonight and he'd only be at the house long enough to take a shower and pick up Wizard.

"Do you know what time Dad's plane is arriving in Grand Forks tomorrow?" I asked him.

"Late, I think he said around eleven. I remember him saying he was hoping he'd be able to sleep on the plane as he didn't want to be tired for the hour and a half drive home."

"I won't worry then about staying up for him tomorrow night. I'll see you at home, we'll have to fight over who gets the shower first." Only one of our bathrooms had a shower, the other had a bathtub.

"I think he's going to beat you," Nick commented as Kirk was already walking to his car.

"I know, but I hope he got the hint and he'll be out of there before I get home. I need to go back to the first fire and make sure everything is okay."

"I'll stop by both fields again on my way over to your place too," Nick offered.

"Thanks, I appreciate it." Nick and I made sure everything was filled with gas and the water tanks full before Nick went home and I drove back to the blue grama field.

I took my time driving around, but saw nothing smoking. I started to drive towards home when my phone pinged again. This time it was Hugh answering my text from earlier. His response was interesting. He said he was happy with everything and had been enjoying all the wildlife. According to the Erickson's he hadn't been at the cabin to enjoy the wildlife. I shrugged; maybe they had been in town or on their walks when he'd been around or maybe he should be added to my suspect list. Then I chided myself, he wasn't even here at the time of the murders. Yet something about the man didn't ring true and he is related to Peter whom Judith named in her journals. As I drove I thought about the wisdom of giving in to my curiosity and letting myself in his cabin to look around. Then I gave myself a mental head slap knowing if I did that and was caught it would be the end of my cabin rental business. Kirk and Wizard were gone by the time I got home. Tabitha was inside waiting for the canned food she was treated to when she was in the house.

"No luck hunting today?" I asked her. She only meowed and rubbed my legs. I fed her and then went to shower. By the time I got out of the shower, dressed, and made it downstairs again, she was ready to go outside. Jessica and James were driving up when I opened the door. I slid on shoes and went out to help them carry in the dishes.

"Can you turn on the oven and stick this pan of pork chops in to warm them?" Jessica asked. "The other two containers are macaroni salads I made for the salad bar today."

"It sounds delicious." I was setting the table when Nick and Faye walked in. "Thanks for coming Faye," I told her.

"I'll do anything to help figure this out. I do wish we had some clue about who killed Christopher. People in town are already starting to look at me weird," she said looking sad.

I gave her a consoling hug, "I'm sorry."

Faye straightened her shoulders and said, "First things first, tonight is about tackling Judith's murder." Then she looked shocked at her words and said, "Did I just say tackle a murder, like we're some sort of super sleuths?"

We laughed and Jessica said, "We are tonight, but first let's eat."

The food was delicious as always, and we had fun visiting. Jessica and James were treated to a lot of jokes at their expense about possible honeymoon ideas and horror stories of what might go wrong at weddings. Faye had a great story about a friend whose aunt got stood up at the altar when the groom's old girl friend showed up in a bikini during their vows. But once the food and dishes were cleaned up, it was time to get down to business.

I cleared my throat and said, "I need to make this clear, tonight is about finding other possible suspects for Judith's murder to pass on to the sheriff and that is all. We need to prove to the sheriff that Judith's death is related to meth and not Christopher, Faye, or Nick. I plan to let the sheriff know who we suspect. I have no desire for myself or any of you to get involved with anyone crazy enough to deal with drugs, especially meth. Sally, the new veterinarian, claimed to be a good friend of Judith's and told me Judith kept journals. Jessica and I happened across a journal and I took pictures of the pages."

"We happened across the pages? That's the story you're going with?" Jessica asked with her eyebrows raised.

Ignoring her I continued talking, "I took pictures of the pages from the last few weeks of her life. She didn't always identify people, but I'm hoping we can figure out who she was writing about, and if anything she wrote indicated she suspected them of being involved with meth. Judith first became aware of a meth problem because of her dental practice, so I'm hoping something in these pages will tip us off to who she may have suspected. With any luck, I can bring the names to the sheriff, and he can follow up to see if one of them killed her." I had made copies of the pages for everyone and passed them out.

Everyone started reading and it was quiet until Nick spoke up, "Here she talks about replacing a filling that had fallen out of someone's mouth and how it wasn't a cavity she had previously fixed. She also noted she thought it was strange as he either ate a lot of sugar or something was going on with his teeth. She wrote it surprised her that someone so young and with dental insurance would have such bad teeth."

"Do you suppose it was one of the new people in town, as it wasn't a cavity she originally filled?" I threw out.

"It could be, how long had she been a dentist here?" Nick asked.

"She's been here since the last dentist retired, and that has to have been at least fifteen years ago," James answered.

"Maybe this person was a possible meth user?" Nick suggested.

"Judith didn't say meth, but it could have been one of the first people that got her thinking about it," I said.

"Who is new to the community?" Nick asked.

"The vet, Sally, is fairly new—about two years," Jessica offered, "but Sally was her friend."

"The high school principal has been here about the same amount of time and Tony's son, Cory, recently moved back home," James said.

"Do we know if anyone else is new in town? Judith talked about Sally and the principal in earlier pages and named them," I said, already feeling disheartened as this wasn't getting us anywhere.

James offered, "I don't know if this makes sense or not, but we do have a new person at the bank. I don't know her name, but Peter Inver is training her, maybe she was at the dental office?"

We looked at Faye, and she asked, "Does anyone know her name? She might have been in, but unless you have a name, I'm not going to remember her. I haven't been here long enough to know who is new to town. Judith does say on the next page she was planning to ask someone about a relative they have that could possibly help her with her suspicions."

"I'll talk to Peter Inver. We've banked with him for years; I can stop by and ask him if Judith had talked to him and find out if he's willing to share anything about the woman he's training," I offered knowing it was a long shot. After a moment I said, "Peter's cousin Hugh is staying in one of my cabins. I'm sure I saw him at the school and he hasn't been spending much time at his cabin. You don't suppose he could be supplying the drugs."

"He wasn't here when Judith was murdered though," Nick stated.

"No, but Peter is here, maybe they are in on it together."

James spoke up, "I can't believe Peter is involved in anything like drugs. He loves this town. He's been known to suspend mortgage payments when someone is undergoing financial hardships."

Jessica had been reading ahead while we talked and interrupted us, "Here Judith talks about someone having a lot more money than other people who have the same occupation."

"That could be anyone," I said.

"What did she say about the person?" Nick asked.

Faye had found the page and was reading it, then said, "This is Al Mitchel."

How do you know that?" I asked.

"Because she says the last time he was in the office, we had to clean the carpets."

"I saw that, but I thought it was a coincidence," I said.

"No, whenever Al comes in we joke that we should add cleaning to his bill as his boots are always full of manure," Faye said.

James added, "Judith may have been on to something. I've always wondered where his money came from too, but he's always had a lot, not just recently. I assumed he inherited a large amount, at least I think someone once told me that."

"He's one of the people we think may have impersonated Dad at the convention and could be Christopher's father," I mused. "Do you suppose it is all related somehow?"

"Anything is possible," James said.

"We'll put him on the list. You did find a reason for me to talk with him once already, but I'll find a reason to stop by there again," I said.

"I'll come with you when you do," James insisted. "You do have a track record of getting yourself in trouble, should he be the bad guy."

"What if it causes you to buy another bull?" I asked laughing.

"It won't, but I could use some hay. I doubt he has any extra, but it might be a reason to stop by, I think he may have paperwork he is supposed to be getting me for the bull I bought too."

"I've got this person figured out," Faye said interrupting us as she pointed at the page in front of her.

"Who is it?" I asked.

"The IPD driver."

"How do you know?" I asked.

"Judith wrote that his normal time to stop by the office is 10:00 a.m. That's what time Darius typically delivers to our office."

"Why was she suspicious of him?" James asked.

"She thought he had an abnormal amount of stops in Arvilla and all the packages were small."

"Using that as a basis feels pretty shaky," Nick said dismissing him as a suspect.

"I agree, but I'll write down his name," I said and added him to the now lengthy list.

"This must be Jill's father," Faye said as she got to the bottom of the same page.

"Jill, the dental hygienist?" Jessica asked.

"Yes. Judith wrote that Jill's father was in but something Judith said must have bothered him. She wrote that he left as soon as she finished the procedure and didn't brag about Jill at all as he was prone to do. She mentions she was going to ask Jill if she inadvertently offended him. It must not have been anything serious as I remember he was in the night before her murder. I left before she finished with him."

"His name is Jed Alman right?" I asked. "I need to talk to him again too." It was quiet as we continued to flip through the pages until after fifteen minutes of silence I said, "I think we're getting sick of this, at least I know I am. It's late and time to quit."

"I agree," James said as he tried unsuccessfully to hold in a yawn.

"I'll take this with me," Faye offered. "I'll study it more tomorrow."

"I won't have any time to look at it," James said. "I need to move cattle to another pasture tomorrow."

"Nick and I won't either; tomorrow is our last burn. Faye, if you have the time; that would be great. You are having better luck identifying these people than the rest of us anyway."

"I'll make the time. Judith was a great boss, and I'd like to help find who killed her."

"Remember anything we come up with goes straight to the sheriff. As I understand it, people using methamphetamine can react crazy and we don't want any part of it," I cautioned.

"I agree," Nick said.

Jessica and James stood up. "We're going to take off," Jessica said as she gathered her containers.

"Thanks again for bringing supper, it was delicious. I'll pick you up Saturday at three for your bachelorette party," I told Jessica.

"You're not going to tell me what you have planned?" Jessica asked.

"Nope," I answered wanting it to be a surprise.

"Can you at least tell me what type of clothing I should wear?" she begged.

"Nothing you would care about if it got dirty," I smiled as I answered her. I had finally decided what I was going to do for her party and had let the others know this morning by text. I had a gap in reservations for two of the cabins on Saturday night and we were going to commandeer one of them for an old fashioned slumber party complete with hiking, four-wheeling, a bonfire, and board or card games. They had acted excited when I told them and I was hoping Jessica would enjoy it too.

"That's kind of vague," she said suspiciously.

"That's all you're going to get out of me," I said as I pushed them out the door. After they'd gone I turned to Faye and Nick who were also getting ready to leave and asked, "Did Judith ever say anything about Dan?"

"Of course she talked about him, but what do you mean?" Faye asked.

"Sally implied Dan and Judith weren't happy together anymore, yet I didn't pick up on anything like that in the journal pages—only normal marital issues."

Faye considered it for a few minutes, then said, "I know there was tension at times, but I wouldn't say they were unhappy. She didn't say much, but I got the impression Dan had a hard time with Judith being the main bread winner. They also disagreed sometimes on how to raise their kids. Judith was laid back and more inclined to let Dan deal with the disciplining. She once said Dan was frustrated about always being the bad parent. I do know they went out weekly for a date night and they were always affectionate when Dan stopped by the office."

"Jessica said almost the same thing. I wonder what Sally knows that makes her think anything different?"

"Sally is the veterinarian?" Faye asked.

"Yes. Why?"

"I remember Judith saying the veterinarian was an old friend from college. She commented on how her friend had changed from when she first met her. Judith hoped she'd eventually find other friends as they didn't have anything in common anymore."

"Sally made it clear she knows something about Dan. Maybe I'll talk to her again. It wouldn't hurt to get to know her anyway. If she moved here on Judith's recommendation and now Judith is dead, I bet she's lonely. I'll have to invite her out one night when a bunch of us go out again," I said.

"And question her more at the same time," Nick added knowing me too well.

"Perhaps," I answered being evasive.

He laughed. "I'll see you tomorrow morning." He gave me a quick kiss and then they left.

The house was strangely quiet after everyone was gone. I felt anxious and wandered around the house trying to relax. I opened the door and called for Tabitha, who surprised me by coming inside. We curled up together on the couch while I turned on the television and found a rerun of an old sitcom I could watch without having to pay too much attention. I pondered my relentless curiosity and wondered about the wisdom of involving my friends in yet another murder investigation. This one felt different though. I knew next to nothing about drugs, not to mention it wasn't a world I was comfortable even thinking about. If I was honest, it scared me. But somehow I couldn't help but be curious. I should be focusing on Christopher as the sheriff was trying to assign his murder to Faye and his death didn't appear related to Judith's but we weren't making any progress with who might have killed him. I had a couple more people to talk to about him, but even if someone did admit they impersonated Dad, why would they kill Christopher? I absently scratched Tabitha's head. The fact that Christopher was a known con man made it probable he was trying to run a scam on someone. Perhaps trying to blackmail someone about them being his father, but as I concluded before, why would that cause anyone to kill him? Unless Christopher knew something about his father that they didn't want anyone else knowing. The sheriff thought one possible theory why Judith was shot was because someone thought she was Faye. Maybe there was some truth to that. Christopher and Faye had been a couple for many years. Maybe Christopher told Faye something she doesn't even remember; something that would be a possible reason to get rid of both of them. If that was the case we were wasting our time with Judith's journal notes as meth had nothing to do with either murder. I didn't know if that was good or bad. I felt safer staying away from that world, yet I did want to see whoever was responsible for either making or bringing meth to our town caught. But as I understood it, meth could be made anywhere, it doesn't have to be brought in and assuming it could only be due to new people is likely faulty thinking. If Judith was killed in place of Faye then Faye could yet be in danger, but Christopher wouldn't have mistaken Judith for Faye. My thoughts were spinning back and forth and I must have fallen asleep as the next thing I was aware of was the noise of Kirk and Wizard getting home. Tabitha must have gone outside when they got home as she was no longer with me on the couch.

Kirk was pouring himself a glass of orange juice when I asked, "How did practice go?"

He jerked and spilt some juice. "I didn't see you laying there. You startled me. It went great. Squirt was even there and appeared sober. Maybe I was mistaken and he's been preoccupied with something else."

"I hope so; his family does have a lot going on. How is Wizard doing?" I asked.

"He's great, one hundred percent back to normal."

"I'm not sure that's a good thing," I responded. I could hear Kirk laughing as I got off the couch and started up the stairs to my bedroom. Halfway up the stairs I remembered I had to check on the fields we burned today and walked back downstairs.

"Did you need something?" Kirk asked.

"No, I just about forgot, but I need to make sure the fires from today haven't relit." As I drove to the last field we burnt I saw headlights at the other end of the field. My heart pounded as I drove closer until I recognized Nick's pickup. I parked next to it, got out and waited until my eyes adjusted to the darkness. Once they did I spotted Nick using a shovel to put out small smoldering clump of grass about fifty feet away.

"You didn't have to check on the fields." I told him when he finished and joined me by our pickups.

"I know, but I was restless tonight, and honestly I was hoping to catch you out here somewhere. We haven't had a lot of alone time together since admitting we loved each other."

I smiled and moved closer to him. Nick wrapped his arms around me and I said, "You could have called me to meet you."

"Something always interrupts us. I guess I was trusting in fate. If I found you, it was meant to be."

I kissed him and he eagerly returned the kiss. We spent the next hour walking in the dark, talking about our hopes for the future and discovering common interests we hadn't known we had. We both enjoyed British murder mystery shows, stand-up comedians, a desire to learn Spanish, and most surprisingly to me—Nick also wanted to find someplace to take ballroom dancing lessons. Now that Nick had shared his past with me he was no longer guarded in his manner. He shared how he continued to struggle with his feelings of anger and loss in regards to his deceased mother. I shared my fears about being able to keep my farm operating profitably and not wanting to be a disappointment to my father. It was a beautiful evening and after I kissed Nick goodnight and got in my pickup to drive home I felt as though all was right in my world. I was cherishing the relationship Nick and I were building.

CHAPTER THIRTEEN

Harebell flowers usually have five (occasionally 4, 6 or 7) pale to mid violet-blue petals that are fused together into a bell shape. Another name it is commonly known as is bluebell, but it was also historically known by several other names including bla-wort, hair-bell, lady's thimble, witch's bells, and witch's thimbles.

As I STOOD IN THE KITCHEN Thursday morning I smiled to myself thinking of last night with Nick. I was confident in the future we were building together. Dad would be home late tonight. I had missed him, but his being gone also reinforced it was time for me to get moving on finding my own place to live. I briefly thought maybe it wasn't necessary as perhaps Nick and I would get married soon, but then I mentally shook myself—I was definitely rushing things. I reconsidered; while it was easy being here, I was also chaffing a bit at the lack of privacy. It was time to move out, but I would miss Dad and the pets. Kirk and Wizard weren't awake yet and as I peeked out the window to see if Tabitha was around an idea started formulating. Developed farmsteads with existing wells and septic systems were few and far between, but there was plenty of room right here to move in a small house or trailer. I left the house with a spring in my step, excited about the possibility of my own place. I decided to swing by the cabins again to see if Hugh was around. After my suspicions of him yesterday I wouldn't mind talking to him, and doing a cabin check with him would be a good excuse. I called Nick to let him know where I was. He was busy with one of the four-wheelers. We must have run over something sharp yesterday as a tire was flat and he was going to check with Tony to see if they had any spares on hand. If not, a trip to Parkville, or Grand Forks might be in order before we could burn. I pulled off the highway turning on to the gravel road leading to the cabins. I was thankful there was no sign of the Erickson's; not only was I short on time but I also would have hated to interrupt yet another day of their stay. Hugh's vehicle was parked in front of his cabin, but there was no movement. I had just parked my pickup when he opened the door, with a mug in his hand.

"Good morning Carmen. Is something wrong?"

"Not at all, I like to check in with my guests at least once. I stopped by the other day and visited with the Erickson's," I said pointing at the cabin where they were staying, "but you weren't around."

"My cousin and I have been busy reminiscing and revisiting old haunts. I haven't had much time to enjoy the solitude. I did get your text yesterday. I answered you and I would have let you know if I needed anything," Hugh said giving me a funny look.

"I'm sorry for interrupting, but I don't feel like I'm doing my due diligence if I don't at least stop by once in person," I replied bothered once again by him. His explanation of his absence from spending time at the cabin was a contradiction to his earlier text about claiming to have been enjoying the wildlife.

"It's okay. I'm glad you stopped by," Hugh surprised me by saying.

"Is there a problem?" I asked.

"Not at all. I'm hoping it would be possible for me to stay on another week?"

"You're in luck, but I should warn you that a bachelorette party will be taking place in cabin B on Saturday night, but then it should be back to quiet. The Erickson's check out Saturday morning and Sunday the other two cabins will be occupied. So it will be no problem for you to extend your stay. I do have your cabin rented the following Sunday though," I responded once again suspicious of him.

"That will be fine, I can't imagine I'll need to be here any longer than that," he answered.

"I'll swing back through later today with another contract to sign for the extended stay and you can let me know about the food."

"I won't be around, but you can leave it on the table. I assume you have a key to get in," Hugh said and took a long drink of coffee.

"I do, as long as it's okay with you," I answered as I excitedly wondered how much I dared snoop now that he had given me permission to go in his cabin without him being there.

"Not a problem, I'm glad it worked out to stay another week," Hugh said turning to go back in the cabin.

"Does Melanie have anything to do with your decision to stay another week?" I asked, my question forcing him to turn around.

He smiled and said, "Perhaps, but I haven't had time to see much of my cousin's family either."

"I should get going, thank you for extending your stay." On my way to the seed plant I considered questioning Peter about his cousin Hugh. I couldn't imagine what it was he and Peter had been doing that kept them so busy they hadn't even spent time with Peter's family. I loved where I lived, but even I had to admit there wasn't that much to do and see other than flat, broad expanses of farmland, with intermittent wooded farmsteads. I smiled—if James were here he would tell me I don't need to stick my nose in everyone's business. When I got back to the seed plant, Nick was standing next to his pickup. "Did you find a tire?" I asked when I parked next to him.

"I was on my way to pick it up. They were busy this morning so it took a while for Tony to get back to me, but he found one."

"I can go get it, if you've got something else to do," I offered.

"That would help. I've been working on the fertilizer spreader; I forgot to tell you I was having problems with a hydraulic hose when I took over from you the other day."

"Is it something serious?" I asked.

"No, I'll be done shortly if you can pick up the tire."

"I'll be back in a half hour." I backed my pickup out of my parking spot. I was glad this worked. I could stop by home and get the paperwork for Hugh's cabin and drop it off. The trip to the dealership would also give me the opportunity to question Tony about his son and verify how Cory made his money. Maybe Cory only told him he flipped houses. I wanted to know if Tony had witnessed it first-hand. I drove home—printed out the contract—started to grab a sticky note and then stopped realizing I could take advantage of technology and save myself a trip back to Hugh's cabin and from the temptation to snoop. I took a few minutes to text the contract to him along with his food choices and ran out the door somehow managing to avoid stepping on Clyde who was hacking up a hair ball on the front steps. I waited a minute until he was done, and with no time to take care of it properly, I kicked it off the steps. As I drove, I reminded myself to be careful with my questioning of Tony; I didn't want to risk offending him. They'd been good to us in regards to fixing our four-wheelers in a timely fashion and I couldn't let my curiosity ruin our business relationship. I pulled into the dealership and was thankful it was Tony standing with the tire.

"Talk about service—have you been standing there long?"

Tony chuckled. "I was rolling it over to the front door. I thought I'd leave it there as I figured you would be in a hurry."

"The addition to your dealership is impressive. It's always nice when a local business is thriving," I said, hoping he would volunteer more information. I was in luck.

"Business is good, but I'm not going to lie, it wouldn't have paid for this. Cory moved back home and paid for these updates. I told him we didn't need the expansion, but he insisted. I guess he got a little finicky about wanting nice conditions to work in."

"I can't blame a person for that," I said as he looked embarrassed his existing shop hadn't been good enough for his son.

"I guess not, and I shouldn't have been surprised. After all whenever I visited him in South Dakota he was living in pretty fancy places."

"How come he stopped?" I asked.

"The friend he worked with was about twenty years older than Cory and wanted to do something else—construction work is hard on a person's body. Cory didn't want to keep on by himself. I had been there a few times to visit, and let me tell you what they did was difficult work. A few of the houses they took on, I would have burned down—but they did it. I was proud of him, but I am glad he decided to move home."

"I'm happy for you, I'm sure you like having him here," I said as he placed the tire in the back of the pickup. "Do you want me to pay now?"

"No, I know you are in a hurry, I'll send a bill."

"Thanks Tony. Have a good day." I got back in the pickup for the fifteen minute drive back to the seed plant. It sounded like Cory had obtained his money by hard work with no drug activity. I was happy to remove Tony and Cory from my suspect list and even happier Cory had joined his dad's business. I had wondered what would happen when Tony retired. I was thankful the shop would continue. Kirk had joined Nick and they both were waiting for me with everything loaded and ready to go with the exception of the four-wheeler with the flat tire. We quickly changed it, got it on the trailer, and were on our way.

"Is everything okay?" Nick asked when I didn't say anything after we'd went a few miles.

"Yeah, I'm just thinking. I hate the thought of not only a meth problem in town, but possibly two murderers too. And I especially dislike that I've gotten nowhere with figuring anything out," I said in frustration.

"I wouldn't say we've made no progress. We are confident

Christopher had to have been killed by someone not wanting anyone else to know he was their son and that can only be one of four people as who else would he even know in this town. You've talked to three of them; did you get any sort of gut feeling from any of them?" Nick asked.

"I don't know. Al was so jovial..." my voice trailed off. Nick watched me as I collected my thoughts. "He was jovial, but menacing too, if that makes any sense. He laughed about the possibility of an illegitimate child, which I don't think he would have done if Christopher was his son and had approached him."

"Unless he's cool under pressure and wanted you to think that," Nick offered.

"It could be. Cord denied talking to any strangers—which doesn't mean anything. If it was him he would deny it. But he sure didn't act at all guilty when I questioned him about the convention. He did say Owen and Al spent a lot of time together separate from the rest of the group. You were the first one to come up with the names of the people that went to the Las Vegas convention. Did you have suspicious about any of them when you first started checking into them?"

"Only that they are all financially well off, which would make them attractive to Christopher. I thought Jed was the least likely as he's done with his farm and his son-in-law is operating it now. Jed wouldn't have any control over the farm's money for Christopher to go after," Nick said as he shrugged.

"Jed could have a huge savings account set aside," I offered.

"I asked a few people—stressing that he was so young to be retired, he must have a lot of money stuck away and everyone responded that Jed lived simple. A couple of people commented that either the son-in-law or his daughter, Jill, must have pushed and Jed was forced to turn the farm over to them earlier than he wanted to," Nick answered. "I didn't get any farther with the rest of the men."

"Cord never had any extra money when he was farming, but he does now that a gravel company is leasing his land. He doesn't have any family, so I can't see what kind of a con Christopher could have tried to pull on him. What would Cord have to lose if an illegitimate son turned up? I plan to talk to Edna about Owen Laterly, I think he was her landlord before she bought the house she lives in and runs her bakery out of. She might have some insight about him. I did ask Melanie—she bought her building from him instead of renting. She indicated she didn't care for him."

"Please promise me you are going to stay focused on Christopher's murder; let the sheriff deal with Judith and the meth aspect—turn the journal pages over to the sheriff. Depending on how big and widespread drugs are here, there could be scary people involved," Nick said.

"I agree, but it did occur to me late last night that Judith's death may have had nothing to do with drugs. After all she hadn't reported anyone yet."

"Her journal pages said she was going to talk to someone in law enforcement," Nick reminded me.

"How would anyone have known that though? Our own sheriff was unaware of the meth angle until we told him."

"The journal you found was missing the last five days of her life—we don't know if she contacted anyone. She may not have had any confidence in the sheriff so she didn't tell him her suspicions," Nick suggested.

"I guess, but another theory that keeps going through my mind is what if whoever killed Christopher thought Faye knew something too and she may yet be in danger."

Nick considered my words and said, "You may be right, but I don't think she's in danger. If your theory is correct, they'd have to know by now she didn't know anything or she would have told the sheriff."

"True, that makes me feel better," I said relieved.

Changing the subject, Nick asked, "Have you heard anything back from the two students about when they can start walking fields for the summer?"

"They are coming in next week after school one day to go through the herbicide training and fill out paperwork. They both plan to start the Monday after school is out for the year. If it works to talk to Edna today, I should also stop by the school and say thank you to April. I hope that's a relationship we can keep going—we always need summer help."

"You're not planning to investigate the new principal when you are there?" Nick asked looking at me with worry in his eyes.

"Maybe, and that's all the more I'm going to say about it." And that was all the more I did say, as we had arrived at the field. I called in my burn permit, notified law enforcement, and we took a few minutes to discuss strategy. It was a long burn but everything went well. We were finished and back to the seed plant by three.

"Do you need to get going?" Nick asked Kirk.

Kirk answered, "If I'm home by six I'll have plenty of time to pack, the band is leaving early tomorrow morning."

"I think your sister is anxious to get to town, despite my warnings her detective itch needs to be scratched," Nick told Kirk.

"Just for that I'm leaving right now. Have fun putting everything away," I said and started walking to my pickup.

I could hear Kirk sputtering as I walked away, "Carmen, this is the last burn of the year, there's a lot of stuff to clean up and put away."

"Have fun." I waved at them as I drove away. I decided to stop by the school first as the school day was almost over and I wanted to catch April before she left. The school buses were lined up waiting for school to get out and a few kids were starting to trickle out the door. I found a parking spot and walked in the building. It was such a difference from my school years of freely coming in and out of the building to now having to stop in the office and sign in. It was sad this was a necessary procedure to keep kids safe. April was standing up gathering files off her desk when I knocked on her open door.

"Hi Carmen, what can I do for you?"

"Nothing, you have been a tremendous help and I wanted to stop by and say thank you. Both the students you recommended are planning to work for us," I told her wondering why she was looking nervous.

"That's great. I'm kind of in a hurry, was there anything else?" she asked.

"No, I'll walk out with you. Did you need help carrying anything?" I offered.

"Sure, it would be helpful if you could take the box on the chair by the door. Thank you."

"How is the new principal working out?" I asked as we walked through the hallways.

"Nolan Richland?" she asked and I nodded. "He's not so new anymore, he's been here for two years now, but I think he's doing okay. He's been focused on helping out the marginal students," April answered.

"What is a marginal student?" I asked.

I must have sounded somewhat indignant as she laughed and said, "That's my terminology for the kids that without some sort of intervention may fall off the beaten path. Nolan tries hard to establish personal connections with them, talking to them in the hallways, letting them know he's available if they want to talk."

"That sounds like a good guy," I said or, the cynical side of me thought, he knows he can influence them into buying drugs.

"He appears to be a good guy, but I'm hoping he's being careful to take care of the rest of his duties. I've heard rumbling that the office staff has been picking up a lot of what are supposed to be his duties," April said.

"It sounds like he cares about the kids, they wouldn't fire him?" I asked.

"I doubt it would come to that, at least not without warning. But maybe it doesn't matter to him, I think this is his third principal position, which for his age, is a lot."

"Maybe he's independently wealthy and doesn't need to keep

a job," I said but I couldn't help think, maybe he's staying one step ahead of law enforcement.

"He must, after all he keeps applying places, but he does drive a fancy car, I assume he needs a job to support that. See, that's his car over there," she said and pointed.

"That new Corvette is his?" I stopped and looked again. Hugh, my cabin guest, was checking out the car too. I hadn't been sure it was him I'd seen before at the school but now I was positive, making this the second time I had observed his presence at the school. I wondered why.

"You can give me the box now Carmen. We're at my car," April was saying as I realized we were standing by her vehicle, which was a slightly beat up blue Ford Taurus. I handed her the box. "Thanks for helping and for stopping by, it was nice of you to follow up with me."

"No problem, I hope I can approach you again next year. We need summer employees every year."

"That would be fine. I'll keep it in mind for next year's seniors," April said and then got in her vehicle.

My pickup was parked on the other side of the parking lot, and as I walked towards it, I saw Hugh standing by a corner of the building watching as a slender, average height, red-haired man, who I guessed was the principal, walked out of the school. At least I assumed it was Nolan as he stopped by the Corvette. He was talking with a couple of kids. He stood and visited with them for a few minutes, then one of them shook his hand and they walked away. Hugh continued to watch as Nolan got in his vehicle and drove out of the parking lot. Hugh noticed me watching him, nodded, and hurried away. That was weird. As I walked to my pickup my mind wondered if the principal was responsible for the meth. He could be recruiting kids to either buy or sell, but what was Hugh's role in this? Maybe Hugh was a drug supplier and the principal was interrupting his business by trying to get the kids on the straight and narrow. I debated about stopping by the Sheriff's Department and letting him know what I saw, but I decided Sheriff Poole wouldn't appreciate my half-baked theories with no proof. Hugh drove by me and I made a spur of the moment decision to tail him—if driving one car length behind someone on a two lane street with barely any traffic can be considered tailing that is. I followed him a couple of blocks until he stopped and parked in front of Melanie's studio. He waved at me when he got out of his vehicle. Feeling foolish, I waved back and drove by. It was time to visit Edna. Her high school employee should be there and she'd be able to visit with me.

There was nothing better smelling than a bakery I thought as I walked inside Edna's. Then I corrected myself, a field of blooming wild bergamot or purple prairie clover was better; but it was close. Edna was standing behind the counter filling a tray with jelly doughnuts. Her helper was running the cash register, but the line was only two deep so I didn't feel too bad about stealing Edna for a couple of minutes.

She looked up, spotted me and smiled, "Good afternoon Carmen."

"Do you have time for a break?" I asked her.

"I was about to take one, you have good timing. You can come back here where we will have some privacy and you won't stink out my customers."

I was puzzled at first and then I realized I smelled like smoke, "I'm sorry. I tend to forget how strong the burning smell is." The smoke smell perhaps explained April's strangeness around me.

Edna smiled and said, "Don't worry, I understand." She looked at her employee, "Tish, I'm going to take a break," and she motioned for me to follow her behind the counter.

She had a small couch and a table set up in a corner amongst her supplies.

"I assume you're sleuthing again?" she asked me with a grin.

"What makes you say that?"

"Because there have been two deaths, not from natural causes, and you tend to be not too far behind when that happens."

I laughed and said, "Guilty, but I am trying to stay out of Judith's investigation as I believe it has something to do with meth."

"That would be wise. So what do you think I can help you with?" Edna asked getting right to the point.

I explained about Christopher, the convention, and our suspicion that one of the four men impersonated my dad and fathered Christopher. I told her we thought Christopher may have been killed because he was trying to blackmail or scam whichever one of them was his father.

"Interesting, but what does that have to do with me?" Edna asked.

"Didn't Owen Laterly used to own this building?" I asked her.

"Yes—I rented from him for five years until he sold it to me after I pestered him for a year. It was easier for him to sell than keep up with the repairs. I'm not so sure he wasn't smarter than me."

"Owen is one of the men from the convention. I don't know him, and I was wondering if you'd offer an opinion on him."

"He's not the friendliest of men, but he was a good landlord. He was quick to address any problems, and didn't raise the rent," Edna replied.

"What do you mean about not being friendly?" I asked.

"He never smiles and keeps to himself. I don't think I've ever seen him with anyone else. He used to sell insurance, I imagine that was why he was with at the convention, or at least that would have been his tie to the other farmers."

"Maybe he got burnt out dealing with the public?" I suggested thinking of the many times I had to bite my tongue when dealing with a customer.

"It could be; I used to get the sense he didn't have time to visit as he was either wanting or needing to be somewhere else."

"What do you mean by that?"

"I'm not sure, but when he would stop by to collect the rent, he continuously checked his watch while he waited for me to write the check. It may have been my imagination he was impatient, but

I did hear somewhere that he had a gambling problem. Maybe he was anxious to be on his way and I was keeping him from the casino. After all the nearest casino is an hour away in Parkville."

"He owns other buildings in town, maybe he has a lot of repairs and he's always running behind," I suggested, but I made a mental note about a possible gambling problem. Maybe he got in trouble with gambling debt when he was in Las Vegas. Perhaps that's what Christopher was going to hold over his head. After all, if he substitutes for ministers in the area he may have been worried Christopher was going to ruin his reputation. "Did you ever get the impression Owen could be violent?"

"I never had that much interaction with him—only when I paid my rent and then when I bought my building," Edna answered. She shrugged and asked, "Is the bachelorette party on for Saturday?"

"It is."

"You know, I thought you were insane when you suggested the cabin, but I'm looking forward to it now. It'll be nice to relax, visit, play a few games and be somewhere private where we can be ourselves without the town watching us."

"I hope Jessica will like it. It's not a very fancy party."

"Jessica's not a fancy person. I think it will be perfect," Edna reassured me.

"Thanks. But I've taken up enough of your time, I'd better get going. But first I'm going to buy one of those jelly filled doughnuts for the road."

I stood on the sidewalk, eating my doughnut, wondering what I should do next. Kirk and Nick could handle putting away the equipment, and it would fill the rest of the work day for them. I could stand to pick up a few groceries before Dad got home. Kirk and I hadn't starved, but we hadn't been cooking many actual meals, only quick things like tacos, cereal, and frozen pizzas. I knew we were almost out of milk, butter and bread too. As I got in my pickup to drive to the grocery store I remembered a check a customer had given me a few days ago when they picked up their seed. I decided to swing by the bank, deposit it, and maybe visit with Peter. I checked the time; it would be open for another half hour. The bank was almost empty of customers when I walked in so I wouldn't offend too many people with the smoke smell on my clothes. I walked to the nearest teller, asked for a deposit slip, filled it out, and gave that and the check to the teller. Peter stepped out of his office as the teller handed me a receipt. I veered his way.

"Hi Peter," I greeted him.

"Hello, Carmen. I can tell you've been burning today," he said as he backed up a few steps.

"Yes, sorry for the smell. Are you enjoying your cousin being in town? He's been staying in one of our cabins and he extended his stay another week."

"He mentioned that. I was glad to hear it; I haven't gotten to see as much of him as I had hoped. I guess he's been keeping busy getting in touch with his old classmates."

Now I was confused; Hugh had indicated to me he had been spending a lot of time with his cousin. "What does Hugh do for a living?"

Peter looked embarrassed as he answered, "I have to admit I don't know. He hasn't kept in close contact over the years and when I asked him he said he was between jobs."

It dawned on me that Hugh could be our mystery law enforcement person Judith mentioned in her journal. Realizing Peter was staring at me waiting for a response I said, "James mentioned you had a new employee you were training. Is it someone you want me to be working with from now on?"

Peter looked puzzled for a moment and then said, "You must mean Paula, no, she was only here for training. She's been gone for a month now. Are Chet and Karla getting home soon? Bev and I wanted to have them over to play cards one night."

"They'll be home late tonight," I answered, crossing Paula off my suspect list.

"I'll have Bev get a hold of Karla tomorrow. Nice seeing you

Carmen, I'm sneaking out early today, but I need to grab a few files first to review at home tonight," he said and walked towards the back of the bank.

On my way back to my pickup I was thinking as I walked; if Hugh was the law enforcement person Judith had contacted he could be working undercover explaining why Peter didn't know what his job was. If I was correct, it would be for the best if I left Hugh alone. I didn't want to mess up anything he might be doing to stop the drug problem. The grocery store parking lot was packed when I arrived. It was apparent 5:00 p.m. wasn't the best time to shop if you were in a hurry. I got in the store and realized why it was so busy, it was senior citizen night. Once a month, the grocery store would have numerous items marked half price for senior citizens. It was Chloe's idea and it was a great help to those who were living on limited social security funds. Local businesses, including ours, donated money to the grocery store to supplement the program. There was an unwritten rule that people who could afford it shouldn't take advantage of the sale items, but as with everything there were people who abused the program. While I was standing there trying to decide about trying a new brand of whole grain bread I overheard someone calling the name Owen. I looked up and saw a stooped man about Dad's age stop, turn around, and greet whoever had been calling to him. Melanie, who I hadn't noticed was next to me, pointed and said, "That's Owen. Watch him take full advantage of the half price items. When you asked me about him the other day, I didn't want to say too much in front of the others, but I don't like that man."

I looked at her in shock; Melanie never said a bad word about another person other than her ex-husband.

She continued, "Something about him bothers me, I haven't figured out yet what it is, but there is something."

"Does he kill bugs?" I asked her with a grin.

She actually laughed. "He does, but that's not it. It's not evil, but something is off with him." She grabbed a different loaf of wheat bread than what I had been looking at and handed it to me. "Try this one," and then she walked away.

I looked at the loaf of bread and deciding to try it; I added it to my cart and I started to work myself towards the aisle I had last seen Owen going down. I lucked out, he was standing in front of the soups, adding every half price one to his cart.

"Are you Owen Laterly?" I asked when I got close to his cart.

"Yes," he answered hesitantly, turning to look at me.

"I'm Carmen Karlaff," I said sticking out my hand to shake his.

"Can I help you?" he asked ignoring my outstretched hand.

"I don't know if you're aware, but I built three cabins on my property as a venture into the tourism industry and I understand you own quite a few buildings in town that you also rent out?" I asked.

"Yes," he answered, clearly wondering what I was leading up to, which was smart, as I had no idea either. I was trying to come up with a reason to have a conversation with the man.

Thinking feverishly, I asked, "Who do you use for insurance? I understand you used to sell insurance, and I thought you might have an idea of who to use. Our farm's insurance policy premium took quite a jump when we added the cabins. I don't think they had any familiarity with that line of work and I was wondering if there was a less expensive company for the cabins."

"You're Chet's daughter I believe?" he asked.

"Yes, I am." I was glad he brought up my dad, I was hoping some familiarity would make questioning him a lot easier.

"He's a good man," he said and then remained silent.

"Yes is he is. Do you have any tips for an insurance company to check out?" I asked again as he continued his silence.

"I only sold crop insurance, and I'm sure your current insurance company would have the best rate out there because of the bundling of all your other assets. A stand alone policy for only the cabins would not be cost effective," he answered.

"Thank you for the information. Dad and I were looking at old photos the other day and I remember Dad pointing you out. You went with on a trip to Las Vegas my dad and a lot of other people having to do with agriculture from here went on many years ago."

His face darkened. "I did," he said tersely.

"Dad had a lot of good memories from that trip, did you also enjoy it?" I asked, as the ability to come up with any intelligent questions had deserted me.

"No I did not. If you'll excuse me, I need to get going." He grabbed his shopping basket and head toward the checkout.

I finished picking out my groceries, paid for them, and drove home. As I drove I felt confident I had come up with my number one suspect for who might have impersonated Dad. Something about the trip brought up bad memories for Owen. But, I cautioned myself, it could be as simple as he might have lost a lot of money gambling. I hauled in the groceries, went outside with Wizard, checked on Tabitha and Clyde—Tabitha was cleaning herself on the front steps and Clyde followed me to his food dish. It wasn't empty, but he enthusiastically helped himself to the fresh food I put in it. I spied a glimpse of our feral cat in the trees behind the garage hunting something. I walked back in the house and was surprised Kirk wasn't home yet. I knew he had to pack. I hoped he and Nick hadn't had any problems putting the equipment away. I put the groceries away as I tried to figure out what to cook for supper.

CHAPTER FOURTEEN

*An early spring burn, before the growth of warm
season grasses, will help control cool season grasses
and non-native plant species, as well as prevent
woody stemmed plants from growing.*

I WAS PULLING LEFT-OVER LASAGNA I HAD found in the freezer
out of the oven when Kirk drove in the yard. While it baked
I had enjoyed a nice long shower and was now dressed in comfortable shorts and a t-shirt. I waited with washing my burning
clothes, knowing Kirk's clothes would need to be washed too, and
I could put them in the same load. I let Wizard out to greet Kirk,
before he drove me crazy with his barks of enthusiasm when he
saw Kirk out the window from the back of the couch where he had
been lounging.

"Have you heard from Dad yet?" he asked when he walked in,
Wizard trotting happily next to him.

"No, I keep meaning to check his itinerary, but I'm guessing
they're on the plane right now. Did you and Nick have problems
that you're so late?"

"No, my agent called and our tour is postponed. I had to let the other guys know so I stopped by their houses on the way home," he answered.

"What happened?"

"Nothing serious, they had a mix up with the dates. It will work out better anyway, we leave in two weeks which means I'll be home for Jessica and James' wedding," he answered not sounding too disappointed. "Plus it will give us more time to work on our new songs, we're getting together to practice tonight."

"True."

Kirk smelled the air, "Did you make lasagna?"

"I did, but I can't take the credit for it, it came from the freezer. I think it was leftover from Jessica's restaurant."

"That's more like it. I was starting to wonder if you had bad news to give me and you were trying to soften me up."

"Aren't you funny—it's ready if you are, or did you want to shower first?"

"I'm going to shower first. You don't have to wait for me though."

"It needs to sit for a few minutes anyway. Go ahead. I'll put together a couple of lettuce salads for us while you shower."

"Thanks, I'll be back in five minutes."

It was closer to ten minutes by the time Kirk came back to the kitchen. We ate in silence, both of us tired out from the day. Kirk helped me clean up the kitchen and then he and Wizard left for band practice. Wizard must be behaving as Kirk was continuing to take him with. I had just started the clothes washing machine when I heard pounding on the front door. When I opened it both Nick and Faye were standing on the front steps.

"I figured out who more people were in the journal!" Faye said with excitement.

"You did? That's great. Come on in," I said as I led them to the kitchen table. Nick gave me a quick kiss as he walked by, making me wish I wasn't so interested in investigating murders and Nick and I could be alone.

Faye sat down, opened her notebook and waited for me to sit

down next to her. Once I did she said, "It wasn't that difficult, in fact I'm not sure why she even bothered not naming people as anyone who worked in the office would know who these people are."

"Maybe she hoped if anyone peeked at her journal and they didn't see names, they wouldn't bother to examine it any closer," I suggested.

"It could be. I guess it doesn't matter why. Anyway, when we left off the other night we were talking about the IPD driver. I think the next person she wrote about is the veterinarian."

"Why wouldn't she use her name?" I asked. "Judith used Sally's name in the earlier pages."

"I don't know, but Judith writes about this person being an old friend and that if it wasn't for the fact that she loved animals, Judith wouldn't have anything more to do with her. Judith talked about her being vengeful, and she wondered why when her occupation was so needed she had worked in three different places the last seven years."

"That does sound like Sally. It is strange she was in so many different vet clinics in such a short amount of time," I said.

"Maybe not," Nick offered. "It could be she didn't like the pay or the communities the clinics were in. Maybe she wanted to own her own clinic."

"I guess." I shrugged.

"The next person she wrote about has to be Owen Laterly. He owns the building the dental office is in. Judith wanted to buy it, but he wouldn't entertain the notion of selling. She also listed him as one of the people she was noticing had bad teeth. She was unsure if it was meth or perhaps a medication he was on, although he hadn't volunteered any medications to add to his file that would harm teeth—yet not everyone is honest when they give us their list of medications."

"That's interesting. I talked to Owen this afternoon at the grocery store. For someone who fills in as a preacher at times, he's a sour individual. I would be skeptical he was a drug addict although I do think he's a gambler."

"It could be possible his gambling is getting him in financial trouble so he started selling meth. Maybe he started using too," Nick said.

"That wouldn't explain damage to his teeth if he recently started using," I said. "I think he's a better candidate for being Christopher's father."

"What makes you think that?" Nick asked.

"When I brought up the Las Vegas convention he made it clear he didn't want to talk about it," I answered.

"That's interesting," Nick said. "We also thought because of the preaching, his reputation would be something he might feel a desperate need to defend."

"Especially if Christopher knew something about his gambling too," I said getting excited. "Although it doesn't appear to be a secret about him being a gambler. Who else did you figure out?"

"I could only find references to two more people in the pages you found. I think one of them was Cory as she wrote about the person having a lot of money, new to town, and that he had excellent teeth—so no meth connection there."

"He could be dealing and not using," Nick suggested.

"I talked to Tony this morning and Cory's money was made honestly by flipping houses. Tony had even visited Cory and saw the houses they were working on," I said.

"It doesn't mean he isn't involved in drugs also," Nick said.

"True, but Tony isn't a stupid man. I think he'd know if his son was up to something," I insisted not wanting Tony or Cory to be involved.

"But would he tell you?" Nick asked.

"I don't think you need to consider him," Faye said. "Judith had the comments about him crossed off. I think she ruled him out. But it did occur to me we could have him mixed up with Nolan, the high school principal. They are both young."

"That could be. She talked about Cory by name in the earlier pages, but I guess she did the same for the principal and Sally too," Nick said.

"I'm getting discouraged, between the notebook the sheriff found at the dental office and the journal pages I found, we keep coming up with the same names, but aren't any closer to having proof of anything," I said as I slumped in my chair dejected.

"We can't give up," Faye said. "I think we've made progress. There is only one person left she wrote about that we don't know who it is. She wrote about calling an old friend for advice."

"I'm sure that was the person she knew who had a connection to law enforcement," I said. I considered whether or not I should share who I thought Hugh was and decided for now I would keep quiet. If he truly was investigating the drugs here in Arvilla I didn't want to say anything that might jeopardize his chance of success.

"Don't you think it's about time to turn this information over to the sheriff?" Nick asked.

Faye looked at him in surprise and said, "But the sheriff thinks I killed Christopher and that there is a possibility I am involved in Judith's death."

"I'm not talking about us giving up on finding out who killed Christopher; I'm talking about Judith's murder. If it is meth related we should be staying out of it," Nick said looking at us with concern in his eyes.

"I agree; I don't want anything to do with the drug aspect of this either. I'll find time to stop by the Sheriff's Department tomorrow and share with him the information we have. He's not going to be happy with me." Faye started to protest and I continued, "But I am not giving up on investigating Christopher's murder. You are positive Christopher didn't have anything to do with meth and there is no way he could be somehow mixed up in Judith's murder?"

"Absolutely not, Christopher was involved in a lot of bad things, but he and his uncle always stayed away from drugs. Their activities were illegal but they were scared of the drug business. They said it was too violent."

"Didn't he beat you?" I asked surprised by her comment.

"Yes. Ironic, I know. He didn't see any problem with physically abusing me, but the thought of someone beating him up was abhorrent and he was scared of gun violence. I don't even think either one of them owned a gun. That's another reason I'm so convinced Christopher didn't have anything to do with Judith's death."

"Unless he hired someone, who mistook her for you," I suggested.

"I've been thinking about that possibility, but I don't believe it. Christopher would have wanted his revenge on me by personally beating me, not by hiring someone to kill me."

As Faye finished talking, I heard a car door slam. I got up, peeked out the window and saw Dad grabbing his suitcase out of the back of his pickup and Karla walking towards the door. James' vehicle wasn't far behind them. He must be coming to pick up Karla, but I didn't know why Dad wouldn't have dropped her off before coming home.

CHAPTER FIFTEEN

*Some believe Native Americans conducted burns
to maintain prairie habitat so bison herds would flourish.
It is thought the fires mimicked the effects of lightning
strikes and kept the prairies healthy, while creating
the conditions needed for good hunting land.*

I RAN OUT THE DOOR, GAVE KARLA a hug, and went to help Dad with his luggage. Nick had followed me out and grabbed the suitcase Dad was carrying. Faye held the door open for us as we tromped through the door with James following us.

"I thought you weren't getting home until late tonight?" I asked him.

"Both Karla and I were tired and looking forward to getting home. We lucked out with an earlier flight having a few open seats. We also wanted to share our news," and as Dad said that Karla held up her left hand showing us a gorgeous sapphire ring.

I covered my mouth to hold in my scream and in a muffled voice asked, "Are you guys engaged?"

"We are." Karla answered as Dad put his arm around her.

I looked at James and was relieved he was smiling, although it didn't surprise me that James was just as happy for them as I was.

We spent several minutes hugging and congratulating them before Karla said, "I hate to break this up, but I'm exhausted."

"I'll take you home, Mom," James said.

As I gave her a hug goodbye I whispered in her ear, "Welcome to the family." Karla kissed my cheek and then she and James left.

"I'm so thrilled for you," I told Dad.

"You're sure? I'm not trying to replace your mother," Dad said as Faye and Nick stood awkwardly listening.

"I know that Dad. No one can replace her, but she would want you to be happy." He nodded in acknowledgement and sat down at the kitchen table. "Did you have a good time?" I asked after Nick, Faye and I sat down at the table with him.

"We did, but I think I'm going to sleep for a week," Dad answered. "But the trip was well worth it, glaciers, calving glaciers, grizzly bears, mountains, orcas, whales; Alaska is a great state. The only thing I wish we would have done that we didn't was fish for salmon."

"Karla enjoyed the cruise also?" I asked.

"She did. She started off a little seasick, but the ship doctor gave her motion sickness pills and she had no problems after that."

"I'm sure the proposal helped too," I teased him. He merely grinned. "I can make you something to eat if you are hungry?"

"I don't think I'll be hungry for a long time. We ate so much food," he answered as he patted his stomach. "I'm looking forward to getting back to my walking tomorrow. What's been going on around here?" he asked.

I looked at Nick and Faye with a question in my eyes.

Dad saw my look and said, "Don't tell me there's been another murder?"

"Two actually," I admitted.

That took the wind out of him, he couldn't even respond, only stared, until he asked, "Who?"

I gave him a quick rundown on Judith, and then Christopher.

"That's awful about Judith; poor Dan and the kids, but I'm not understanding about Christopher? I know you called and told me about his tie to Faye and about him believing I was his father, but how did he end up here?"

"It's kind of a long story; would you rather wait until tomorrow when you've had some rest?"

"I'm fine, go ahead."

Faye told Dad how Nick had moved her to California when Christopher was put in jail the first time for fraud and how Christopher found her and beat her again when he was released. She told him about Nick coming to help her and how Christopher was arrested a second time, this time for beating her and how Nick finally convinced her to move to Arvilla. She finished up by relating how a friend had let her know Christopher was out of jail again and was looking for her, but before he found Faye he was discovered dead in our field.

"And I imagine Sheriff Poole believes either you or Nick is responsible," Dad said shaking his head. "By the way, I can't believe you thought I would have cheated on my wife," Dad said to Nick looking hurt.

"I did until I met you," Nick acknowledged. "I should have known better than to believe anything Christopher ever said."

"But we do believe whoever Christopher's father is—he's from here. As I told you when I called, someone impersonated you when you went to that convention in 1993. We've narrowed it down to Owen Laterly, Jed Alman, Cord McCaster, and Al Mitchel. We think Christopher found out which one was his father and tried to scam or blackmail them leading to his death."

"It couldn't be Cord McCaster," Dad said confidently.

"Why do you say that?"

"I don't always remember things right away. After you called me I recalled Cord being very uncomfortable in a big city. He stuck close to your mom and me the entire weekend—it couldn't have been him. I do remember Al and Owen spent most of their free time together but I can't say I have any recollection of Jed from the trip."

"It sounds like Jed was the only one who had time that wasn't accounted for," I commented.

"I wouldn't say that, everybody kind of paired up and did stuff together. I don't happen to remember Jed. But although I remember certain people doing things together, it doesn't mean they were attached at the hip. The meetings only lasted from noon to four, and evenings were on our own. We typically had supper together as a group but we didn't stick together all night—other than Cord. We were there for three or four days I believe, plenty of time for people to get themselves in trouble. Come to think of it, Al and Owen were good friends at the time, and I always wondered if something happened between them on the trip. They never appeared to get along after we got back."

"That's interesting," I said, starting to be suspicious.

"Don't get your Nancy Drew going too much, Owen stopped selling crop insurance after the trip and it could have been as simple as they didn't have anything in common anymore. Al would have been one of Owen's biggest customers. Maybe Owen didn't like Al, and once he didn't have to rely on him to buy insurance they drifted apart," Dad said.

"Can you think of anyone else from the trip I could talk to that might know if something happened between the two of them?" I asked.

"Not tonight, my brain is tired, my body too. Maybe something will come to me when I sleep." Dad stood up and started to pick up a suitcase.

"Do you need that brought to your bedroom?" I asked,

"No, I'm going to dump it in the laundry room."

"I'll take care of it. I need to do laundry tonight anyway," I offered. I didn't, but I knew Dad wouldn't take me up on my offer if he thought I was doing something extra for him alone.

"Thanks, Carmen. How's your brother doing, isn't he leaving tomorrow with his band?"

"There was a change to his schedule; they won't be leaving for another two weeks. He's been helping with the burning, but tonight the band and he are practicing. Wizard on the other hand, he's had several adventures."

"Those are stories for another day. I'm going to bed." Dad said goodnight to Faye and Nick and then grabbed his toiletry bag and walked down the hallway to the bathroom.

"We'd better get going too," Nick said. "What do you want me to work on in the morning?"

"I'd like to spread fertilizer, but there isn't any rain in the forecast." If we spread granular fertilizer and there wasn't any moisture, it would dissipate before it was absorbed by the soil. We didn't have the right equipment to inject liquid fertilizer.

"I could at least do the field that is irrigated," he offered.

"That would work, we can run the irrigation to incorporate it, but first we need to install the pump in the gravel pit," I reminded him.

"How long will that take?" Nick asked as this was a new part of our operation to him. In his previous work experience with irrigation they had wells and it was only a matter of turning on the system in the spring. We had one irrigation system with a well, but the rest had pumps in gravel pits.

"An hour or two, the pumps are there, but we lift them out of the water in the fall. I forgot you didn't help with that, Dad and I did it while you finished the leadplant combining. I'll meet you at the shop at seven tomorrow and we'll tackle the pumps."

Faye let herself out the door, giving Nick and me a few minutes alone to say a proper goodbye. Nick reluctantly pulled away after a lengthy enjoyable kiss, said goodnight, and left. I wasn't tired so I sat down on the front steps and enjoyed the night. I could hear frogs croaking and an owl hooting. Clyde came over to greet me. Tabitha wasn't around, and after Clyde walked away—he could take only so much attention—I decided to walk around the yard to look for her. I knew I wouldn't sleep well if I didn't verify she was okay.

Kirk laughed at me when I did this, he said Tabitha had been with us for six years and she knew how to stay safe. I had never observed her wandering out of our yard, but we did have outbuildings and if we didn't pay attention she sometimes got locked in one of them. I got halfway around the house before I spotted her staring up a tree. I looked up and saw Wizard's squirrel friend studying her. I smiled and decided I didn't need to worry about her tonight. As I walked towards the door I could see headlights coming down the driveway. I assumed it was Kirk and I waited by the door for him. Wizard came barreling out of the car first, running with excitement towards me as fast as his little legs could take him.

"How was practice?" I asked Kirk when he got closer.

"Good and bad."

"What does that mean?"

"Kyle found us a replacement for Squirt and he's working out well," Kirk answered.

"I wasn't aware you'd kicked Squirt out of the band?" I asked. "I thought you said he was better at your last practice?"

"We haven't kicked him out, but remember I said I was going to talk to the sheriff about him?"

"Yes, didn't you do that?" I questioned him.

"I didn't have to. Squirt went and talked to the sheriff on his own."

"Do you know what he told him?" I asked.

"I don't, but somehow Kyle heard that Squirt told the sheriff who his dealer was and afterwards they found a rehab place for Squirt somewhere in southern Minnesota. I hope it works. I called Squirt's sister tonight and told her he was welcome back whenever he finished treatment."

"Did the sheriff arrest anyone?" I asked, realizing my avoidance of the sheriff while I tried to figure out the journal pages had left me in the dark as to what his investigation was coming up with, although I was sure he wasn't bothered too much by an absence of visits from me.

"Kyle didn't know, but he did hear a rumor that a DEA agent is supposed to be showing up in town. I don't know how it could be true, as I don't think the Sheriff's Department would let that information be public, but Kyle thought it was true."

"That can't be good. It would appear drugs are a bigger problem than I was hoping they were if our local law enforcement can't handle it." I started to believe I might be right about Hugh's identity.

"There was a murder," Kirk reminded me.

We had walked in the house and sat down at the kitchen table by now. Wizard head to his cushion and spun circles trying to make a comfortable spot to sleep.

"I think you better stay out of this Carmen. People who deal with drugs aren't people you should be messing around with," Kirk cautioned.

"I already came to that conclusion. I'm only trying to figure out who killed Christopher," I assured him.

"Maybe they are connected though."

"I don't think so," and I explained about Christopher's tie to someone in this town and Faye's belief he avoided anything to do with drugs.

"How do you feel about Nick keeping his family a secret from you?" Kirk asked, impressing me with his insight as to how that might have hurt me.

"I'm not sure why he felt the need to keep it a secret, everyone has somebody in their family tree they're not proud of," I answered.

"We don't have anyone in our family we are keeping from people because we're ashamed of them," Kirk stated.

"What do you mean?" I asked.

"Faye has been pretty open with people about her and Nick's past. I've already heard a few people making comments about how you better be careful, or Nick will wind up owning your farm."

"Oh no, sometime I forget how awful some people can be," I said.

"I've heard plenty of people defend him too, so it's not everyone. But I can understand Nick not being anxious to share the past.

I could tell from his first day here he had fallen for you. I don't imagine he thought he had much of a chance if you'd have known about his history. I think it's a good thing you got to know him for who he is before you heard about his family," Kirk said.

"Am I that shallow?" I asked feeling ashamed.

"I wouldn't say shallow, but I think you would have put up boundaries and it would have taken a long time before you would have lowered them for him."

I looked down at the floor acknowledging the truth of his words. I didn't like it, but Kirk may be correct. "You know what the worst thing is?" I asked him.

"What?"

"I'm getting wise advice from you," I told him as I shook my head.

Kirk smiled, "I never thought I'd hear those words from you. It's kind of scary, I'm not sure I want to be a grown up?"

"I think it's too late," I gave him a hug and said, "Dad is home by the way."

"I figured that out when I saw his car," was his smart aleck reply.

"He and Karla got engaged on their cruise," I retorted.

He grinned, "I knew he was going to ask her."

"He talked to you about it?"

"He did, and before you get hurt that he didn't talk to you, he had a last minute attack of the nerves when he was leaving and I was here. Are you okay with it?"

"Of course I am. They are perfect for each other. I'm just astounded that you managed to keep it a secret."

"You didn't think I had it in me, did you?" Kirk answered as he grinned at me.

"I have to admit I'm surprised. Whether you like it or not you have grown up. I'm going to bed. You don't have to help tomorrow so enjoy your day off," I told him as I turned to walk out of the kitchen.

"I think I better help," he said sounding sheepish.

"Why?" I asked wondering what was up.

"I forgot to tell you our custom seeder called this morning after you left and ordered another 600 acres for a seeding project. I'm guessing you'll need my help to mix the seed in the morning."

And just like that, things were back to normal. "You didn't think to tell me about it until now?"

"Sorry, I forgot. Goodnight." He hurried to his bedroom before I could chew him out, Wizard trotting behind him.

I walked upstairs and set my alarm for 5:30 a.m., I was going to have to get to the seed plant computer and figure out the seed mix before I met up with Nick. I changed into my pajamas and then fell down on my bed. My mind was swirling thinking about Squirt and drugs. I knew I'd better get my butt to the Sheriff's Department tomorrow and let him know about Judith's journal. I wasn't getting anywhere, and I wasn't sure I wanted to. Drugs were out of my league. My mind turned to which of the four men, well three now, could have been Christopher's father. Dad was confident Cord had nothing to do with it. I did need to find a reason to talk to Jed and Al again. I hoped Dad could think of someone who might have insight about what went on at that convention and at some point in my thinking I must have fallen asleep.

CHAPTER SIXTEEN

Prevention of woody growth is a key factor in managing prairies. Controlled burns remove woody plants, preventing the land from turning into a forest habitat.

D AD WAS UP READING HIS NEWSPAPER and sipping coffee when I walked downstairs rubbing my neck.

"What's wrong with you?" he asked.

"Kirk must have let Tabitha inside when he let Wizard out last night. She wormed her way on to my pillow; I think I slept with my head turned all night. You're awake early, I thought you'd sleep in," I said as I poured a cup of coffee for myself.

"I think my sleep will be interrupted for a few days until I get back in a routine. Who knew a vacation could mess up your sleep patterns so much? It looks like the sheriff hasn't made much progress with either Judith's or Christopher's murder," he said.

"What are you looking at?" I asked him peering over his shoulder.

"The newspaper has an article. The sheriff had nothing to say, other than no comment, for any of the reporter's questions. Which reminds me," Dad said, "you could ask Mauve Johnson what she remembers about the convention."

"Who is Mauve Johnson?"

"She was a reporter who came along for the trip."

"Our local newspaper sent a reporter to cover an agronomy convention in Las Vegas?" I asked incredulously.

Dad laughed. "Her husband worked for the agronomy company and the owner of the newspaper agreed to give her the time off to go with as long as she wrote an article about it."

"That explains the picture we found in the old newspaper, but I didn't see an article with it," I said.

"I wondered about that myself at the time, but I assumed it was too dull of an article to publish—anybody who would have been interested in the convention would have been with. I haven't seen Mauve around in a few years. I think she was about fifteen years older than me, but I haven't heard of her passing away. She was an observant person, if anyone was up to something on that trip, she'd have known."

"I'll see if I can find her," I said as I put a piece of bread in the toaster and fried myself an egg. "Did you and Karla talk about a date for your wedding?"

"We didn't want to decide anything until James and Jessica have their day; but we both agreed it would be low-key. We kind of sprung our engagement on you last night. Are you sure you are okay with it?"

"I couldn't be happier for the two of you—honestly," I continued, "and that's the last time I want to hear that question."

Dad nodded as he studied my face and then asked, "So what's going on with the farm? Do you need help with anything today?"

"No, I'm on my way to the seed plant to work out a seed mix and then Kirk is going to mix it while Nick and I work on getting the blue grama irrigation pump installed. We can fertilize that field and then irrigate it in as there isn't any rain in the immediate forecast. Were you looking for something to do?"

"Not really," Dad yawned, "but I thought I'd offer."

"Thanks anyway. I better get going." I put my dishes in the

dishwasher and filled my coffee mug. I could hear Kirk and Wizard moving in his bedroom, so he wouldn't be late to mix the seed. I walked out to my pickup and drove to the seed plant where I spent a couple hours computing a seed mixture. I checked inventory and then called a few other growers I knew who would be up early and ordered the wildflowers we were getting short on. Nick and Kirk arrived at the same time. I gave Kirk the seed mix and Nick and I went to work on the irrigation pump. We had a few unforeseen problems and it took longer than I had expected. We worked through dinner, and by 1:00 p.m. we had the irrigation pump working, fertilizer spread, and the irrigation system set to put on a half inch of water.

"If we hurry we could make Jessica's restaurant before she closes for the day," Nick said.

"That sounds good to me; I wouldn't mind a Reuben sandwich." I jumped in with Nick and we drove to town. I called Kirk on the way to make sure he had finished the seed mix.

"All taken care of, the custom seeder picked it up at ten. I'm home now but did you need me to do anything else?" he offered.

"No, you can take the rest of the day off."

"Okay, I think I'll see if I can locate where Squirt is and find out if I can visit one day or at least call him."

"Good luck." We parked in front of the restaurant as I hung up. It was empty with the exception of a table of four that was lingering over their coffee.

"Hi guys," Jessica greeted us. "James told me about Karla and Chet. I'm so excited for them."

"Kirk and I are too. You aren't cooking today?" I asked her.

"I had so many phone calls for wedding related details; George finally kicked me out of the kitchen. Phyllis just left—she wanted to leave a little early today so you've got me waitressing." Phyllis was Jessica's longtime waitress and known for her legendary memory—she never had to write down an order.

"What can I get you?" Jessica asked us.

"The dinner special on your board was chicken pot pie with a breadstick. Do you have any left?" I asked changing my mind about a Reuben sandwich.

"I do."

"I'll take that," I said.

"I will too," Nick chimed in.

Five minutes later she brought us our plates and sat down with us while we ate. After I had eaten enough to settle the starvation part of my stomach and could slow down, I asked Jessica, "Do you know Mauve Johnson?"

"I do, Mauve was a good friend of my mother's when she was alive."

"Do you know where I could find her?"

"She lives in the nursing home. She had a stroke about three years ago and is now starting to show the effects of Alzheimer's."

"Is she cognizant enough to question her?" I asked.

"I haven't been to see her for about six months, but at that time she had good and bad days, it depended on the day you saw her. I don't know about now. Why do you ask?"

I explained what Dad told me. "Do you think there's a chance she would remember the convention?"

"Doubtful, but you never know. I've heard remembering events from the past sometimes goes better than recent events," Jessica answered shrugging.

"I think I'll try anyway. I have time today—I'll stop by this afternoon."

"Let me get you a piece of banana cream pie to take with, it was her favorite." Jessica got up to get the pie.

Nick had been listening to us and after Jessica left to get the pie he asked, "Sleuthing again?"

"Yes, but not anything to do with Judith, and before I go see Mauve I'm going to stop by the Sheriff's Department, tell him about the journal, and give him the notes we came up with."

"Good, but you know he's not going to be very happy with you."

"I know, but he never is when it comes to me, I'm used to it. I am hoping when I tell him I'm going to stay out of Judith's investigation it will gain me a couple of brownie points."

"Worth a try," Nick said, though I could tell he doubted it was going to make any difference.

We both finished our plates as Jessica came back with the pie in a to-go container. She set it down and turned to leave. I stopped her when I said, "Don't forget about tomorrow night."

"How could I, I'm looking forward to it—last girl's night out."

"I hope not," I laughed.

"I should amend that, last girl's night for me as a single woman," she said correcting herself.

"That's better. I'd have quite a talk with James if you weren't going out any more with us girls."

"Especially as I'm planning on men's nights out whether he's married or not," Nick said. Then he asked Jessica, "Do you have the bill?"

"I do," and she pulled it out of her apron pocket.

Nick looked at it and put money on the table.

"Do you need change?" Jessica asked.

"No I don't. Thanks for a delicious dinner. That was a great potpie."

"It was my grandma's recipe," Jessica said as she started clearing our table.

"Do you want me to go with you to the Sheriff's Department?" Nick asked when we were outside.

"That's not necessary, besides I left the stuff in my pickup at the seed plant. After you bring me back to my pickup you can take the rest of the day off if you want," I told Nick.

"An afternoon off is a good idea. My dishwasher has been acting wonky; I can take it apart and see if the parts I need are available in town before the hardware store closes."

Nick let me off at my pickup. "Good luck with the dishwasher," I told him.

On my way to the Sheriff's Department I realized I was dreading the upcoming visit, knowing Sheriff Poole wasn't going to be happy with me. I parked, gathered the copies of the journal pages, our notes, my thoughts, and walked in.

"Is Sheriff Poole available?" I asked the dispatcher.

"He is. We've had a betting pool going as to how long it was going to take you to visit the sheriff." She smirked and said, "It looks like Deputy Rogers wins." The dispatcher motioned for me to go back to the sheriff's office.

"Carmen, what can I do for you today?" Sheriff Poole asked as I rapped on his open door.

"Well, it's more like what I'm hoping I can do for you," I said. I sat down and explained the journal pages, who we thought Judith was referring to, and how we couldn't figure out who the last person was—the one she was going to ask for help from, although I was convinced this was Hugh. When I finished I stared at him waiting for the explosion.

"This is helpful. Thank you very much," the sheriff responded in a calm manner.

"What?" I sputtered; shocked I wasn't getting chewed out for how I obtained the copies of the journal pages.

"I know it may surprise you, but I am capable of handling an investigation."

"Well, yes I know that," I admitted. "But. . ."

The sheriff interrupted me and said, "You're wondering why I'm not mad about you finding the journal, taking pictures of it, and not telling me about it?"

"That—and also wondering if you continue to think Judith was shot mistakenly for Faye?"

"I don't, and believe me when I say we are close to making an arrest for the murder of Judith and for who's responsible for the meth in this town, at least as they pertain to Judith's murder. I am under no illusion that drugs won't continue to be a problem as they are everywhere."

"What about Christopher's murder, is Faye your main suspect for that?" I asked, dreading his response.

"Either her or Nick, but I am confident neither of them is responsible for Judith's death."

"That's not very reassuring. They aren't murderers," I said reminded once again of how dealing with the sheriff sometimes felt like you were banging your head against a brick wall.

"I wasn't trying to be," he responded.

Trying to divert his attention from Nick and Faye I asked, "Do you think the journal pages and what we deduced from them will be helpful?"

"It correlates with a lot of information we had accumulated already." He grinned and said, "Dan found the journal and brought it to us a couple of days ago."

"Oh," I said deflated.

"We can solve a murder without your help," Sheriff Poole said. "By the way I do know who it was Judith was contacting for help."

"Are you sharing that information?" I asked, knowing he wouldn't but hoping he verify my belief that it was Hugh.

"Not with you. Carmen you need to stay out of this."

"Trust me, I have no desire to interfere with a drug investigation," I told him, keeping to myself I had every intention of continuing to look into Christopher's murder. "Good luck, I hope to hear soon that you've made arrest for Judith's murder."

"You will," he replied already looking down at the paperwork on his desk.

I walked out of the sheriff's office, checked my phone for the time, and decided it was early enough to visit Mauve before the nursing home served supper. I didn't want to interrupt their meal time. As I drove the six blocks to the nursing home I belatedly wondered if I could walk in without calling ahead. I knew Covid had changed the public's access to nursing home residents and I wasn't sure if those rules continued. When I walked in the building there was a sign asking you to please wear a mask if you had a cough or any cold symptoms, but there was no indication you couldn't visit someone. I walked to the nurse's station and asked for Mauve Johnson's room number.

"Are you family?" they asked.

"No, does that make a difference?"

"Not whether or not you see her, but if you aren't family we want you to be aware that sometimes she is lucid but she can also be very uncommunicative, and is sometimes angry."

"I think it's hard for her to talk since her stroke and it frustrates her," one of the nurses piped up.

"Is it okay if I visit her?" I asked.

"Visitors are always good, and sometimes she has good days, we only want you to be aware."

"Okay, thanks," I responded hesitantly. As I walked down the hallway toward her room I couldn't help but wonder if this was a complete waste of time. The door was open and I knocked as I pushed it open farther. A gray-haired, thin woman I assumed to be Mauve was sitting in a wheelchair looking out a window.

She looked up and said in a distorted slow voice, "Do you have my supper? It better not be soup. I'm sick of soup."

"I'm sorry, I don't work here. I do have a piece of banana cream pie for you," I said handing her the container.

Her eyes gleamed and she said in her gravelly voice, "My favorite. Who are you?"

"My name is Carmen Karlaff. My father is Chet Karlaff, do you remember him?"

She gave me a puzzled look for a few seconds and then it looked like fog cleared from her eyes. "I do."

"He told me you were a reporter with the local newspaper," I said.

"I was," her gravelly, distorted voice responded.

So far it appeared I was lucking out with a good day. "Do you remember going with my Dad and your husband to a convention in Las Vegas?"

"That was a stupid trip. They wouldn't let me write the good story, only the picture," her answer taking a lot of effort.

"What was the good story?" I asked getting excited.

"No proof they said."

"No proof of what?" I asked.

"No proof, too upstanding of a citizen. No one else witnessed. I always thought better of Owen." She mumbled starting to get agitated, "all that money, gone." She started shaking as a nurse walked in.

"What's going on in here?" the nurse asked.

"I was asking her questions about an article she wanted to write many years ago."

"It must not be a very good memory. I think you should leave it alone," she said as we both watched Mauve rock back and forth.

"I agree—I'm so sorry. Will she be alright?"

"Yes, every once in a while something agitates her, she'll be okay in a few hours."

"Sorry again, I'll leave," I said as I started toward the door.

"Should I let Owen know you stopped by?"

"Owen Laterly?" I asked.

"Yes, she didn't have any children and while Owen never visits, I assume too busy with the buildings he owns, he does call and check on her. He helps pay for anything she needs that Medicaid doesn't pay for. I imagine there must be some sort of family connection."

"No, you don't need to let him know I stopped in. Thank you again, I'd better get going." As I walked out of the nursing home I wondered what was going on. Why was Owen taking care of her and what story did she want to write about the convention? I had to find out who was in charge of the newspaper in 1993. I was almost positive the newspaper had been owned by the same family for as long as I could remember so I didn't think it would be difficult to find out. I know Kathy, a girl that was three years behind me in school, was operating the newspaper now. I was sure it would have been her family then too. Someone might remember what this story of Mauve's was. Dad hadn't said, but I'm assuming because Owen was taking care of Mauve, her husband must be dead. I decided to stop by the newspaper office and see what I could find out. I checked the time and saw I had about thirty minutes before they closed for the day. I drove to the newspaper office and parked in front of it.

"Hey Carmen, can I help you?" Kathy asked looking up from an overflowing desk when I walked in.

"I was wondering if it was your family who owned the newspaper in 1993?"

"It was, my family started this paper in 1945 and one of us has been running this thing ever since. Unfortunately for me my brother escaped the legacy and lives and works in the California sun, while I'm stuck here working with our parents."

I could tell by her expression she wasn't at all upset by this turn of events. "Do you know if anyone who was involved in running the paper in 1993 is available for questions?"

"That would have been my grandparents, but they've both passed away. Is there something I can help with?"

"I doubt it, I was talking to Mauve Johnson at the nursing home and she indicated a story she was working on. . ." my voice trailed off as I didn't even know where to go with this explanation.

"Are you sleuthing again?" Kathy asked.

I looked at her in surprise, "Why would you ask that?"

"I'm afraid your reputation precedes you," she paused, "or maybe I should say you're name has come up when I've questioned the sheriff at various times. What did Mauve say?"

"Long story short, I'm looking into the body we found in our burned blue grama field, and I think it ties into an agronomy convention people from here attended thirty years ago. Mauve went with, and when I asked her about the convention she indicated there was a big story she wasn't allowed to publish when she got back."

"She is a little out of it now—how do you know anything she said is real?" Kathy asked.

"That's a legitimate question, and the answer is, I don't, that's why I wanted to talk to someone who worked here at the time."

"We do have some old files I can take a peek at. If she wrote the story, even though they didn't publish it, I'm sure it's saved. My grandparents saved everything. My mom did clean out a lot of it when they took over the paper though. But," she continued, "if I do find something, you have to agree to tell me the whole story right away, I don't want to wait until the sheriff issues a statement. I only publish once a week and depending on the timing, often when the sheriff makes an announcement; it's old news."

I hesitated, "I can't tell you before he makes an arrest."

"You can at least tell me your side. I promise not to release the story until the sheriff has made an arrest, but the story would be ready to go, and I can hold the newspaper for a day or two or move it up."

I considered for a short time and then agreed.

As I was walking out the door she asked, "Have you considered checking out the major newspapers? Perhaps something significant happened in Las Vegas. Maybe you'll find out Mauve's story had no local ties at all and that's why it was axed."

"That's a good idea, thanks." It was too late to head to the library now, but it was time to go home for supper anyway.

CHAPTER SEVENTEEN

Humidity and wind direction are important factors
in determining the effectiveness and safety of a potential
burn. Relative humidity determines how hot a fire will burn
and wind affects the smoke's movement and the effectiveness
of the firebreaks. A change in wind direction can present
challenges by causing the fire to become unpredictable.

O N THE DRIVE HOME I DECIDED I would visit the library tomorrow morning. I should have time before checking the Erickson's out of their cabin, cleaning it, and getting Hugh set up for another week stay. He had text me back earlier with the updated contract. I had to go to town anyway in the morning to pick up stuff for the bachelorette party so stopping by the library wouldn't take a lot of extra time. When I walked in the kitchen door I was greeted by the smell of a pot roast in the slow cooker and Dad asleep in his recliner with Wizard on his lap. The only acknowledgement I got from Wizard was him opening his eyes as I tiptoed past them to my office. Sometimes slow on the uptake, I realized on the drive home I could research if anything happened during the convention on-line. After numerous hits for crimes that happened in Las Vegas on the days in question in 1993, I decided I'd better narrow my search down a little. I tiptoed past Dad and Wizard again and went upstairs to get the copy of the picture I had. If my memory was correct, they were standing in front of the entrance to the casino hotel they stayed at. That should help narrow my search. Rather than risk waking Dad again by going downstairs, I sat down on my bed and used my phone to search. After putting in the dates, and the casino hotel name, three different incidents came up. The first one was a brawl involving visitors from New Jersey, which I didn't think pertained, but the next two sounded promising. One was an elderly lady who claimed she was mugged after winning a $50,000.00 jackpot and the other was a bag of high stakes poker chips worth over $200,000.00 that had been inadvertently misplaced. It was never found and a security guard was fired. But I couldn't read any more than the headlines and the first couple of sentences without buying a subscription to the newspaper. The library was back on my schedule. I heard noise downstairs and I hurried down to help Dad with supper.

"Were you able to find Mauve?" Dad asked me as I was mashing the potatoes.

"I was, but other than a few rambling sentences she didn't make much sense." I told him about visiting her in the nursing home and about her claim there was a big story she wasn't allowed to print about the convention when she got back and how Kathy from the newspaper was going to check old files to see if they had the cancelled story on hand. "Do you remember anything significant happening?"

"I don't, but it was a long time ago. The convention itself was kind of dull, we enjoyed the accommodations and the nice weather, but other than that, casino life wasn't for us and your mom and I were glad to get back home."

I told him about the articles I found but nothing rang a bell with him. Kirk walked in as we were putting the food on the table. "I thought you had practice tonight?" I asked him.

"Squirt was gone again and nobody knew where."

"I thought he was already gone for treatment and you had a replacement?"

"We thought so too, but the replacement couldn't make it tonight and Squirt asked if he could come to practice since he hasn't left for rehab. I was hopeful a change had already started—especially as they hadn't sent him away yet."

"Maybe he had an incident and they got him admitted early," I suggested.

"It could be, but no one notified us," Kirk said with a shrug. "It's okay. I think everyone could use a night off anyway. Should we play Pinochle tonight?" he surprised me by asking.

"That sounds like a good idea," Dad said. "It's been a long time since I've played."

"Me too," I agreed and we spent an enjoyable evening playing cards. I couldn't remember the last time the three of us had done anything fun together. We broke it up at 10:30 p.m., with Dad handily beating both Kirk and I.

I woke up Saturday morning excited for Jessica's bachelorette party. Marcy, Faye, Edna, Melanie, Frankie and Chloe, were meeting up with Jessica and I at the cabins at three this afternoon. First I had to visit the library, then on to Chloe's grocery store to pick up junk food and drinks, and then to the seed plant to get the four-wheelers loaded up on a trailer and drop them off at the cabins. Knowing I would need another vehicle to accommodate all eight of us I would then take the empty trailer back to our house and pick up Dad's Polaris Ranger side-by-side. I decided to check with Edna to see if she could pick up Jessica to save me time. I called her bakery phone number and was glad I caught her instead of her voicemail and she agreed to pick up Jessica. That would free up some time to check the Erickson's out of their cabin and clean it while I waited for everyone to show up. While I was thinking of it, I went to the closet we used to store the linens and supplies and grabbed clean sheets, towels and various toiletry items like toilet paper and Kleenex to restock the cabins. I put them in a tub so they'd be handy to grab when I came back. Dad and Kirk weren't around, but the coffee was made so they weren't too far away, probably out walking Wizard. I grabbed a granola bar, filled my coffee mug, and drove to the library. I was surprised to see Marcy working.

"I thought you weren't working today?" I asked her.

"Beth, my library assistant, called in sick this morning. Don't worry I won't be late this afternoon, we close at two on Saturday. What brings you by?"

I explained to her about the articles I wanted to read, how the newspaper required a subscription to read them, and that I was wondering if the library would have access to the articles.

"Do you remember the name of the newspaper and the dates you are interested in?" she asked me.

I gave her the information and she checked. "Sorry we don't have a subscription to that one. I'll check elibrarymn.org." After a couple minutes of typing on the keyboard, she said, "No luck there either. I do know a friend of mine who is a librarian in Nevada. They might have a subscription and if so, I'll have her send copies of the articles to me."

"That would be great, I sure appreciate it Marcy," I told her.

"I don't know if she's working today, but if she is, and can find the articles I'll bring them with me tonight."

"Thanks. Are you bringing your fabulous artichoke dip?"

"It's already made. I only have to heat it up in the oven tonight," she replied with a grin knowing how much I loved it.

"I'm looking forward to it. I'll see you later." I left the library to head to the grocery store. It was obvious I hadn't eaten enough for breakfast as I was starving and thus committing the horrible sin of shopping when hungry. By the time I got to the till, my cart was full of more snack items then we could ever eat. The next stop was the seed plant to load the four-wheelers. When I arrived Nick was there loading the three four-wheelers for me.

"You didn't have to do this," I said happy he had though.

"I know, but I wasn't busy and I thought I'd save you time today. I know you have to clean the cabins too."

I kissed him and said, "If you really wanted to help you could come clean the cabins with me."

He kissed me back and answered with a smile, "I don't want to help that badly."

"Thanks a lot. What are your plans for the evening?"

"James and I are driving to Grand Forks, he has parts to pick up and depending on what films are showing we may take in a movie."

"Have a good time; and thanks again," I said as I leaned in to him and gave him another kiss, which turned into an unplanned but gratifying interlude. We broke apart, I hopped in my pickup, backed up to the trailer, and Nick hooked me up. I drove out to the cabins to drop off the four-wheelers and noticed the Erickson's were loading suitcases in their vehicle. I stopped by their car.

"Did you need help?" I asked Marge.

"No. Alex has almost everything loaded, but thank you for offering."

"I hope you're not rushing out on my account, you don't have to check out until one," I told her.

"Our granddaughter has a piano recital this afternoon so we're hoping to get home in time to attend that. Do you need us to do anything for checking out?"

"If you could sign this receipt," I got out of my pickup and handed it to her, "and I'll email you a copy, along with a short survey you can fill out if you choose to. If you do, please be honest with anything I can do to improve things."

"I don't think we'll have any comments. We had a wonderful, relaxing time—other than the bear visit. We also saw a lot of wildlife, which is what we were hoping for," Marge said looking happy.

"Thank you. Have a safe drive home." I got back in my pickup and drove to the cabin we were going to be staying in tonight to unload the four-wheelers and drove back home for the side-by-side. Dad and Kirk offered to share their dinner, but I passed knowing I was going to be eating a lot of junk food tonight and it wouldn't hurt me to miss dinner. I grabbed the tote I had packed earlier and loaded the side-by-side. The Erickson's were gone when I got back. I parked in front of their cabin and spent about thirty minutes cleaning, changing sheets and restocking towels and toiletries. My next stop was Hugh's cabin to drop off more clean towels and restock any supplies he needed. I had hoped he'd be there to prevent me from giving in to my urge to snoop. I grabbed the garbage from the can outside the door and put a new bag in it. I decided to leave the clean towels and supplies on the counter along with a note telling him if he wanted clean sheets to let me know and I would change them for him. As I set the clean towels on the counter I couldn't help but notice a piece of paper with names and lines drawn on it. To be honest, I saw the corner of the paper under a magazine and 'accidently' pushed the magazine aside. I didn't get more than a glimpse of Sheriff Poole's and Squirt's names when I heard a vehicle coming. I replaced the magazine and walked out of the cabin just as Hugh got out of his vehicle.

"I hope you don't mind but I let myself in to leave clean towels."

He looked at me while I tried to look innocent, and said, "That's okay."

"I also left a note asking you to let me know if you want clean sheets or anything else," I said feeling more awkward the longer I stood there.

"That's not necessary," Hugh said.

"Okay, if you need anything, let me know," I said knowing I was repeating myself.

"No worries," he responded sounding impatient, "As I mentioned before I'm not spending much time here."

"Well if you do think of something, I'll be staying in the cabin over there tonight with friends."

"I won't be home until late," he said bluntly.

Not knowing a good way to end this difficult conversation I said, "Have fun," and got back in my pickup and drove to the cabin to unload the side-by-side and the groceries. The encounter with Hugh felt strange. He hadn't acted that way in any of my previous encounters with him. I couldn't help but wonder if having the Sheriff and Squirt's names verified my belief he was an undercover law enforcement officer. I considered calling the sheriff and then decided to stay out of it, at least for tonight. I hoped for Melanie's sake Hugh was a good guy. It was now two o'clock, there was enough time to go home and grab the change of clothes I had forgotten earlier. By the time I got back to the cabin site, Marcy, Melanie, and Chloe were already there.

"I picked a top bunk," were Melanie's first words to me. "There was a small spider web in the corner and Marcy told me she would kill the spider if she spotted it so even though I don't like heights I'm not risking her sleeping there and killing an innocent spider."

Marcy looked at me, rolled her eyes, and said, "It looks like you have enough food for us to stay a week."

Chloe chimed in as she grinned, "I didn't say anything to you when you were in the grocery store; I assumed you were buying a few things for home too, but it looks like I was wrong."

I looked at the stacks of food and had to agree with her, I had overdone it. "I like to munch," I said in my defense. "Did you hear back from your librarian friend?" I asked Marcy.

"Not yet, but I'm sure I will on Monday," she responded as she helped herself to a bottle of water.

I heard more vehicles and stepped out of the cabin, Jessica and Edna were parking and Faye and Frankie were coming down the road behind them. The next few minutes were chaos as everyone piled in, picked their sleeping spots, and stashed their belongings. Jessica appeared excited which gave me hope she thought this was good idea. After a quick snack we took off on the all-terrain vehicles. The first stop was a gravel pit located far in the southwest corner of the property. The water was cold, so not ideal for swimming today, but we took off in the kayaks we had stashed there for our guests' use. I had been skeptical when Kirk had suggested buying them, but I had to admit it was a good idea. After an hour of paddling around, with only one kayak tipping, and a beaver sighting, we got back on the all-terrain vehicles. We took another short ride around the outskirts of the property being careful to avoid disturbing the hiking trails, then back to the cabin for a supper of grilled hamburgers and roasted vegetables. After the huge meal we took off for a hike, and had the incredible experience of coming across a bull elk. It was only a quick glimpse before the elk was gone, but a breathtaking experience. By the time we got back to the cabins it was dusk and we were all exhausted and ready to sit around a campfire and visit. I had brought board games, but by the time we got back inside the cabin around midnight, no one had the energy. We crawled into our beds and the rustling eventually subsided as people fell asleep. I couldn't help but think we were getting old—a few years ago we would have stayed up all night. I was starting to fall asleep when I heard a car. I hadn't noticed Hugh's vehicle all day, so I assumed it was him getting back. I had to get up to use the bathroom and I peeked out the window. There were no lights on in his cabin yet, and I couldn't see where the vehicle went. Remembering the scratches on the door of cabin C, I decided to check it out. I didn't want people who didn't belong here coming on the property. I was putting on my shoes when Jessica stirred.

She rolled over and whispered, "What are you doing?"

"I heard a car, but I don't know where it went. I want to check it out."

"You're not going out there alone. There have been two murders that haven't been solved." She tiptoed over and got her shoes too.

We opened the cabin door, snuck out, and closed it as quietly as possible. The night was warm, with a breeze rustling the leaves, which I hoped would mask any noise we might make. We stood listening for moment and when we didn't hear anything I decided to walk towards Hugh's cabin. I motioned for Jessica to follow me and we walked through the prairie. I was thankful the moon wasn't bright enough to illuminate us. Then I stumbled in a gopher hole just about falling on my face and rethought that, but I didn't dare use the flashlight app on my phone. I don't normally spook easily, but it felt like someone was out here somewhere. Jessica and I crept up to the propane tank behind Hugh's cabin. We crouched down behind it and listened. As I started to stand up, I saw another set of headlights coming down the road and I heard rustling from behind the cabin to the left of us. Jessica grabbed my hand, squeezed it, and I crouched back down, chest pounding. I heard the car shut off and saw the silhouette of someone standing on the porch of the cabin before the dome-light went off when the car door shut. Whoever it was lit a cigarette and I stared at the person. Their shadow looked familiar and I finally figured out it was Squirt. What was he doing here? Then I saw another set of car lights heading our way. Squirt asked in a loud trembling voice, "Are you there?"

A voice off to our left from behind the cabin answered, "I am."

I stood up again despite Jessica tugging on my shirt trying to make me to crouch back down. I wanted to see if I could get behind the person who was off to our left, in an attempt to find out who it was. I made it about twenty feet before the headlights of the second car almost illuminated me. I dropped to the ground. The car shut off, the lights went out, and the car door opened and shut. I was starting to stand up again, when I was grabbed from behind and a hand went over my mouth.

"Be quiet please," a whispered voice said.

I felt myself start to panic, but somehow the please calmed me. I was thankful again for the darkness so Jessica couldn't see me, or she'd get herself in trouble too as I knew instead of going to get help she would try and rescue me. I couldn't fault her; I'd do the same thing.

"Do you have my money?" I heard an unfamiliar voice asking from the front of the cabin.

Squirt answered in a stammering voice, "I do. Do you have any more for me?"

The voice laughed, and said, "You addicts are all the same, the minute you scrape up money to pay what you owe; you want more. I don't suppose you have the money to pay for your next fix?"

Squirt answered his voice a little stronger, "I do. Do you have the meth?"

"I do."

The arm holding me tensed, I heard a car door open and then, "Here it is, how much money do you have?"

Lights came on from the left side of the cabin, the arm around me let go, and the person who had been holding me ran to the front of the cabin. I dropped to the ground in relief and I heard, "Freeze, you are under arrest." Two shapes came from behind the vehicle lights. I stumbled my way over to Jessica.

"What's going on?" she asked.

"I have no idea," was my perplexed answer. We stayed crouched behind the propane tank until the noises settled down and I heard the sheriff's voice say, "You can come out now Carmen."

Jessica and I stood up and walked cautiously towards the front of the cabin.

Hugh was there smiling at me. "The sheriff warned me you'd find a way to stick your nose into this."

"What's going on?" I asked feeling confused.

"Hugh is a DEA agent. He was a friend of Judith's. She called him to come here and look into the meth problems," Sheriff Poole answered.

"I thought so!" I blurted out. "Did Judith tell you she was going to call him?"

"She did, and I thought it was a good idea. Hugh already had a lead on Nolan Richland. He had suspicions from the last school he was employed at."

I noticed for the first time they had the principal of the high school in hand cuffs with Squirt standing talking to a deputy.

"What does Squirt have to do with this?"

"It took a lot of persuading but he agreed to tell us where he was getting the meth and in return for no jail time, he agreed to this set-up. I understand this place has turned into one of the sites that are routinely used for drug deals," Sheriff Poole told me.

My shoulders slumped and I felt sick to stomach, "How have I not known what was going on?" I asked.

"According to Squirt the location of your trail cameras are known and they make sure to avoid them. If it makes you feel any better this is the first time an actual cabin was used. Typically they stay in their vehicles on the road in case they have to make a fast exit. You should be happy you have good locks on the cabins as they did try to get in one for more privacy. Squirt came through for us and convinced Nolan to meet him at a cabin so we'd have room to hide. I'm surprised Nolan agreed to it, but Squirt owed him a lot of money and he was enough of a regular customer that Nolan agreed."

"You keep saying they. Do you know if more people are involved?" I asked.

"A few suspicions, Judith's journals have helped. Hugh and I are confident Nolan was the primary person behind it. I'm hoping he'll be persuaded to tell us if he is working with anyone else."

"What about the murders, do you have anything tying Nolan to them?" I inquired.

"Not yet. We'll have to see what happens when we question him. Now why don't you head back to your cabin, Hugh almost had a heart attack when he heard you folks were going to be staying out here. It was too late to change the plan so we hoped nothing would interfere, somehow I knew you'd show up though."

"What about. . ." I said starting to ask another question.

The sheriff interrupted me and said again, more insistent this time, "Go back to your cabin."

Jessica grabbed my arm and we walked back to the cabin. "Wow, what a night," she said.

"Some bachelorette party, everyone asleep by midnight and a drug deal," I said and sighed.

She snorted, "Life is never predictable with you around."

With our nerves relaxing, her words caused us to collapse into giggles and when we got ourselves under control we tip-toed back in the cabin. I crawled back in bed thinking I was going to have a tough time falling asleep, but I must have passed out as soon as my head hit the pillow.

CHAPTER EIGHTEEN

The rich soils created from tallgrass prairies
are one reason for our nation's agricultural success.

S UNDAY MORNING I WOKE TO A shriek. I sat up, forgetting I was
in a top bunk and bonked my head on the ceiling. "What in the
world is going on?" I asked Jessica who was the only one left in the
bedroom as I rubbed my head.

"No idea," she said already out of bed and halfway to the door.

I jumped off the bed, wincing when I landed on a small rock
that must have come in on someone's shoes. This day was getting
off to a good start. I followed Jessica into the small kitchen area and
saw Melanie staring in horror at Frankie, and Chloe doubled over
in laughter by the window.

Frankie turned and looked at us, "I'm not sure what happened.
I got up early and thought I'd wash the dishes. She came out of the
bedroom and freaked out."

I looked at Melanie. You could see she was making an obvious
effort to calm herself.

"I rescued a monarch chrysalis I found attached to a stick lying
in the road. I was going to put it in an aquarium I have at home,

hoping it would hatch and I could release it. Frankie must have thrown it out as it's not here anymore."

"Is that all," Frankie said, and then seeing the glare Melanie gave her she continued, "I wouldn't throw it out, I knew what it was and who most likely brought it inside. I put it by your bag over there." She pointed to the area by the couch where we had stacked most of our belongings.

Melanie sagged in relief, and then apologized, "I'm sorry, I guess I overreacted."

"You think?" Frankie answered with a smile.

Peace restored, we gathered around the kitchen table and enjoyed a breakfast of scrambled eggs and caramel rolls.

After a few minutes of eating, Marcy said, "I vote we make this an annual event. I had such a good time getting away for a night, and best of all it was free."

"I agree," Frankie said, while everyone else nodded. "But I guess you lose income if we are staying here," she commented looking at me.

"I can spare one night a year for my friends. I think it's a great idea," I said happy my friends had enjoyed themselves.

"By the way, where were you and Jessica last night?" Faye asked. "Did we wake you up?"

"No, I was barely conscious but I vaguely remember seeing you both sneak in at one point during the night," she answered.

I explained to everyone what had happened. When Melanie heard what Hugh's part in the adventure was she grinned happily.

"I can't believe we slept through that," Edna said and continued to speak, "but I'm glad they caught who was responsible for the meth."

"At least this time," was Chloe's jaded response.

"The school isn't having much luck with principals; remember the last one had two DUI's. Thank goodness he resigned," Frankie said.

"Do they know if he killed Judith?" Faye asked.

"Not as of last night but I'm going to stop in at the Sheriff's Department this afternoon," I answered.

"Will you let me know what you find out?" Faye asked.

"Sure." I got up and started clearing the table. "Is anyone up for one last hike before we head home?" Everyone agreed and we went on a short half hour hike before coming back to pack, clean the cabin, and go home. I decided to get it over with and stop by the Sheriff's Department on my way home, knowing I didn't have a lot of time as Nick and I planned to help Jessica and James with cleaning out the farm building at James' they were going to hold the reception and dance in. Hugh's vehicle was there along with the sheriff's car. The dispatcher didn't even talk to me, only pointed for me to go back to the sheriff's office—I wondered briefly if I should be concerned I was this familiar to the Sheriff's Department. Hugh and Sheriff Poole were sitting in his office looking at paperwork. They both looked up when I walked in.

"Good afternoon Carmen," Sheriff Poole greeted me and indicated I should sit down.

I sat down next to Hugh and asked, "Did you find anything out about Judith's or Christopher's murder?"

"Nolan claims he didn't do it. He's been giving up his associates and admitting to the drug charges, but insists he had nothing to do with any murders," Sheriff Poole answered.

"Who are his associates?" I asked.

"That isn't anything we're going to share with you," the sheriff said as Hugh nodded in agreement. "He hasn't named anyone local," the sheriff relented sharing that tidbit.

"Do you believe he didn't kill Judith?" I asked.

They looked at each other, and Hugh said, "We do. He was genuinely shocked when we told him Judith was suspicious of him."

I slumped in my chair, disappointed.

"I'm sorry Carmen, but this leaves Faye as my primary suspect. She had ties to both of them."

"I admit, Christopher's murder would benefit her, but what

possible reason would she have for killing Judith?" I asked.

"Perhaps Judith deduced she killed Christopher, or saw them together?" the sheriff suggested.

Hugh had been studying me, and then said, "Who do you think did it?"

I explained about the trip and someone impersonating my father. "Christopher was the son of somebody in this town. I think it was either, Owen Laterly, Al Mitchel, or Jed Alman."

"Why would they kill a son they never knew they had?" Hugh asked.

"I haven't figured that part out yet."

Sheriff Poole interrupted, "I'm sorry but Faye is the best suspect."

"Christopher was a known con man. . ."

"As I understand it your hired man and Faye are too," Sheriff Poole interjected.

I rolled my eyes and continued, "Dad suggested I talk to Mauve Johnson, she went to the convention also, and see if she remembered anything of significance happening. She indicated she had a story but the newspaper wouldn't print it."

"Doesn't Mauve have Alzheimer's?" the sheriff asked.

I ignored him and kept talking, "I think something happened in Las Vegas. Maybe one of those men, along with Christopher's mother, committed a crime and Christopher knew what it was and was trying to blackmail them about it. Marcy is helping me obtain a couple newspaper articles about two incidents that occurred at the time they were there. One was an elderly lady who claimed she was mugged after winning a $50,000.00 jackpot and the other was a bag of high stakes poker chips worth over $200,000.00 that was misplaced and never found. I don't have the actual articles yet, I didn't have a subscription so I could only read the headlines, but I think our murderer and Christopher's father is the same person. If one of those men obtained the start to their wealth by illegal means and Christopher had proof, now that would be a motive for murder. My only problem is I don't know how or even if Christopher found out his father wasn't my dad—I'm assuming he came across a picture and somehow discovered the name of the person wasn't Chet Karlaff."

They had been listening to me and when I finished Hugh said, "That does sound promising."

The sheriff interrupted, "but how would that explain Judith's murder?"

I deflated again. "I don't know, maybe her murder was for another reason entirely that we don't know about. I only know Faye wouldn't kill anyone."

"I've heard that refrain from you before," the sheriff pointed out.

"And I haven't been wrong either," was my snapped back response.

Hugh interrupted our tiff and said, "When you get the articles, why don't you drop them off and we'll check them out."

I gave him a look, "Aren't you DEA?"

"Yes, but I'll be around for a few more days. It wouldn't hurt to have another person take a look at them as long as the sheriff doesn't mind?"

Sheriff Poole surprised me by saying, "That would be helpful."

"I'll bring them by as soon as Marcy gets them to me." I got up and left the Sheriff's Department. As I was walking to my pickup, my phone rang.

It was James, "Hi James. Did you and Nick have a good time last night?"

"We did, but that's not why I'm calling. I have to go over to Al's this afternoon after we are done cleaning out the building. I had called him about the possibility of buying hay from him, he didn't have any extra, but he did have the registration paperwork on the bull I bought from him ready. I know you wanted to talk to him again, do you want to come with me?"

"I do, I'm on my way to pick up Nick right now. We'll be at your place in ten minutes."

"Don't stop for food, Jessica is planning to feed you as a thank you for your help," James said. "Chet and my mom are here also."

As I drove to Nick's, my mind was working fast and furious on how I could bring up anything concerning the convention with Al. I wasn't any wiser by the time I got to Nick's place.

CHAPTER NINETEEN

*It is believed native prairies, those that have never been
planted or plowed and contain mostly original plant
communities, are among the most endangered ecosystems
in the world.*

NICK WAS WAITING FOR ME BY his pickup when I drove in the
yard. He got in, buckled his seatbelt, and said, "Faye had a
lot of fun last night, but it sounded like you and Jessica had an
adventure."

"We did." I spent the drive to James' telling Nick about Hugh,
the arrest, and how the sheriff doesn't believe Nolan was responsible for either murder.

"So I assume Faye continues to be his primary suspect?" Nick
asked sounding discouraged.

"Yes, but I think we have Hugh on our side. He said he was willing to help look into our theory."

"That sounds encouraging," Nick said as we pulled in James'
yard.

After eating we walked out to the building which James was
using to store items such as snowmobiles, riding lawnmowers,

lawn furniture and a couple old tractors.

"Does any of this stuff start?" Nick asked.

"That's the problem," James answered, "it used to, but nothing has been used for years. We may luck out and get a few things started but I'm sure we're going to have to tow the majority of it out."

While the guys messed with trying to start things and towing what didn't; Jessica, Karla, and I worked on removing everything we could carry and sweeping where we could. By four o'clock we were finished with the exception of one tractor Dad and Nick continued to tinker with.

"I have to admit I'm amazed at how well this went," Jessica said as we sat on the front porch resting. "The decorating will go fast on Friday."

"Are you ready to head over to Al's?" I asked James when he joined us.

"I am, but I wish I didn't have to," he answered.

"Why is that?"

"I don't know, something about him bothers me, or maybe I'm only jealous," James said with a shrug. "But let's get it over with." We got up, said goodbye to Jessica and Karla, and waved to Nick and Dad as we walked to James' pickup.

"Why would you be jealous of Al?" I asked when we got in his pickup.

"Only the fact that everything about his place screams clean, new, and modern, while I'm continuing to pay off the loan for the last eighty acres of land I bought six years ago, and by the time I pay off my operating loan each year, there isn't a lot of extra. Cattle prices haven't exactly been through the roof."

"Maybe Al is overspending and has loans right and left."

"No, I don't think so. Mom heard Al had a wealthy aunt who passed away many years ago who left him a pile of money. As the story goes it was quite timely too as the bank was planning to foreclose on him."

"That's interesting," I said and I told James about the thefts at the casino which happened at the same time as the convention. "I wonder about the timing of the inheritance and the convention. Maybe my banker, Peter Inver, would tell me about the foreclosure and when Al got his inheritance."

"I doubt it," James said. "I'm sure that's confidential information, but Mom might remember more. You can ask her when we get back. What are you planning to ask Al about today anyway?"

"I've been racking my brain, trying to figure it out all day. So far I haven't come with any great ideas. Maybe I'll bring up Christopher's murder and see how he reacts."

"I'll try and work the murder into the conversation somehow and then you can take over."

"Thanks James. You know I just realized you're going to be my step-brother when our parents get married."

"I don't have to buy you a Christmas present, do I?" James jokingly asked.

"Only the biggest item you can afford," I retorted.

He laughed and asked, "How was the bachelorette party by the way?"

"I think it went well, haven't you talked to Jessica yet?"

"Only briefly, she said there was too much to tell and we'd talk about it tonight when we could relax."

"Well, not to steal her thunder, but it was an interesting night." We spent the rest of the drive over to Al's talking about the party and the drug arrest.

James was astounded and then commented, "They're positive Nolan didn't kill Judith?"

"Faye is now the sheriff's main suspect," I answered shaking my head.

"You'll figure it out, you always do," James reassured me.

As we drove onto Al's ranch, and with James' words fresh in my mind, I paid attention to the buildings, fencing, yard, and house. I had to admit, everything was immaculate and new looking.

Even if his start-up money was obtained due to an inheritance or illegal means, he was putting in the time and reinvesting money into taking care of things. As I was admiring a smaller red barn I assumed was used for calving, my attention was caught by two men standing next to a large white barn angrily gesturing, and then the larger man shoved the other. The thin, stooped man who was shoved, stormed to a car, got in, backed up, turned around, and spun its wheels causing gravel to fly as it sped by us. I was surprised to see it was Owen Laterly. We parked near the white barn and I realized it was Al himself Owen had been arguing with. He walked towards James' pickup.

"Good afternoon James, Carmen," Al said nodding at us. "I have the paperwork in the barn," he said, ignoring the incident we had just witnessed.

I, however, was too nosy to not mention it. "Was that Owen Laterly, your old insurance agent, you were fighting with?" I asked.

Al looked at me with narrow eyes. "Yes it was," he said as he turned to walk to the barn.

Not one to give up, I asked, "Was something wrong?"

Al stopped, turned around, looked at me, and said, "Not that it's any of your business but Owen is an old friend, and he's having financial problems. I already bailed him out a few times, and he didn't take kindly to being told no today."

Feeling put in my place, I looked at James who shrugged, and then we followed Al inside the barn where he took a left and walked in a room set up as an office. I don't know much about cattle, but I was impressed by the charts, pictures, and data on the walls tracking the lineage of bulls. His aunt's money may have given him his start but it appeared Al had figured out a way to make a success of selling bulls and semen. I could see invoices lying on the desk showing shipments of both semen and bulls all over the country. Al was successful, but like James I felt there was something about him that prevented me from admiring or even liking him.

Al picked up a packet of papers off the desk and handed them to James saying, "Sorry I didn't get these to you before."

James accepted the papers saying, "It wasn't a problem. To be honest I wasn't even aware I needed them. I've never bought a bull of this quality before."

"Stick with me son, and we'll turn your herd into a first class one," Al said slapping James on the back.

James hid it well, but I could tell he was bristling at the man's comments. James must have decided to give up any pretense of being civil as he asked Al, "Did you hear the body that was found in Carmen's field was the long lost son of someone around here?"

Al was visibly startled and said, "What?"

I chimed in, "Yes, someone pretending to be my dad had an affair at the agronomy convention in Las Vegas a bunch of people from Arvilla went to in 1993. The affair resulted in a son, Christopher, who came here looking for his real father." I decided to lie and continued, "He discovered it wasn't my dad and the sheriff believes Christopher's real father must have killed him not wanting to acknowledge an illegitimate son."

Al was either a very good actor, or he truly had no knowledge of any of this as he only stood there with a puzzled look on his face and said, "That's quite a story. Is this tied to Judith's murder somehow?"

I lied again, "The sheriff thinks so." I waited a second and then said, "I'm not so sure."

"That's right, you fancy yourself a detective don't you," Al said with a sneer. It appeared he was done with pretending to be nice.

Not wanting to show his words stung me I replied, "I wouldn't say detective, more like curious."

James interjected, "She has a way of finding out the truth though."

Al stared at me. I decided to push more, "Weren't you with on that trip?"

"I was," he said after hesitating a bit.

"Do you remember anything that would help identify who might have impersonated my dad?"

Al shook his head, "That was a long time ago. I'm sorry but I do need to get going." He walked away ending our conversation, but stopped, turned around, and said, "You know Jed Alman was with on that trip also and his daughter worked for Judith. If I were you I'd start there." He walked away again.

James and I looked at each other and then went back to his pickup. We drove in silence for a few minutes until I said, "I understand what you mean about not liking that man."

"There is something about him isn't there? But he didn't react at all when you mentioned Christopher. I don't think it was him."

"I agree, but I wish it was."

"Someone being a jerk doesn't make them a murderer," James commented.

"But it's so much more satisfying when they are," I replied laughing. "Do you think he was serious about the idea of checking into Jed?"

"I have no idea—the only thing I know about Jed is that his son-in-law operates his farm now. I think Al was only trying to deflect your attention from him."

"I believe the sheriff is wrong and Judith's murder must have something to do with drugs. If Al is correct about Jed or Jill being responsible for Judith's death; then they must have something to with meth. But even if they had something to do with Judith's death, they would have had nothing to do with Christopher's."

"Except Al referenced the convention so maybe there is a connection you're missing. At least your suspects are disappearing. Your dad helped you rule out Cord, and it doesn't appear Al has anything to do with Christopher either. If your theory about the motive for Christopher's murder is correct, you are only left with Jed and Owen," James said as we drove back in his yard.

Karla was outside planting flowers in a flower bed. She looked up when we drove in. We parked and walked over to her. "Hi guys,"

she said as she stood up and wiped her hands on her jeans. "Chet
went home a half hour ago. Nick got the tractor going and moved
it behind the barn, he's inside helping Jessica with something. How
did it go at Al's?"

"I got my paperwork for the bull," James answered.

"Did you get your questions answered?" Karla asked me.

"He wasn't the most forthcoming person I've ever talked to but
I don't think he has anything to do with Judith's or Christopher's
murders," I answered.

"You know, I've never liked that man," she surprised me by saying. Karla rarely said anything bad about anyone.

"Why is that?" I asked. "Not that I disagree, but what make you
say it?"

"He's always acted like he's way better than the rest of us, just
because he lucked into money years ago. Maybe if he would have
had to earn it, he would be a little more humble."

"Do you know for sure it was an inheritance?" I inquired.

"Fairly sure, why do you ask?"

I explained to her my theory of Christopher's father being connected to something illegal that happened during the convention
and how I thought Christopher had tried to use the knowledge of
it for blackmail and wound up getting murdered instead.

"Wow, that's quite a story. I can tell you that Al and Owen were
up to something. They rarely joined the rest of us, and when they
did, they spent their time huddled in a corner talking to each other.
I always did think something bad must have happened between
them, as by the time we got back from the trip, they were barely
speaking to each other."

I told her about the newspaper articles and asked, "Do you
think one of them could have stolen the money?"

"I suppose one of them could have. Owen was and continues
to be a gambler, although everyone pretends they don't know.
I've also never thought of either one of them as being very honest
but I am almost certain Al's windfall came from an inheritance. I

happened to be in the bank the morning Al came skipping in with a big fat check crowing to everyone around him that his money troubles were over. He paid a lot of people off the next few weeks and his bills were significant, plus he built his fancy white barn. Even if he had stolen the $200,000 it wouldn't have paid for even a portion of all that."

"What about Owen?" I asked.

"It's possible, but the buildings he owns in town to my knowledge were bought over long periods of time. If he did steal the money, he didn't make a big splash with it."

"Maybe he gambled it away," I suggested.

"Could be," Karla said. "I have always wondered if Owen knew something about Al, the rumor around town is that Al has bailed Owen out financially quite often. But I heard the sheriff made an arrest, I didn't hear the details, but I assumed it had to do with the murders."

"No, it was a drug arrest and they don't believe it had anything to do with Judith or Christopher's murders," I told her wondering if I should add Al back on my suspect list.

"That doesn't seem possible," she said.

"I agree. I've been trying to stay out of Judith's murder as drugs aren't anything I want to get involved in, but now the sheriff doesn't think her murder is drug related so Faye is back as his primary suspect."

Karla laughed at that, "Poor Sheriff Poole. He finds a way to almost invite you to every murder investigation, doesn't he?"

"I'm beginning to think I should stay out of this one. My suspects aren't turning out to be viable," I answered with a shrug.

"You'll figure it out. In the meantime, what's been happening with the wedding planning? I don't want to bother Jessica, and James is pretending to be ignorant. I think he is scared I'm going to start meddling, but I only want to help if I can." James rolled his eyes and walked away. I spent a few minutes updating Karla before going in the house to get Nick. It was almost six and I knew I had to get to the cabin sites. It had been a busy day and it was fortunate the guests were checking in late today. Both cabins were being rented by members of a large family and they were going to arrive around six. I dropped Nick off at his house, feeling bad we didn't get to say a proper goodbye but I was running late. No one was at either cabin when I arrived. I did notice Melanie's car at Hugh's cabin. I was happy for her, now that I knew who he was, but regretted not questioning her about their relationship during the bachelorette party. As I parked I saw a dark blue SUV coming down the road with a greenish Jeep following behind it. They stopped at my pickup and introduced themselves. The Jacobson's were in the dark blue SUV and the Humphries were in the Jeep. I wasn't sure which was which, but the husband of one family and the wife of the other were siblings. I directed them to their respective cabins, helped them with their bags, and made sure Edna had delivered the food. By the time everyone was settled, my stomach was growling and it was time to head home for supper.

I arrived home to find Kirk and Dad sitting outside, each with a cat on their lap and Wizard happily digging a hole in the spot we had hoped to plant a garden. "What are you two doing?"

"Enjoying the late afternoon sun while supper cooks in the slow cooker," Dad answered stroking Tabitha who was staring at me with a gleam in her eye, thrilled to be in Dad's lap and not trusting I wouldn't ruin it for her.

Wizard came running over to greet me and came to an abrupt stop when he noticed Clyde in Kirk's lap. He barked loudly in protest. Tabitha merely flicked an ear but Wizard was successful in startling Clyde enough that he jumped out of Kirk's lap. Wizard trotted over and sat down next to Kirk with a satisfied look on his tiny doggy face.

"How is the investigation going?" Dad asked as I sat down on the front steps next to them.

"It is going nowhere. The sheriff said the new principal, who was the source of meth in town, didn't kill Judith and my theory of Al or Owen keeps getting weaker."

"Why is that?" Kirk asked.

"I thought either Al or Owen impersonated Dad, becoming Christopher's father and was responsible for one of the crimes I discovered happened at the casino hotel you guys stayed at in Las Vegas. I assumed Christopher knew about it, either because his mother told him or he found something in her possessions after she died and he attempted to blackmail one of them. But according to Karla, Al inherited his money, and Owen has never appeared flush with a windfall of money; although he is known to be a gambler so he could have lost it all. Karla thinks Al helps Owen out with money and Al inferred the same thing when James and I talked to him today."

"I've never known too many people who think they have enough money. Just because they obtained money other ways, doesn't mean they were averse to more if an easy chance presented itself," Dad advised.

I pondered for a few minutes, "That is true Dad. I guess I'll keep them on my suspect list, or maybe I should give up. I don't feel like I'm getting anywhere. If it wasn't for Sheriff Poole wanting to pin this on Faye I would give up."

"I know you are discouraged, and I'd love to agree with you so you'd quit trying to figure this out, but I know you and you won't stop. It's been a long day. Let's go in and eat supper." Dad set Tabitha down and Kirk, Wizard, and I followed him in the house.

It was a quiet meal, as we were all tired. Dad went to his recliner, while Kirk and I cleaned up the kitchen. Kirk and Wizard disappeared into his bedroom and I went upstairs to mine. I tried organizing my thoughts on a piece of paper, before giving up in frustration, and deciding to lose myself in a book for the rest of the evening.

CHAPTER TWENTY

*Native plants are better adapted to the local climate and soil con-
ditions. They provide nectar, pollen, and seeds that serve as food
for native butterflies, insects, birds and other animals. Non-native
common horticultural plants are not as hardy and often require
insect pest control to survive.*

I HAD STAYED UP LATE READING AND woke up Monday morning with a definite lack of ambition. There were a million things
I should be doing, scouting fields we burned last week for any
quack grass that may be starting to grow, checking seed inventory
to ensure we weren't getting short of any species, catching up on
accounts receivable and payable, helping Nick repair equipment as
something was always breaking down, and the list goes on. But with
the busy weekend I was feeling lazy and other than a 500 acre seed
mix to put together it could all wait until tomorrow. If the prairie
blazing star I ordered last week didn't show up this morning even
the seed mix would have to wait. If it did come Nick and I would
have the mix ready in plenty of time before the custom seeder was
picking it up at noon. Either Kirk or Dad must be awake as I could
hear noise coming from downstairs. I stretched one more time,

crawled out of bed, and dressed. When I walked down the steps I discovered it was Dad. He had coffee ready and was working on making waffles.

"Good morning," he said as he poured the batter in the waffle maker. "Would you like one?"

"I would." I grabbed myself a plate, silverware, a glass, and went and stood by Dad waiting for the waffle. "Did you eat already?"

"I did. I was up early. I think moving the equipment yesterday aggravated my back and I couldn't lie in bed anymore."

"Are you okay?" Dad didn't often complain so I sometimes forgot he had back issues.

"Yes, I took a couple of Tylenol and went for a walk with Wizard. I'm doing okay now."

"That explains why Wizard isn't around; you must have tired him out."

"He went right back in Kirk's bedroom to sleep," Dad said as he sat down next to me to drink his coffee.

I decided it was the perfect time to bring up the idea I had about moving out of the house. I said, "I've got an idea to run by you."

"What's that?" Dad asked.

"I think it's time I got out of your house. . ."

Dad interrupted me, "You don't have to move out."

"I know I don't have to, but I think it's time, especially with you and Karla getting married," I responded.

"We haven't decided which place we'll call home or even set a date yet. Either way Karla was insistent that there was no reason you should move out."

"That's nice of her, but what would you think about my moving a small modular home into the yard? That way we both have our privacy, yet I'm close for any help you might need and I don't have to leave the pets."

Dad was silent as he considered, until he said, "If that's what you want, I think it's a good idea, but I want to reiterate that you don't have to, but I do understand you wanting a place of your own. You will take Wizard with you when Kirk isn't around won't you?"

I laughed, "As long as I can stop in here for breakfast in the morning it's a deal. Thanks for understanding Dad." He looked like he was getting teary eyed so I said, "Nothing will happen fast. It takes forever to find a contractor and by the time I have a place ready, who knows, you and Karla may be married, she'll be moving in, and you won't even miss me."

Dad retorted, "Or maybe you'll be married and moving into Nick's house and you won't need to construct anything here."

Not knowing how to respond I changed the topic and we visited for a few more minutes while I washed my dishes. I filled my coffee mug, gave Tabitha a scratch as she was proudly sitting next to the front steps with a dead mouse. I got in my pickup and drove to the seed plant. Nick was opening the large box of prairie blazing star that had just been delivered. We spent the rest of the morning putting the mix together. As we finished, my phone pinged. It was Marcy—she had the newspaper articles I had been waiting for. I sent her a text telling her I would pick them up around noon.

Nick asked, "Is something wrong?"

"No, Marcy has the newspaper articles I've been waiting for. I'm going to stop by the library around noon and pick them up." As I finished talking the custom seeder drove in. Nick started loading his trailer while I gave him his invoice.

After paying me, the custom seeder said, "I heard on the radio this morning the veterinarian was arrested."

"What?" I asked in amazement.

"I guess she and the high school principal were involved in the meth that's been showing up around here."

"Wow, I hadn't heard," I said knowing my curiosity would make a stop by the Sheriff's Department necessary when I was in town. Maybe Sally had killed Judith—she certainly acted odd about Judith and Dan. Nick finished loading the trailer and gave the custom seeder the bill of lading to sign.

As he started to drive out with his trailer full of seed bags, he stopped and rolled down his window, "I may need another 400 acres later this week, but I don't know for sure yet."

"Call me when you do. We only need a few hours notice."

"Thanks Carmen. I'll talk to you later," he waved and was on his way.

I told Nick what the seeder said about Sally and that I was going to stop by the Sheriff's Department after I went to the library. "Would you like to come with?" I asked Nick.

"No. I plan on getting the rogueing van ready. I'm going to change the oil and make sure their equipment is ready and loaded in the van."

"That's a good idea, they'll be starting in two weeks, which reminds me the kids we hired will be coming by on Wednesday after school to fill out their paperwork and get trained on herbicide use. If you think of it, will you check the file cabinet for the training folder?"

"I will, and good luck sleuthing," he said and winked.

I grabbed a chicken salad sandwich from the convenience store when I filled gas and then drove to the library.

Marcy was helping someone when I walked in, but she handed me a piece of paper. I took it over to one of the couches and sat down. Her friend had emailed links to files of the articles and a password to use. I logged-in to the first one and started reading. Fifteen minutes later I was feeling foolish. Along with the original articles, Marcy's friend had sent the follow-up articles to the thefts. The missing poker chips had been found after the police reviewed the security footage and discovered it was one of the casino's card dealers and they found the chips at his house. The person who had stolen the old lady's jackpot ended up being her own grandson. I had based all my theories about Christopher's murder on one of those cases. I was contemplating not stopping by the Sheriff's Department after all when Marcy walked up to me.

"Ruth, the friend who sent me this stuff, wasn't sure, but she had one more link for you to look at. It happened at the same time as the other incidents and wasn't reported as a headline, but was in the back pages of the same newspaper. She thought because you were interested in thefts that occurred during that time—maybe it would be of interest." Marcy handed me a sticky note.

Feeling discouraged I almost didn't look at it, but logged-in again and read. I started to feel excited. This sounded like the kind of thing Christopher's mother would have done. There were numerous pick-pocket complaints for three days matching the dates of the convention. Police interviews of the people who had lost money and valuables claimed it was a woman using crutches accompanied by her husband. The woman with crutches would bump into people causing them to drop things, crutches would fall, and by the time everyone had gathered their dropped posses-sions and were on their way, they discovered missing credit cards, jewelry and money from wallets and purses.

"Do you know if your friend had a follow-up article to this? The other crime articles I was looking at, she found later articles about them being solved."

"I can ask her," Marcy said, and she pulled her phone out of her pocket and sent a quick text. She noticed someone needing help at the circulation desk and said, "I'll be back as soon as Ruth answers."

While I waited I thought to myself, this could be it. Perhaps whichever of the men we suspected was with Christopher's mother posed as the husband in this scam. If Christopher's mother told him about it and kept proof of some type he might have decided to use it for blackmail. That would provide a reason for killing Christopher. Neither Owen nor Al would want that to come out. They both had reason to protect their reputations, but which one of the men? I needed to talk to Owen and Al again. Maybe that was the reason for the fallout between the two of them; one or the other knew about it and covered for their friend initially but regretted it later. Or maybe Owen knew Al was responsible and has been using it as a hold over his head to help with gambling losses over the years. Although why not kill Owen I wondered? Maybe Christopher was the last straw, and if that was the case, then Owen could be in danger as he would know Al killed Christopher. Or perhaps it was Jed as it sounded like he kept to himself during the convention and no one has had any input as to what he did with his free time—while Owen and Al had hung out together.

Marcy approached me interrupting my musings. "Ruth had checked, but didn't find anything. She cautioned as it wasn't big news—if it did get solved it maybe didn't warrant the space to write about."

"Thanks Marcy, and tell your friend thanks too. I think her information may be helpful." I left the library and drove to the Sheriff's Department next. I walked in and once again the dispatcher motioned for me to go back to the sheriff's office without checking with the sheriff first. Hugh was again in Sheriff Poole's office. He looked at me with a big smile while the sheriff only looked up and grunted.

Hugh asked, "You heard about Sally Stewart's arrest?"

"I did. I'm hoping she is responsible for Judith's murder?"

"I'm afraid not," the sheriff responded, "whether you like it or not, Faye remains the best suspect."

I sat down on the last open chair in his office, the other was stacked high with over-flow files from his desk. "I don't accept that. Why is Faye the only suspect?"

Hugh answered, "Both Nolan and Sally have alibis for the time of Judith's murder."

Sheriff Poole said, "In fact we let Sally go."

"I thought she was a partner of Nolan's with the meth?" I asked confused.

"She didn't know about the meth. She simply rented Nolan the old house that was on a piece of the veterinary clinic's property far back in the woods. It was in tough shape, but Nolan talked her into it by claiming he needed a spot for he and his dog to live as the dog was disturbing the neighbors in town with its barking. He got the water and electricity hooked up and she had no clue he was using it to make meth."

"You believed that story? Wouldn't she have wandered out there at least once to check on the property?"

"I don't know if you noticed, but Sally walks with quite a limp. She has a bad hip, and is waiting for her health insurance to approve a hip replacement which they won't yet because of her age. She made Nolan take her out there once to verify the dog had adequate shelter, which it did. He paid the rent on time, and she didn't think any more of it. And before you ask, yes, we are positive Sally had nothing to do with it."

"What about Darius the IPD driver? Judith said in her journal she was suspicious of all the small packages he was delivering."

"We talked to Darius and he confirmed Judith had talked to him. Of course he couldn't share package information with her, but we checked it out. Turns out Melanie ordered and shipped to each business in town informational packets on the importance of insects to the ecosystem and a sample of an eco-friendly deterrent spray they could use in their places of businesses instead of killing bugs with insecticides," the sheriff said with a snort of derision. "We are confident only Nolan is involved at least in regards to other locals. Hugh has been after him for a few years now. When Nolan felt people might be getting suspicious, he'd leave his job and move to the next town needing a principal. He'd look for a person naïve enough to rent him land and set up his lab. That's another reason we believe Sally, he used the same dog excuse the last two places."

I looked at Hugh for confirmation and he nodded. Debating whether or not to bring up my theory again, I started to say, "I continue to believe something from the convention has to do with at least Christopher's murder..."

The sheriff held up a hand and stopped me, "I looked into the thefts you told us about that occurred during the convention. They were both solved."

"I found that out," I admitted and tried to tell them about the stealing by the man and the woman on crutches which also coincided with the dates of the convention. The sheriff looked uninterested while I talked, Hugh was at least giving me the courtesy of actively listening but I could tell he wasn't buying my theory either. I stopped talking and decided it wasn't worth wasting my energy trying to convince them until I had more information. I was beginning to think Judith's death did have something to do with Christopher's. Something important was on the edge of my thinking, but I couldn't grasp what it was. I said goodbye to both of them and walked out the door. As I stood on the sidewalk I debated what my next step should be. I noticed Sally sitting on a bench in front of the bookstore. I crossed the street and sat down next to her.

"What do you want?" she asked.

"I wanted to say sorry for how Nolan deceived you," I answered. "I'm glad the sheriff let you go."

"I feel like such a fool. I can't believe I had a meth lab on my property and I didn't know it. I should have been more suspicious of someone willing to rent a dump to live in, yet never ask for anything to be repaired," she said shaking her head and staring at the sidewalk.

"Do you mind telling me why you blamed Dan for Judith's murder?" I asked.

She looked up at me in anger, and then deflated in front of me, "I was jealous. Judith was my best friend in college and when I heard Arvilla needed a veterinarian I decided to buy the clinic and move here, but it wasn't the same. Judith was busy with Dan and her kids and didn't have much time for me. She did mention her concern about meth when we went out for breakfast one day, so when she was killed and Dan blew me off and wouldn't let me help with her funeral arrangements I guess a part of me wanted revenge. When you were in the clinic that day with Wizard I decided to mention Dan to you. It was stupid and childish I know, but I wanted him to get in trouble, not arrested or anything—only be suspected and maybe questioned."

"You didn't think the loss of his wife was enough to deal with?" I couldn't help but ask.

"I think it's obvious I have anger issues. You can see why I stick to animals; I'm not a likeable person, but I am a good vet."

"I'm sure you are." I sat in silence for a few more minutes, before getting up and deciding I would go talk to Owen. I said goodbye to Sally, not quite sure what to make of her, got in my pickup and drove towards his run-down office. I was in luck; his vehicle was in front of his building. As I looked at the disrepair his building was in, I mused that his gambling wasn't doing him any favors. He was sitting at his desk rubbing his forehead when I walked in.

He looked up and said, "Now what do you want?"

Deciding to go with the direct approach I said, "People believe Al bails you out of your gambling debts. I think Al did something at the convention a bunch of you went to in Las Vegas, something he doesn't want anyone to know about. You must have been holding it over his head all these years. Does it have something to do with either of the murders that have happened?"

Owen surprised me by bursting into gut-busting laughter. He finally wound down, wiped tears from his eyes, and said, "You aren't much of a detective. Do you think if Al had done something he didn't want others to know about he would have allowed me to live all these years and then decide to go on a killing spree?"

I hung my head in embarrassment but proceeded to press my theory in dogged determination, "Did Al cheat on his wife and father a child with a woman during that trip? I think Al and she stole money and their son, Christopher, knew about it and Al got rid of him when he showed up here."

"Seriously Carmen, you have an active imagination."

"Al did something illegal on that trip, why else does he keep giving you money? Mauve Johnson must have known something too, what are you to her that you are her contact at the nursing home?" I asked him.

"I help out Mauve because she was my wife's Godmother and a faux grandmother to my daughter. Mauve doesn't have any other family, and because my daughter lives too far away to help, Mauve became my responsibility. And in answer to your question about Al, he is simply a good friend. Now unless there is something else, feel free to leave."

Feeling foolish I turned around to walk out the door, when Owen said, "I did see Jed with a woman at the convention."

I stopped and asked, "You saw him with a woman, like in a compromising way, or only talking to someone?"

"I didn't pay much attention," Owen said. "I didn't want to know, and to be honest I thought he deserved to have a little fun, his wife was a lot like his daughter is; mean. Maybe you could leave Al and myself alone and consider him."

Not sure if he was intentionally deflecting attention away from he and Al by falsely accusing Jed, and knowing he wasn't going to talk to me anymore, I gave up and left. I called Nick and invited him to supper which he accepted and then I called Dad to let him know I was bringing supper home. I stopped at the grocery store and picked up a bucket of chicken and a couple of sides from the deli. As I walked past the bakery shelves on my way to the checkout I couldn't resist and grabbed a carrot cake for dessert.

Dad and Kirk were both home. I stuck the chicken in the oven to keep it warm while we waited for Nick. He showed up thirty minutes later. I was embarrassed about my visit with Owen and purposely made no mention of murder while we ate. After the kitchen was cleaned up Kirk left for band practice and Dad, Nick, and I sat around the table enjoying the carrot cake. I finally relayed what the sheriff had told me about Nolan and Sally and how Faye remained his primary suspect for the murders.

Nick said, "We know she didn't, so what other information have you gathered to steer us in another direction?"

"I was convinced it was Al or Owen, but when I stopped to talk to Owen today, he laughed at me. He made a good point about Al having left him alive all these years and yet he murdered two people now? I have to admit he made me feel foolish as what he said makes sense. He did say he remembered seeing Jed with a woman, but I think he was trying to divert my attention. I'm sure the two of them were up to something at the convention, but I'm not so sure it has anything to do with the murders," I said spinning my fork around my empty plate, frustrated at my lack of progress.

"I don't think you're wrong Carmen," Dad said. "Those two weren't around much, and now that I think about it, I believe they even rented a car for one day. Looking back I wouldn't be surprised if they were up to something, but I can't say one way or the other about a woman being involved with either of them. I never saw Owen, Al, or Jed with a woman. In fact I rarely saw any of them. Did you ever find out what the article Mauve referred to was about?"

"No. In fact I kind of forgot about it. I'll ask Kathy right now." I found her name in my contacts and sent a text.

"Why don't you and Nick take a walk, relax, and enjoy the beautiful evening. I'm going to give Karla a call and then head to bed," Dad said as he walked out of the kitchen.

"I think that's a good idea, what about you?" I asked Nick.

"Some alone time with you sounds like the best thing I've heard in days."

I whistled for Wizard and we walked out the door heading for the well worn trail we walked on the edge of our sideoats grama field. There was a big tree stump leftover from a huge cottonwood that had fallen down and it was the perfect spot to sit on Nick's lap and relax while Wizard ran around smelling possible rabbit trails.

Nick said, "You're frustrated aren't you?"

"I am."

"I may be way off base, but I don't think the sheriff suspects Faye any more than you or I do."

I leaned away from his shoulder and looked at him, "What do you mean?"

"I think he has no idea either, and by saying he suspects Faye, it makes you keep asking questions. He hasn't even questioned Faye other than right after each of Judith's and Christopher's murders. I think if she was his only suspect he would have been bothering her a lot more."

I considered his words and said, "You may be right. But he's always telling me to stay out of his murder investigations for my safety. Why would he want me nosing around?"

"Because he has nothing, and he's certainly not going to ask you directly for help."

"I should have picked up on that." I stood up, agitated now.

"So much for a relaxing walk, sorry I ruined it," Nick said ruefully.

"You didn't ruin it; the best times of my days are spent with you," I said. "Oh wow, that sounded corny didn't it?"

"Maybe a little, but I feel the same." Nick stood up and held me close as we kissed.

We were interrupted by the ringing of my phone. I looked at caller id and saw it was Kathy from the local newspaper. "What's up Kathy?"

"I found the article you were looking for a couple of days ago, but it was kind of explosive and I needed to talk to my parents first to find out the reasons why they didn't print it. It may help your investigation. You can look at it tomorrow if you'd like."

"I do, but couldn't you text or email it to me?"

"I'd rather not—we might be liable for a lawsuit if the information in it got out."

"That sounds intriguing. I'll be there tomorrow," I told her as I disconnected the call.

"What was that about?" Nick asked.

I told him what Kathy said as we walked hand-in-hand back to the house. We discussed work plans for tomorrow. The custom seeder had placed an order for another 400 acres. I would go in early to get the seed mix computed, and Nick would mix it when he got to work. While he was doing the mixing I had to check on my cabin guests and then I'd go to town to look at the article. Nick and I shared a long goodnight kiss and then Wizard and I walked inside. I put Wizard in Kirk's room and went upstairs to set my alarm.

CHAPTER TWENTY-ONE

The deep roots of native grass species bind soil particles together, helping with soil stability which is crucial in preventing soil erosion.

I WAS AWAKE WELL BEFORE THE ALARM went off anxious to get to the newspaper office. I tried to calm down knowing Tuesdays their office didn't open until late morning due to putting out the week's edition on Monday and I did have plenty of things I had to get done before then. I spent around three hours at the seed plant computing the seed mix and physically checking inventory. We were again getting low in a few of the wildflowers we use in mixes so I sent an email to two of our suppliers asking about their availability and price. I waved at Nick as we passed in the driveway of the seed plant. I drove to the cabins. I didn't plan on waking anybody up if they were sleeping in, but it was nine o'clock, so I was hopeful someone would be up. I only wanted, as always, to make my presence known and check if they needed anything. The Jacobson's cabin had one person standing outside when I drove up. As I got closer I recognized it was one of the Humphries. If I had the families figured out correctly it was the sister of the father of the Jacobson family. I stopped quite a distance from the cabin trying to not wake anyone up that might yet be sleeping and walked to the cabin to ask if everything was going well. Fifteen minutes later I was on my way feeling satisfied that at least in the cabin world I was accomplishing something positive. She had been effusive in her praise, exclaiming over the quietness and how they had been making a lot of quality memories with their kids. I'd have to be sure and let Kirk know his kayaking idea was a hit.

I walked in the newspaper office, sat down in front of Kathy's desk, and waited impatiently for her to get off the phone.

She hung up, picked up a file folder and said, "The reason this wasn't printed was because there was no proof, and the person that is mentioned in this article had and continues to have considerable power in this community. If this gets out, we'd be sued. In fact I have to admire Mauve's professionalism for never saying anything to anyone over the years. If it turns out this has bearing on the murders, of course we'll have to say something to law enforcement, but for now this is between the two of us. Do you agree?"

I agreed, hoping I could indeed keep it to myself. She handed me the folder, I opened it, and started reading Mauve's hand written note.

Across the top of the paper in cursive she had written—I would like to pursue an article based on the following information—and underneath she had the following typed up:

On February 20, 1993, I had the misfortune to visit with a very inebriated Owen Laterly at a casino in Las Vegas, NV. He told me Al Mitchel had pulled off an amazing con. Al had a wealthy, elderly aunt who lived in Henderson—approximately sixteen miles from Las Vegas. She had never married and given up a child for adoption in her thirties. She contacted Al, her only remaining relative, gave him some money to hire an investigator and locate this long lost child before she died. She wanted him to handle it as her health was poor. Owen said Al used the money for himself and never did pursue finding the child. He planned on being her only surviving relative in order to inherit her money. When she was diagnosed with terminal

pancreatic cancer she begged him again to find her child, and per-
haps knowing the type of person Al was, she told him if he didn't find
her child she was leaving her money to charity. Al convinced Owen to
pose as the child and they both went to visit her in the hospital while
at the convention. Al had arranged for a less than honest lawyer he
knew to be there to change her will the same day they went to visit
her. Owen didn't want to proceed but Al forced him by threatening
to confiscate his property as payment for the gambling debts he had
incurred which Al had covered. Owen was relieved when the aunt
accepted Al's story without requiring proof. She was going to leave her
money equally to Al and Owen. Owen told her he had more money
than he knew what to do with and was just happy to get to know her
before she died and that Al was more deserving of her money. The
will was signed and witnessed. They visited her one more time before
she passed away. I could tell Owen was obviously distressed about his
part in the deception.

"Wow!" I said when I finished reading. "Why didn't they let
Mauve pursue the article?"

"I asked my mom the same question and she said my grandparents did tell Mauve she could pursue it, but with caution. Mauve
approached Owen again when they were home from the convention
but he denied everything. She tried tracking down the aunt's care-
takers, but had no success. She found a copy of the will, and got the
lawyer's name, but he wouldn't talk to her. Mauve wanted to write
the article anyway, but my grandparents talked to their lawyer who
told them it would be in their best interest to not pursue it, or they
would have to spend a lot of money defending themselves in court.
Without collaborating information they were sure to be sued. Mom
said Mauve visited with Owen a couple more times with no luck.
Mom thought it was around this time his gambling debts starting
piling up in earnest with Al doing his best to keep Owen solvent."

"Interesting," I said once again discouraged. "This confirms Al
Mitchel is a jerk, but it doesn't help with solving either murder. At
least Owen is making Al suffer."

"I didn't think it would help," Kathy said, "but I thought I'd let you know in case this fit in with something else you've ascertained."

"It doesn't, but it leaves me with only one suspect left on my list."

"Care to share who that is?"

"No, I've been wrong about everything else so far. I better not malign someone else's name until I find proof. Thanks for finding this."

"It was kind of fun, I run into Al every once in a while and he tends to treat me like I'm not worthy to even talk to him. He intimidates me, but not anymore. I think it's going to be a lot more fun to talk to him the next time I see him." She grinned.

I high-fived her and walked out of the newspaper office. Jed was the last person on my list. I wondered where I could find him. The dentist office was a couple blocks down the street. I decided to walk there and see if Jill would know where I could find her father.

Faye looked up when I walked in. "Are you having a problem with your tooth?" she asked.

"No. I was wondering if Jill was available?"

"She's with a patient right now, but she should be done in about ten minutes. Would you like me to have her call you?"

"No. If you don't mind, I'll wait." I sat down and started scrolling through my phone. It had been a while since I had read any national news. I put my phone back in my pocket when I heard Jill's voice coming down the hallway. She escorted her patient to the front desk telling Faye to schedule them the next time the dentist from Parkville would be here. She turned to walk back down the hallway.

"Jill, do you have a minute?" I asked stopping her before she got too far.

"Sure, what can I do for you Carmen?"

"I'm sorry to bother you, but I was wondering if you could tell me where your dad is. I don't have his cell number and I didn't want to drive out to your farm if he wasn't there."

"Why do you want to talk to my dad?" she asked, her eyes narrowing.

"The sheriff doesn't agree, but I'm sure the man who was found in the field we were burning has something to do with the convention your dad and others from Arvilla went to in 1993. I'm starting to believe Judith's death has something to do with it also. I wanted to talk to your dad to see if he remembers anything that might have a bearing on the murders."

"You aren't a detective Carmen. You don't need to bother my dad, you already talked to him once before and upset him. If the sheriff thinks there is a reason to talk to him, he can question him. Now if that's all, I need to get back to work." She walked away.

Faye had over-heard us and said, "That was kind of nasty of her."

"She's not wrong," I said. "I don't have any right to talk to him."

"Are you giving up?" Faye asked.

"You know me better than that. But I don't think I'll try to talk to Jed for a while. At least not until I somehow get more information. Owen indicated to me he'd seen Jed with a woman at the convention. I'll give Owen more time before I talk to him again, maybe he will have remembered something else. I'll talk to Karla and Dad again too, maybe with a nudge they'll remember seeing Jed with a woman also."

"You'll figure it out," Faye told me.

I left the dentist office and got in my pickup. I didn't start it right away, my mind was busy thinking. I was now sure Al and Owen had nothing to do with the murders, despicable people, both of them, but apparently not murderers. My only suspect left was Jed, but I was stymied on how to find any proof. I wondered if there was any way I could convince the sheriff to test Christopher and Jed's DNA—but disregarded that thought as I knew Sheriff Poole would never go for it. If Christopher's mother was the woman with the crutches, and it was Jed with her, maybe law enforcement from Las Vegas would have physical descriptions on file—but unless the sheriff supported me I doubted they'd even talk to me about a thirty year old case—especially one that might have even been solved for all I knew. I'd have to think of a way to find the information on my own. But for now I was going to head back to the seed plant and get back to my business, which I hadn't been paying much attention to the last few days. I spent the rest of the day scouting fields for quack grass. It was early yet for the fields we had recently finished burning, but the fields we burned over a week ago had a few spots of quack already growing. The roguers would start next week and now I knew where to send them first. Supper was a quiet affair, Dad was over at Karla's helping her pack for her eventual move into James' house, Kirk was at band practice, and Nick was changing the oil on Faye's car. I spent the rest of the evening reading outside with Tabitha stretched out on my lap while Wizard enjoyed running around the yard. Nick text me as I was getting ready for bed and asked if I'd like to meet him for breakfast at Jessica's restaurant in the morning. I answered I'd meet him there at seven and I went to bed.

Wednesday morning dawned to a cloudy, dreary day. I checked the forecast on my phone and saw there was an eighty percent chance of rain late tonight. Perfect, we could get the fertilizer spread on the rest of the fields today. There was no sign of Dad, Kirk, or Wizard, but the coffee was made so somebody was awake. I filled my mug and head out to my pickup. Nick was waiting for me in a booth when I got to Jessica's restaurant. I debated for a brief second and then slid in next to him on the same side instead of sitting across from him.

"Good morning," Nick said as he moved over to make more room for me.

Phyllis came over to take our order; over-easy eggs, hash browns, and wheat toast with peanut butter for me; and a Denver omelet, wheat toast, and bacon for Nick. We were enjoying our food when Jessica took a break and came over and sat with us.

"George took over cooking for me—I saw you guys sitting here and wanted to say hi. Was everything good?" she asked.

"Delicious," Nick and I answered in unison.

"How are you doing? I can't believe your wedding is in three days. Are you having any last minute second thoughts?" I asked knowing what her answer would be.

"Not a one! I can't wait to be Mrs. Jessica Harmen," she answered smiling.

"And when Dad and Karla get married you'll be my step sister-in-law!" We laughed together and then spent the next few minutes discussing last minute wedding details. Neither one of us had been able to find someone to style our hair for the wedding. Fortunately Jessica had mentioned it to Chloe at their book club last night and Chloe offered to do it. It turns out she loved to style hair and apply make-up, she had even considered a career as a beautician. Nick was starting to look bored so I said, "We'd better get going; I think Nick has had enough of wedding talk."

Jessica retorted, "If you're sick of it, think of poor James."

"Somehow I doubt he minds too much," Nick said as we got up and out of the booth leaving Phyllis a generous tip. Jessica went back to the kitchen and as Nick picked up the bill I noticed Jed sitting at a table by himself. I asked Nick to give me a minute and I went to sit down next to him.

He looked at me in surprise and said, "Hello Carmen."

"Good morning Jed—I was wondering if you'd given any more thought to the convention in Las Vegas, maybe you remembered something about who may have fathered the man we found in our burned field?"

"I have more important things to do than worry about something that happened thirty years ago," he answered as he gripped his coffee cup tightly.

Ignoring him, I persisted, "I've talked to quite a few people and most of them can account for who they spent time with, but no one remembers you being around a lot."

He glared at me and said, "I'm not sure anyone's memory is good enough to remember who was doing what, but if it matters, I'm a loner and I spent most of my free time going to shows and spending time in the casinos. I don't gamble, but I enjoy watching people."

"Owen Laterly mentioned seeing you with a woman. Did you meet someone there?" I asked.

"I wouldn't believe anything gambling Owen says. Are you done interrogating me now?"

"I guess I am; enjoy your breakfast." I stood up and walked to where Nick was waiting for me by the door.

"Did you find anything out?" he asked.

"Nope, other than I'm fairly sure the man hates me," I answered shrugging.

"What's on the schedule for today?" Nick asked as we stood outside on the sidewalk.

"There's rain in the forecast tonight, so we should get the last of the fertilizer spread. I need to pick up cleaning supplies from the hardware store if you want start getting the equipment ready. The high school kids will be coming by after school today and I'd like to clean up the break room before they come," I said.

"I'll call and see if I can get the fertilizer delivered yet this morning and start hooking up the equipment," Nick said as he walked me to my pickup.

I backed out of the parking space and drove to the hardware store. I realized I only had today and tomorrow left to get any work done on the farm. Friday would be spent getting things ready for the rehearsal supper, decorating the church, and setting up James' building and yard where the reception and wedding dance would be held. Monday the roguers, with the exception of the high school students, would be starting and seed order pick-ups would get busy. So far it had been primarily the custom seeders, but after the farmers got their normal row crops planted, CRP plantings would get started. The front of the store was packed so I went around to the alley, parked, and ran into the hardware store. I found cleaners and paper towels, charged them to my account, and went back out to my pickup. I drove back

to the seed plant where Nick was waiting for me with the tractor and fertilizer spreader hooked up and running. I unloaded
my cleaning supplies in the break room and then walked over to
Nick. I was about to ask when the fertilizer would be delivered
when the truck turned in on our road. Thirty minutes later Nick
was spreading fertilizer while I cleaned the break room. When he
finished, I took his pickup and followed him three miles down the
road to the last field that needed fertilizer. It was an eighty acre
big bluestem field and it was one o'clock before we were finished.
Breakfast had worn off and we both were starving. Once we were
back to the seed plant I offered to go on a food run for us, but
Nick didn't need anything as he had packed a dinner. He took the
equipment over to the shop to rinse it out and put the spreader
away for the year. I parked Nick's pickup and walked back to the
break room where I had left mine. As I got in my pickup I noticed
something on my windshield. I got out and found an envelope
stuck under the windshield wiper. I looked around to see if I
could spot who might have left it, but I didn't see anyone either
walking or driving away. I opened it and was surprised to find
it was from Owen. He asked me to meet him at Al's at two this
afternoon. He said he and Al were ready to talk about what had
happened at the convention and that Al had information about
Jed. He also asked if I would come alone as the information was
of a personal nature.

I looked at my phone and decided I would have enough time to
run to town, pick up food and get to Al's. But the more I thought
about it, something felt wrong. My choice of reading material was
cozy mysteries, and I always found myself yelling at the main character when they went alone to meet with their primary suspect, yet
I couldn't believe there would be any danger in broad daylight, plus
I was sure neither of them was responsible for the murders. I was
now confident Jed was the best suspect for at least Christopher's
murder and I wanted to know what information Owen and Al had
about him. I couldn't imagine what Judith could have said or known

that would have caused Jed to kill her but I suddenly remembered Jed had been to see Judith for a tooth emergency the night before she was murdered. Yet, it didn't seem feasible Owen would have driven all the way out here to stick a note on my pickup, but to be fair I wasn't here and neither he nor Al had my cell phone number. I got in my pickup and drove to town to pick up something to eat from the convenience store. I debated the wisdom of going by myself to Al's the entire drive to town, either way I'd have to let Nick know I was going to be gone in case I wasn't back before the high school kids arrived for their training. I picked up my phone and dialed Nick.

I arrived at Al's a couple of minutes before two o'clock. The place appeared quiet, but as I drove past the red barn I saw a vehicle I didn't recognize parked next to a hay storage shed. I parked, looked around, and then hesitantly walked towards the shed. When I got close, Jed stepped out holding a gun.

"Where are Al and Owen?" I asked.

"Not here obviously," he chuckled. "Owen won't be coming as he doesn't know anything about this and Al, his family, and his hired men left for a bull sale early this morning. With you running around town asking questions about Al and Owen; trying to find motives for why they killed Judith and that idiot Christopher, I think the sheriff will be more than willing to blame one or the other for your death when your body is found here."

I started to edge farther away from him but he grabbed my arm with one hand while holding the gun in the other pressed against my side. "Let's move behind this shed. I don't want anyone finding your body too fast, and if you're looking for your friend Nick, I already took care of him."

I looked at him in panic, and he said, "Oh don't worry, I didn't kill him, yet. I only knocked him out. I've got him tied up in the back of my pickup. His body will disappear and he'll be another suspect for your murder, but it's much easier to make a live person move than to lug a dead body around. I thought you might not come by yourself, so I watched and sure enough I saw him coming across the field on a four-wheeler. Now move to the back of this hay shed," he said as he started pushing me.

"At least tell me why you killed them? Judith didn't know anything and Christopher was your own son."

"My daughter is my only child. Christopher was a blackmailer exactly like his mother. I was only looking for some fun and the next thing I know that woman was forcing me to help her steal or she'd tell my wife."

"What difference would that make? You told her you were my dad."

"She had someone take a Polaroid picture of us together. I knew if she did ever contact your family it wouldn't be long before it was discovered it was me instead of Chet. So I went along with her little scam, she'd pretend to use crutches, then run into people on purpose and while they helped her up, I'd be helping pick up their stuff taking whatever I could. I have to give her credit; it was a pretty good plan. Between the jewelry, poker chips, and cash, we pocketed around $20,000.00 that weekend. I got the last laugh though; I gave her a couple of strong slaps, stole the money, and forced her to turn over the picture." He grinned as he said forced her and continued, "I told her if she ever tried to find me, I would not only use the photo to prove she was blackmailing me to help her steal but I would hurt her too. You can imagine my surprise when Christopher happened to run into Jill on the street with a picture of Faye and an old newspaper clipping of all of us who attended the convention. At some point his mother must have said something. He asked Jill where he could find Faye Banning and Chet Karlaff, but pointed at me circled on the picture. Jill knew something was up, so she told him she knew Chet well and if he'd wait with her she'd call Chet to come meet with him. I drove to town and thinking I was Chet he told me he wanted the $20,000.00 I had stolen from his mother or he was going to law enforcement. He said DNA would prove his story. Jill distracted him while I clobbered him with a shovel and knowing he was looking for Faye too, I put the body in your field to implicate either Nick or Faye."

"Your daughter helped you?" I asked, not believing what I was hearing.

"I told Jill years ago about my impersonating Chet at the convention so she'd be prepared if anyone ever showed up looking for me. I didn't expect it to be her son though."

Not daring to point out again that Christopher was his son too, I asked, "Jill knew about you cheating on her mother and the money you stole and she didn't care?"

"My daughter is a chip off the old block and I've never been more proud of her. It was her idea to get rid of him by killing him and my idea to put his body in your field," he said proudly as I fought my nausea.

"Why did you kill Judith?"

"Wouldn't you know the very next day I had a tooth ache. Judith fit me in, but she was asking me all kinds of questions wondering if I'd seen any strangers around town. I figured she had seen Jill and me with Christopher. She needed to go."

"Judith was only trying to figure out who was behind the meth problem in town. There was no reason to kill her," I said starting to struggle attempting to get away.

Finally I heard the voice I had been waiting for, "Put your hands up and step away from her."

Jed was distracted for a brief second and I took the opportunity to hit him as hard as I could in the gut, screaming, "That's for Nick."

Jed dropped the gun and doubled over. I put my hands together and smashed them down on his back causing him to fall to the ground, while I asked, "Did you think I'd be so stupid as to come here without law enforcement?" I took off running to Jed's pickup where I found Nick dazed, but awake and trying to untie himself.

"Some hero I am," he said when he was loose.

"You are, but you were supposed to be a decoy and only let him see you so he wouldn't expect anyone else to be with me, then you were supposed to drive away. What if he had killed you?" I asked holding him close.

"I didn't spot him anywhere, so I got off the four-wheeler to walk around trying to make sure he'd seen me and then all the sudden it went black. He must have somehow got behind me and knocked me out," Nick said as he rubbed his head.

"I'm so thankful you are okay," I said in relief as the sheriff walked by leading a handcuffed Jed who glared at me.

"Will you be picking up Jill as well?" I asked the sheriff.

"I will. Thanks for your help Carmen. I thought you were on a wild goose chase, but I have to admit your instincts were correct. You can come by the Sheriff's Department tomorrow and make a statement."

"Okay." I looked at the time and realized I only had a few minutes before I was supposed to meet with the high school students. I called Kirk and explained what had happened, told him I needed to take Nick to the hospital, and asked him to take care of the students. He could do the training as well as I could. Nick was sputtering in the background about being fine and that he didn't need to go to the hospital. I ignored him, hung up, gave him a big kiss, led him to my pickup, and drove him to the hospital where he was diagnosed with a concussion. They agreed to send him home if someone could watch him overnight. I ignored his protests that Faye could watch him and I could go back to work. I told him I was going to take care of the man I loved and he had no choice but to accept it. He was stunned into silence, so I kissed him. As I sat with Nick that night, I wrote a note informing James about Al's secret which I planned to add to his and Jessica's wedding gift. I knew they would never tell anyone, and I felt James deserved to know he had no reason to feel inferior to Al.

EPILOGUE

SATURDAY AFTERNOON I STOOD AT A church alter and watched as my two best friends were married. I looked around in appreciation at the people I loved. Dad and Karla—the next to be married—with proud smiles, holding hands as James and Jessica exchanged their vows, Kirk grinning as he played the organ doing what he loved most—making music, and Nick, the best man, standing on the other side of James looking at me with love in his eyes. I closed my eyes and imagined what it would feel like if it were Nick and I exchanging vows. I decided it would feel absolutely right. I opened my eyes, smiled at Nick and glanced out at the packed church, full of all our friends and neighbors. I felt blessed.

TARA RATZLAFF LIVES IN THE NORTHWEST corner of Minnesota (just about in Canada) with her husband of twenty-nine years, daughter, five fat cats, and one rescue dog who fiercely greets family, friends and strangers the same—as if she wants to eat them. Tara graduated from North Dakota State University with a degree in Civil Engineering and became the first female County Highway Engineer in the state of Minnesota. She retired early from her career as a Civil Engineer when she and her husband purchased a native grass and wildflower seed farm/business which they operated for over twenty years before recently retiring. With her daughter busy in college and the seed farm no longer keeping her busy, she decided it was time to pursue her dream of writing cozy mysteries. Her hobbies are reading (mysteries only, of course), long walks, swimming when the pool isn't frozen and being amused by the antics of her pets.

* 9 7 8 1 6 8 4 9 2 3 1 6 8 *